myself am hell
A Novel

HENRY WRIGHT

Copyright © 2023 Henry Wright

All rights reserved.

ISBN: 9798854192767

For Betty

CONTENTS

	Acknowledgments	i
1	Part One: Quentin	1
2	Part Two: Ali	17
3	Part Three: A tap on the shoulder	26
4	Part Four: The Japanese Garden	40
5	Part Five: Meet Cute	50
6	Part Six: The Soldier	56
7	Part Seven: Tokyo 1975	100
8	Part Eight: Comings Togethers	145
9	Part Nine: Sanatorium Journal	171

ACKNOWLEDGMENTS

The title is a quotation from John Milton's 'Paradise Lost'. All quotations from John Milton's works are taken from 'Milton The Major Works', ed. by Stephen Orgel and Jonathan Goldberg (Oxford: Oxford University Press, 1991). The following works were also consulted: Fraser, Antonia, 'Cromwell Our Chief of Men' (London: Weidenfeld and Nicolson, 1973); Hill, Christopher, 'Milton and the English Revolution' (London: Faber, 1977); Tanner, Stephen, 'Afghanistan a Military History from Alexander the Great to the Fall of the Taliban' (Cambridge, MA: Da Capo Press, 2002); Rashid, Ahmed, 'Taliban The Story of the Afghan Warlords (London: Pan Books, 2000); Farrell, Theo, 'Unwinnable Britain's War in Afghanistan 2001-2014 (London: Vintage, 2017)

Part One: Quentin

'Thou canst not touch the freedom of my mind'

John Milton, 'Comus'

<u>Outside The British Library, August 2012</u>

Grinds you down treatment Harder and harder to ignore because you do it for the short-term relief of relief of Standing here near people worst thing for me me near people to touch them and go near them and never never just switch yourself off and shut the mind down

all the people in this queue I can't I can't stay in the flat all fucking day I have to go out and then you're near people and not go never go near people and for God's sake make me feel better about this I will make lists and write and and never touch and to never go near anyone because why Just please to stop all this

See that picture of Milton You just raped and murdered him That's not possible Then then how come The Onslow portrait National Portrait Gallery You did this you you did this I'm telling you and I know I I know but not possible there were people around and how can you rape and murder a portrait of myself am hell Why would you No desire to do these things at all it's just

Say it out loud say it out loud say it out loud say it out loud

Don't touch don't hurt never go near

I never would

I had to check I had to you can know but that doesn't always help you it's the fucking condition Here's your solution but you can't always be that strong against Sin and now against Death and

Standing in line for the computers on my last visit here and look up Obsessive Compulsive Disorder and read about it for hours and hours and busy and productive and healthy like the people around me I used to do this before I've gone back Can I go back *Why can't you just*

fucking function? Can you feel everyone looking at you Quentin They can probably smell you too I'm going back and doing a procedure to cut the thoughts out of my head and undo the damage I've *What you're talking about is a time machine*

A time machine An imagining leap to take me back and restore me to how I am I mean I will be I will be journeying there and become again Be alive in a different moment in time I will take a deep breath and start again again I am here but my mind in four months ago and To rewrite and reform myself re-form myself my

Fuck you fuck you I'll kill you I'll smash my fucking head in against a computer screen *Look at what's become of the great scholar Write a masque about the whole sorry fucking situation write and think and think and then write because it's just what you do*

Sitting at a computer in a public library or internet café or British Library like today When it closed I would slope back to my flat and cry and shout and didn't do any of it did I I Milton Milton and my life was just this and only

What if I could change places with the girl in front of me here or this guy sneaking up behind her with a big grin? Could not be any worse for me *never never won't do it and then say it and then*

The time you missed the time you weren't present listening to the fun events unable to

the time when you just weren't anymore easeful death you are not present anymore to *I'm not gonna touch anyone I'm not gonna hurt anyone I'm not gonna go n...* **THUMP**

Crunch.

I open my streaming eyes and I'm on the floor with blood flowing from my extremely painful nose. Great. Just great.

Christ's College Cambridge, September 2001

Mother is making my bed, having neatly folded away all of my clothes. Bless her. Dad is sizing up my room in that engineering-focused way that Dads seem to have. He's testing out cupboard doors and knocking on walls, presumably to see if they're hollow? Freedom and untold pleasures are ahead of me, but my parents are still very much here and cramping my style.

'Very posh indeed,' says Dad of my en-suite bathroom. 'Look at us, love,' he says to Mum, 'the parents of a genius! Christ's College Cambridge! Christ! Who would've thought it?'

'I got all of my brains from you, didn't I Mum,' I say to her as she begins unpacking my big Milton and Wordsworth and Spenser and Chaucer collected volumes.

'I don't know about that, love,' she says, 'but you must've got them from somewhere.' We both turn to Dad as he fiddles with the showerhead.

'Pressure's not very good on this,' he says, with a thin trickle of water coming out. 'Might need to speak to the caretaker before we go. Look.'

'Dad,' I say, 'that's really not necess...'

'Aaaaaaarcgh!' Hot water covers Dad.

'Guess the pressure's okay after all,' I say to Mum.

Mum and Dad have finally departed. We have something called orientation in half an hour, followed by dinner in the oh so posh Christ's dining hall. I'm going to skip all of that and head into town for a drink or two by myself. It's five forty-five and the light is still bright outside. It's things like neat lawns and matriculation ceremonies, and students from Eton (not poor Grammar boys like myself) that people love about Cambridge, about the idea of Cambridge. I can't help imagining a young John Milton walking through here. Twelfth of February 1625, even he couldn't have foreseen a summer of plague. I move under the arch and past the porter's office and a balding man in uniform calls out to me.

'Excuse me, young man.'
'Yes?'
'Are you a new student here?'
'Yes, sir,' I say, 'my name's Quentin Carter.' We shake hands.
'Delighted to meet you, Quentin, my name is Raymond Burnage and I have been head porter here at Christ's for fifteen years. I'm sure you and I will get to know one another well over the course of the year.'
'I'd like that very much,' I say.
'Are you venturing into the town already, Mr Carter, by yourself?'
'Yes, Mr Burnage,' I say, 'I've never been keen on meet and greet sessions. I thought I'd just pop into town and have a walk around, soak up the atmosphere.'
'Try not to soak up too much atmosphere on your first night here, Mr Carter. Remember also that there is a ten o'clock curfew for all residents to be back on college premises on Sunday nights. You will soon realize that at Christ's we care about our students as if they were our family.'
'I won't soak up too much atmosphere, sir, just the right amount.'
He laughs. 'Good. See you later then, Mr Carter.'
There's a little notice on the counter of the porter's reception that says: 'Please ring bell for ATTENDANT'. Speaking Latin to his tutors and fellow students; choosing the life of the mind and soul over that of the Church. Groups of undergraduates swarm around me. They seem to be bosom friends already. A few of them try to jostle me as I sail against the tide. All part of the atmosphere of the place, I suppose. I'm never gonna soak up too much of the atmosphere. Unnecessary physical contact to be avoided. There's a foot bridge about fifty metres down the road from a pub positively spilling over with freshers. Never going to. The handrail is cold to the touch as I lean over. The river rumbles on through the city as the students come and go every year. Has it ever given a damn about any of us? And Milton and Lycidas and

leaving your mark somewhere. And what of the life of the Church? The ultimate source of salvation for all of us sinners. There's a dank aroma in the air that warns against an excess of poetically inclined musing on my first night here. I hear chanting coming from the vicinity of the pub. The water wends its way through thick clumps of river reeds, feeding and moving them. I was worried at one stage that I might be asked to share a room. Privacy and routine. Tennis team tryouts next weekend. The full life and keeping it all going.

    When will my debut student salting take place? The things we utter in the safety of our own minds. The secrecy if not the safety. Don't go on about Milton and the history of the place to the other freshers, they'll think you're some sort of weirdo. The fearfulness that unites the herd. I haven't had the loftiest upbringing, but then neither had Milton. The son of a scrivener, with a career in the Church mapped out for him, but young John had other ideas. He saw tyranny all around him. Time was not unlimited in an atmosphere wherein the Second Coming was anticipated any day. How do you stand out in a place where knowing things isn't enough? Is it even advisable to try?

    The water dances with river nymphs who frolic and dive and beckon me to join them in the river and on down into the depths. I could be sweet Lycidas, tumbling to a sweet subterranean death, a quieting

    I have my copy of *The Sound and the Fury* in my pocket. I never go anywhere without a book, and this one is always my comfort blanket of choice when facing new situations. That sounds so pathetic. I wonder how the guys are getting on at uni? Haven't heard from any of them yet. Everything breaks down at these times of transition.

    The river nymphs are writhing a sensuous dance; they beckon me to lay my head on a soft pillow; the reeds will support me; the nymphs will give me oxygen - the 'black-eyed angels' of the Pyramid Song played by Miles Davis on a trumpet removed from a brown paper bag

    I have an urge to throw my book into the Cam as a salute

to my literary heroes, but I can't bring myself to part with it. There will be no watery grave for this prodigy. I scream at the top of my lungs:

and / lo! from all his limbs Celestial...

But of course I only scream inside my head. That's the kind of thing I would do with the lads back at home after a few pints: spouting poetry at the top of my voice. I move along the side of the river towards a particular drinking joint I have in mind for tonight. I light my first cigarette of the evening and send my meditations floating away on a sea of the bluest smoke...into the river...

The Spread Eagle. I walk in and there's jazz filling the air. I sit down at the bar, order a double scotch, and take out my book. I light another cigarette. The bar feels solid and gives me a pleasing sense of permanence. My life at home was ordered because it had to be. The shelves behind the bar hold bottles of every spirit one could think of. The proprietor is a black American named Henry Lawes. He places my drink down on a red napkin with a bowl of peanuts to keep it company. I have a strange, a funny mind you might say.

'Here you go,' he says in a voice that is cooler than cool and sounds like it's been mainlined directly from a Miles Davis recording session. I bumped into a guy who was in the year above me at school over the summer. He'd just finished his first year at Cambridge and the thing he really wanted to tell me about was this pub and this man, Henry Lawes.

'Thanks very much,' I say.

'You a student?' he asks while wiping down the bar.

'It's the book, isn't it?' I say. 'It gave me away.'

He laughs. 'The book and other things,' he says, 'you just give off that vibe. No reason you should hide it. Which college?'

'Christ's,' I say. He pours himself a drink.

'Cheers,' he says. We clink glasses. I have an overwhelming

wish that this man should continue to like me. 'The college of the poet.'

'Yes,' I say, with too much enthusiasm. He puts down his cloth and leans towards me.

'What's your name?'

'Quentin.' I've finished my drink.

'Can I tempt you to another?'

'Please.'

He fixes my second scotch. 'The way I see it,' he says as he faces away from me and produces the always pleasing sound of a bottle being uncorked, 'when you're a jazz man you really got all the poetry you need from the music, but that don't mean you don't look for the jazz in other things, know what I mean?'

I sit up straight. I'm the young John at one of his university debates. 'Milton worshipped Virgil and Shakespeare, but he'd have wanted to BE Miles Davis. They both had that fearless, fuck you attitude to art and to life.' Stop talking. Never open your mouth too much. Never going to.

Henry serves another customer so I take a drink and think about what I've just said. Genius would surely know and appreciate genius regardless of a few hundred years; be it Joyce, or Faulkner, or Milton, or Davis. The golden locks of the scholar Milton and the big shades of the late era Miles. Miles Milton and John Davis, Miles Milton and Sir John Davis ... The junkie Miles battling hard to kick his habit; the women, the chaos, the drugs, but always that fierce desire to move forwards, to be better, to innovate. Two men living and creating according to their own rhythm. Two boxers making the other guy dance to their tune. I used to manage things very carefully. I never talked to anyone about this. Not a single soul. People assaulting each other. Never never never go near.

'Be careful of that thirst, young sir,' says Henry.

It takes me a moment to realise he is talking to me.

'Sorry, I was away and awash with the river nymphs, Henry.'

'That's what I thought.'

'What did you mean about thirst?'

'Just that there's good and bad thirsts and good and bad

ways of quenching them.'

'Yes, I suppose you're right,' I say. 'Are you playing tonight, Henry?' Stop using his name.

'Oh yeah, I'll be bringin' the horn out just after ten.'

'That's a shame, I have a curfew.' The tiredness of the day seeping into my bones.

'You can sleep here in the bar if needs be,' he says.

I fill up with warmth celestial. 'That's a lovely gesture, Henry, but I was expressly reminded of the curfew by the college porter.'

'Just keep it in mind,' he says. 'A few drinks, some jazz, an opportunity...' He leaves this hanging and walks away.

The jangling rhythm of the jazz combines with the sharp sweetness of the liquor to move me into a fine mood. The place has filled up as my third scotch dwindles. I crunch a handful of the salted nuts. I put the drink down on my book and then pick it up again and swill it around. I should remember the words of the porter and be a wise rather than a foolish fresher. There's a lady with a dog sitting in one of the booths and sipping a gin and tonic.

Never never never go go go Ever ever never go near anyone at all ever

My thoughts, my thoughts. I look around and take notice of the other staff in the place, and one member of staff in particular; she's tall, with peroxide blonde spikes gelled into extreme states that flash and flow about her partially shaven head. She wears denim shorts with a light blue t-shirt. Her navel is pierced and her stomach toned. She has a tattoo of a snake coiling around her right arm, and there are sharp and dangerous-looking objects sticking out of her ears and nose. She comes out from behind the bar with a round of drinks and leans in to me:

'Take a fucking picture, love, it lasts longer.' Her accent is decidedly plummy.

'Madam!' I call after her.

She swings around without disturbing any of the glasses on the tray. 'Did you really just call me madam?'

'Yes, sorry,' I say, 'I don't know your name, I'm Quentin Carter.' I extend my hand, which she ignores.

'How formal of you, Mr Carter.'

'Well, let's dispense with the formalities. I'm Quentin, and you are?'

'Busy.'

And with that she's back behind the bar, chatting to customers who are presumably regulars. I hear a bearded gent at the bar call her 'Derby' when he orders a whisky sour. The scotch is flowing, as is the atmosphere. Henry is on stage giving a passable impersonation of Miles Davis as he plays 'Spanish Key' with the band. I let the music wash over me, this track that I've heard countless times but am hearing for the first time here tonight. Derby sits down beside me at the bar.

Never never ever Never not touch will not ever Never go near

'Hello Derby,' I say.

'What are you looking for?' she says.

'Tonight or in general?' She shrugs.

'Well, tonight I think I'm just looking to relax and have some fun.' She raises an eyebrow. 'Speaking more generally, I have my ambitions and plans.'

'You seem to have an excess of ambition to me. You seem to want an awful lot for yourself.'

'No more than is due to me, I wouldn't say. No more than anyone else wants for themselves, commensurate with their abilities. Show me a student at Cambridge who professes not to have ambition and I will show you a liar. But I have thoughts that rove about.' Did I say that last part out loud? Please stop talking, Quentin.

I will never go near to

'And what of your ordinary people, your people who work to survive, without notions of Milton or ambition?'

'I don't understand the question.'

'Of course you don't, young man, because you are high on the liquid academic air of Cambridge. But you will understand that soon enough. You think the mind is all, don't you. May I quote to you from your favourite poet?'

'By all means.' You can't stop someone when they want to quote poetry.

Touched her. Didn't touch her didn't

'thou shouldst not know / More happiness than this thy present lot.' She sits back on her stool as if her point has been made.

'Comus,' I say. 'How does that apply to me?'

Murdered and raped or raped and murdered them both of them. But simply look around you; it's all you have to do. We're in a public place and everybody's fine. You simply could not have done it.

'You will see, scholar, in time. I bet you were head boy, weren't you?'

'Hold on a moment, you don't even kn...'

'Answer the question.'

'Yes, I was. Is that a crime?'

'Academic star, good at sport, popular?'

'If you say so.' I don't want to play this game.

'But won't everyone be like that here?'

I just shrug. *Punch her in the face.*

'You'll need to find out who you really are now. Beyond all that Cambridge application stuff, you know?'

'How do you know all this?' I say.

'Give some thought to what I said.'

It seems the conversation is over as Derby turns to watch Henry exit the stage amidst considerable applause. *Smash her in the face with the glass*

Touch not and go near Never

I jump down from the stool and clatter straight into Henry and Derby.

'Whoa there, horse,' says Henry, taking my arm.

'Thank you, Henry. I'm gonna call it a night after a quick detour to the gents. I wish you both a pleasant evening.'

I have to turn back at the door to the toilets to make sure

they are both fine. They are both fine. They are talking and laughing. There is no blood anywhere. Everything is normal and as it should be. Take a few breathes. I feel so tired.

I arrive back at the college but to my surprise and no little degree of alarm the porter's office is closed and the gates are locked. I guess he was serious about the half-ten curfew. What would Milton do in this situation? Better find a hotel somewhere. Better start budgeting from tomorrow. Is that a rumble of thunder in the night air? I light a cigarette, and I'm off. *A beaten and bloodied Derby crying for help.* But she was fine when I left. I could go back. Don't be ridiculous.

Eighteen months later

The university's day service for students experiencing psychiatric difficulties. They must be used to seeing despair in their consulting rooms, so matter of fact. A way of carrying on studying while you recover. Take the pills. Mum and Dad are with me. What about my Milton tutorial? I can't sit down to read or do the work, so what do I do? Just do your best and things will get easier. On Monday I catch a bus to the service, having sat in silence through my two-hour Milton tutorial. Everybody looking at me and waiting for me to speak. I sit in the day room and answer questions from one of the members of staff. Each of his attempts to make conversation falters with me. We have a group session. I never believed in this sort of thing. From one group to another. I won't touch him and I didn't. The day room is downstairs while the doctors' consulting rooms are upstairs. On Tuesday I'm feeling desperate so I wait for one of the senior members of staff to see me after the group. We talk and he tells me to relax and go easy on myself. He says on Thursday the doctor will see me. What about today? He says take care of yourself, have a good meal tonight, don't worry about studying, and the doctor will see me on Thursday. The shepherds and the flock. One thought replaces another. You raped, you murdered, you hit them, you touched them. When Thursday comes, I'm late for my appointment because I don't get to sleep till the early hours of the morning. I'm late so I have to wait. I see the staff and then eventually I see one of the doctors. He writes me a new prescription and I tell him I'm going to be late for a tutorial, having missed another one this morning.

'Will it be difficult for you to walk in halfway through?' he asks. I don't understand the question so I shake my head. 'Go and catch your bus then,' he says.

He begins to quote Milton but the door slams behind me and cuts him off. Keeping up appearances at the tutorial. Was the doctor okay when I left him? I'm forty minutes late and this draws a raised eyebrow from my tutor. Letters from the university are building up. Warnings regarding non-attendance. Invitations for me to meet with the Dean to discuss my absences. I do not communicate but I do talk. I talk away at the centre to no end or purpose. This is what they call the talking cure. At this time, I am either numb from the depression or high from the respite of release. A never a never a never in my head.

What I realized in the years after the 2003 crash was that when your mental health deserts you it feels like all is well with the world apart from you. By any standards 2003 was an horrendous year; an illegal and unjustified invasion of Iraq motivated by nothing other than pure greed; the largest ever peaceful demonstration in the history of British democracy ignored; Bush and Blair responding to the terrible events of September 11th 2001 with the politics of fear and hatred, descending to the level of the terrorists. And yet during 04 to late 06 I would look back on 03 with a sort of yearning.

I experienced 9/11 as millions around the world did, through the tv screen. I was three weeks away from starting at Cambridge. I felt tears welling up on that day for the plight of the innocent people in those two towers. There was an eerie atmosphere in the days immediately after, as if the world might come to an end, but it didn't stop me from going out drinking and clubbing with my friends from school as if nothing had happened. The little thoughts always happened on those nights out. The next morning: You did this last night; you caused harm.

Nothing ever affected me like my first OCD crash. It affected me far more than 9/11 or the wars in Iraq and Afghanistan. If I had lost a friend or relative on September 11th or serving in Iraq or Afghanistan, would that still be the case? When your fog lifts, the fog of the world lifts with it. I had returned to Cambridge after a pleasant Christmas break. I had exams but wasn't unduly worried about them; I'd studied a lot over the holidays amidst nights out in London with old school friends. As soon as my parents dropped me off at the house I shared with five friends, I felt ill at ease. I saw friends, I spoke to them, I went through the motions. I went out and walked around and breathed the air but Cambridge no longer seemed to have the same magnificence that it had just four short weeks ago. Everything felt distant, nothing felt real somehow. What comes back to me from that time is the strange odor in my room from all the time I spent in there; unwashed, hungry, and not wanting to face any of the other people in the house. Every act was a sin. Every memory a torment. Every thought a crime to be punished. A couple of days before the Easter break it dawned on me that my mind was now different. Changed utterly. A numbness had set in that I had no way out of. My mind told me that I had done all of this to myself.

I sat down in the library and tried to study. I tried some Chaucer, then some Gawain, but to no avail. The words were the same but the meaning had gone. The grasshopper cannot jump. I got up and went for a walk for no other reason than to escape my books. I felt surrounded by people. I decided to go to the toilet and lock myself in the cubicle. If I could just get there without...

Three girls walked past me. I squeezed up as close to the wall as I could. I was hot, uncomfortable, and starting to perspire. The thought that I had just raped one of the girls blasted into my mind, implanting itself in my consciousness, booked in for a nice long stay. It had an almost physical impact, a knockout blow.

Paralysis and analysis. Research has shown that repeated checking is not an effective method of calming anxiety or reinforcing factual acceptance in the OCD mind or the non-OCD mind. I didn't know that then.

I made it to the toilet and locked the cubicle door. The wall was covered in scribbled student graffiti. I knew the game was up; I could feel my heart thumping through my chest. By the time I returned to uni I was a year behind and my friends had moved on. Did I think I could just pick up where I left off, keep the monster at bay? Monsters don't really respond very well to being contained, do they? And they certainly don't take kindly to being treated lightly and neglected. Nine months of hell? Something tells me it won't be so easy this time. I want to fucking kill myself. Split infinitive.

Saturday February 15th 2003 was a momentous day on which people made their feelings known. Hundreds of thousands marched in the name of peace, while others enjoyed squash and lovely fish stews. I was holed up in my room having not eaten for days. No one noticed the unwashed figure I was cutting when I did venture out of doors. Would I have been one of the marchers on that day? No. There would have been far too many diversions to occupy a healthy Quentin. I might have watched on the news and sympathised, but then again I might not have done. And would I have noticed if a friend of mine stopped going out, stopped eating, stopped washing? I'd like to think so. But university is about fun. And the fun has to go on even if one of the gang is no longer along for the ride.

When the OCD takes hold, it doesn't really matter what's going on in the world. The sufferer's head is the world and it's a crumbling, perhaps already fallen empire. It's impossible to be immersed in the moment or in something bigger than yourself because what you are experiencing is not the moment or the world as you used to know it. Looking back, looking back, that's what you're doing all the time. If you can be said to live anywhere, it's in a romanticized, golden past in which you could cope with life and from this distance you had no problems at all.

I remember lying in my room, hearing footsteps go by outside. I would call my parents and talk and talk until I realized it did no good, and I think they did too. I would have the radio on or play the same dvd over and over, the barest, most tenuous connection to the outside world. As the war drew closer, I remember listening to a phone-in for families of the troops; they told stories and requested records. But I was only listening in an abstract way. I shut myself away in order to escape from people, to escape from those OCD flashes. I was in a prison of my mind's making. The room began to smell unpleasant.

I'm not gonna hurt anyone, I'm not gonna touch anyone, I'm not gonna go near anyone. Fuck off.

Exit. Pursued by a bear. Comus and his rout of monsters are dancing through Quentin's head; perform a compulsion, perform a compulsion, perform a compulsion. Do it do it do it. Check check check check check... Where is my Attendant Spirit? Not in Attendance. He doesn't attend to the sick, only the mentally well...

Fade to black.

Part Two: Ali

'till she reviv'd / And underwent a quick immortal change, / Made Goddess of the River.'

Milton, 'Comus'

London, August 2012

'Hey, fancy a coffee?' says Andrew, my new flat mate.

'Yes please, you read my mind.' He brought the coffee machine with him when he moved into this previously all-female flat.

'What can I do for you? Cappuccino, latte, americano?' His darkly bearded face breaks into a big smile.

'I would kill for a cappuccino please.'

'No murders will be necessary. Have a seat at the breakfast bar.' I do as instructed and watch as he gets milk from the fridge and works away at the machine. Ritual and ceremony wherever I go.

'Tough day?' he says.

'Just long and tiring,' I say with a forced smile. So many days like this one.

'Are you working tonight?' says Andrew.

'No, thank God. Night off tonight.' I have two part-time jobs as well as my uni studies. Satan makes work. 'You are good at that. You could work in a Soho café.'

'I might just do that if the whole uni thing doesn't pan out.'

'What were you doing today?' I ask these things because they are expected.

'Looking at rocks, as per.' He gives the impression that he would rather be a barista if it were up to him. We students criticise our own subjects a lot, but woe betide anyone else who does so.

'What are you reading this week?' he asks.

'The Mill on the Floss,' I say.

'Any good? Here you are. May all your troubles melt away.'

He places the drink in front of me on a saucer. He has even dusted it with chocolate. I feel like crying.

'You like chocolate on top, right?'

'Of course,' I say. I take a sip and it is delicious. 'Mmm, thank you. This is just what I needed.'

He begins to clean out the coffee grounds in preparation for the creation of his own beverage. Another one of our flatmates comes into the kitchen and we say hi to her and exchange pleasantries. Andrew and I fall silent while she fixes herself some cereal, doubtless fuel for a night of intensive studying. We are all mature students. It is more like sharing with other adults than a real student flat. We even have a cleaning rota that everybody adheres to almost religiously. I do not really know this girl, but then I do not really know Andrew that well. I have at least begun to talk to him fairly regularly. She leaves and we resume our conversation. It does strange things to your mind when you go too long without talking to anyone, without really talking to anyone. Your heart begins to value even the most basic daily interactions.

'Are we all drop-outs here?' I say.

'I'm sorry?' he says.

'I mean what is your story? Did you drop out of uni before?'

'I never went to uni before. I was caring for my Mother and working after I did A-levels. I never really had the chance to go to uni back then. I always wanted to, though.'

'So what changed for you?' I sip my lovely drink. It is a strange for me to take the role of the inquisitor. I am usually on the receiving end of incessant questions from my Mother and seemingly everybody else. I have to call her tonight.

He looks away for a moment and rubs at his beard. 'My Mother died,' he says.

'I'm sorry,' I say.

'It sounds horrible to say it but I'm free to do as I like now.' He rubs his beard again then puts his hands in his pockets.

'Sorry for bringing it up.' I turn away from him and rest my head on my hand. He continues to make his drink in silence. The evening darkness is falling and I am beginning to feel hungry. He seats himself next to me at the breakfast bar.

'I don't mind you asking about my Mother,' he says. 'It's nice to meet someone who actually cares.'

'I was primary carer for my Mother at one time, before uni — the first time, I mean. She was hit by a car.'

'What did you have to do for her?' I am about to correct him but I stop myself as I know this is just a figure of speech.

'Everything. My Dad had died two years earlier. She was in a coma for several weeks. When she came to she had incurred brain damage and was confined to a wheelchair.'

'God,' he says.

'We were close before the accident and even closer afterwards.'

'People think caring for someone is so hard, but it's also a way of coping. You can keep busy and tell yourself that you're okay.'

'I think you may be right,' I say. 'I'm not sure a lot of carers ever ask the question of whether they're okay.' My mouth feels so try so I take a sip.

'If you don't mind my asking, what's your story?' he says. 'You tend to keep yourself to yourself.'

'I was not always like that,' I say. 'I dropped out a few years ago. Because of a boy.'

'Are you still together?'

'I'm sorry, but I cannot even begin to answer that question right now.' He takes a big gulp of his drink, as if filling the awkwardness with physical movement. 'Listen, I think we both need a night off. How about we get something to eat?'

'I really should work,' he says.

He is wavering, I can tell.

'My treat to say thanks for the coffee.'

'Okay, sure, why not?'

'Give me half an hour?' I say.

'Great.'

'Hey Mum.' My desk is filling up with nik nacks and little souvenirs that I would rather not look at. There is all manner of smoking paraphernalia from ashtrays to cigarette tins and different kinds of lighters. I also have a couple of pipes. How would I ever explain these objects to another person? Not that other people ever come into my room.

'No, I have not and I will not be anymore.' What is the term for a collector who cannot even look at their collection? I have many books piled up on the floor. 'Please don't spend so much of your time worrying about him...Can you please simply do as I ask for a change?'

I surprised myself by reaching out to Andrew, if that indeed is what I just did. I open my wardrobe and look for an appropriate top to wear for a – what? It is not a date. A human contact and warmth.

'Mother, I know very well what his condition is. The situation has changed now ... no it is not in the past ... it makes no difference if it was before this happened ... Why does it matter how it looks?' But of course it always does seem to matter how things look. 'The two situations are so different that there is simply no comparison, Mum...Well, you did not betray me over and over and break my heart. How would you have felt if Dad had done this to you?' I can feel the tears waiting for their moment again. Why did I say that. Hurting myself and hurting her. 'What have you been up to anyway?'

Her social life is far busier than mine, not that that is at all difficult. I like to hear about her friends and the various clubs and societies she belongs to. She is learning to love books again for the first time since the accident.

'Try The Mill on the Floss, Mum. Yeah, we can compare notes...Great...Yes...I will call you in a few days to find out how you are getting on...Yes?...Okay, if you must...I know I need to do something about it but it's not that simple, is it...Yeah, love you too...God bless you too. Bye.'

This top one will do fine. I pick a lighter from my collection and place it in my pocket with a shudder. I just have time to change. I touch the beads and the Bible on my night table before I leave. I always seem to do this now. God bless you – those words on my lips. Is He watching me right now?

We avoid any further personal conversations as we munch our way through a pizza and a couple of bottles of lager. We are content to keep to small talk.

'Here we are then,' I say as we reach the front door of the flat.

'Yes, yes indeed,' he says. 'That was really nice. We should do it a...'

I kiss him on the mouth. He looks as if his mind has gone blank. I kiss him again and there are tongues involved. He places his hands on the sides of my head. Then he pulls away.

'Hey, hey, Ali, er what is this?'

'Nothing,' I say, 'nothing.' I am not lying. We kiss again and this time his arms are around me. We go in and I lead him to my bedroom. 'Close the door,' I whisper. I am quickly standing before him in my underwear. I have never done anything like this. He begins to take his jumper and t-shirt off.

'What about your boyfriend?'

'That is for me to worry about.' Never was a truer word spoken. I help him to remove the rest of his clothes.

'I don't have any you know whats,' he says.

'No need to worry about that,' I say.

'What about our friendship?' he says while kissing my neck.

'We barely know each other,' I say. I push him onto the bed and get in after him. Thou shalt not...

One foot in front of the other, this is how to survive. I am up early and moving. This is what I tell myself to do and it feels good. I have uni seminars later so my bag is packed with today's books. Reading is my escape from reality and I think it always has been; a way of immersing myself in worlds far removed from my own: Hardy, Dickens – those big books with their big ideas. I have washed my hair, selected an outfit for the day and am tastefully made up. What one might call keeping up appearances. Doing these things because I am meant to do them. On my way out of the flat I slip a scrawled note under Andrew's door saying I hope he has a good day and I will see him later. Will we sleep together again?

The usual whistles from the apes working in high-vis jackets on one of the seemingly never-ending construction sites on Berwick Street. They seem a little disappointed not to get any response from me. How did you guys meet? Well, you know, it was the funniest thing, this one here wolf whistled at me as I was walking past! He shouted "all right, darling?" at me and my heart simply melted. What exactly goes on inside those heads inside their hard hats?

A triple espresso and fruit scone in My Place, a little Soho café. I usually do a bit of reading here but today I find it difficult to focus this early. I gaze into the deep black liquid for a little while and then I spread my butter and jam on the scone. I keep myself dosed up on caffeine every day; I try to maintain regular habits just because. There is a shop around here on Old Compton Street that sells beans from every coffee-producing country in the world. Nowadays I pay little attention to the beans and the flavours. I simply require a morning espresso or two to provide me with some clarity until lunch. They have a pile of free copies of a local arts newspaper. There are some lively things going on but I struggle to take any of it in. I am along the wall by the window and there is a bag on the bench seat beside me. I look around then pull it towards me. It is an HMV bag. I look inside and see a cd of Miles Davis' *Kind of Blue*. I am familiar with the name of the artist but this music leaves me cold. It is a sin against musical orthodoxies. The bag is now on the table. The tables will be split and the Lord will put them together again. I slip the bag into my leather jacket pocket. I sip the coffee and read again a feature on graffiti art: roses springing up through cracks in the pavement throughout the city. How lovely. It is eight thirty. Time for me to be going. There is no one at the counter as I swing my bag up onto my shoulder. I have no time to wait; I will hand in the bag with the cd in it tomorrow.

    I light a cigarette outside My Place, my first of the day. I do not have time to linger over my cigarette. I can hear birds and the sun is already beating down ... 'sun-clad power of chastity'. Snippets of verse popping in. The cigarette is still warm as it consumes itself between my ringed fingers. Chastity does not mean a great deal to me after my recent discovery. I have nearly a full pack of Camels for the rest of the day. God, my hair is a mess. It is sticking out all over the place. Final drag. Crunch it underfoot. The violence of destruction and just wiping it all away.

    I am in the churchyard now so no more cigarettes. I walk the long path among the gravestones. The path is covered with bird poop. There are a couple of people standing by gravestones and a man pushes a wheelbarrow along with gardening tools. St George's Catholic Church, Sansome Street. Who would ever have thought that I would be setting foot in a church again after school? We always go back, every one of us. We go back to our earliest learnings. We return to our Mother.

    The door clangs shut. Choose a pew near the front for closeness to God. The pew creaks when I sit down. Mother always says they made them uncomfortable, that you were not supposed to be comfortable in Church. Somebody is playing a hymn even at this hour of the day. The priest is near the altar. I estimate that he is in his mid-to-late thirties. He sits down. Beams of light fall upon me. Am I about to receive a communication from God?

There are beautiful colours illuminated by natural light. To Church and school as a child: scenes of the Passion, of Christ carrying the cross, Christ on the cross. Inside a church you could be anywhere.

'How are you today, Ali?' His face is kindly. His question is honest. He asks like he wants to know the answer.

'No change.' I have to answer honestly. I see myself as selfish, but I do not wish to appear so before this man who sees the good in everybody. What to make of that.

'Does coming here help you, Ali?'

'It's peaceful here. There's no judgment here.'

'Do other people judge you?'

'I have no one else to talk to. I talk to my Mother, but that is different. I slept with one on my flatmates, which obviously only adds to the feelings of guilt.' Is this too much? Stop being a child; he's a priest not my parent.

'Are you still in communication with your boyfriend?'

His tone is neutral. I can take his language at face value. Asking if it helps; not assuming it does.

'No, I find it too difficult. I just go from anger at him to hatred of myself and round and round,' I say. Wondering if this is indeed how I feel as I'm saying it.

'You are judging yourself. You've had a terribly hard time. Coming here every morning seeking God's help shows that you're a good person.'

Is that really what I'm doing here? I hadn't thought about it like that. Is there a point to being a good person, or trying to be one? Give me the grace of the Lord and I shall be fine.

'Are we not being judged by God all of the time, though?' I need the beads in my hands for this.

'Leave such things in God's hands. Open your heart to Him and He will do the rest. His ways are mysterious to us.'

The door clangs again. Welcome to another pilgrim seeking solace from the world; the sanctuary offered to all by The Church.

'I ditched my faith like I'm ditching him. I only came back

when I was desperate.'

'But you did come back, Ali. God has been with you throughout your life. He never closes the door or abandons one of His flock. He is aware of our frailty and He still loves us. I will just be one moment.'

Frailty. He moves off to tend to his lost sheep. I kneel on the cushion. I look over to my right and see a window made up of long, thin images. There is Christ with an angel looking down on Him. Crowds come to Christ to be healed and he takes them in his arms. This is the space between heaven and earth, with Christ having a foot in both worlds. What can the Church offer me? Please God tell me what to do. A tear rolls down my cheek and crashes onto the cushion as I clamber to my feet. The cheating should surely make this easier? Why do people continue to believe when God never answers their prayers? We expect forgiveness from God, but why can I not forgive? My head begins to spin and my eyes close up. He could not possibly answer the prayers of every believer. The long-term believers probably have as little chance of being heard as I have, and yet here I be. Every morning.

I open my eyes and look around. The priest and his sheep have disappeared from view. I walk towards the altar and stand before it. So many times. The priest and the lamb of God and me. Back in His favour? I see the gleaming and gold of a large candleholder, beautiful in the daylight from the stained-glass windows. Set the table thusly. I pick it up and feel its weight. My place in the Lord's book. The top of it is encircled with miniature depictions of Christ on the cross that sit beneath a jewel-encrusted crown. I place the candleholder in my bag and swing it over my shoulder. Is my Lord a jealous God who blots the sinful from His book? I glance at my watch – it is 9:30. A Lord who send locusts and slays the first born as if it were nothing. Time for a morning session at the British library followed by an afternoon tutorial on The Mill on the Floss.

Part Three: A tap on the shoulder

'Gentle swain, at thy request / I am here!'

Milton, 'Comus'

Outside The British Library, August 2012

I saw her in the distance, towards the front of the queue for the bag check. I'd always enjoyed the little ritual of having my bags checked by serious but friendly men in white shirts and black ties. It gives one a slight feeling of importance. I'm afraid we're going to have to speak to you privately, sir. Please come with me. The suspect is armed and highly dangerous. I recognized her from the elective I was doing in Victorian Lit. I actually giggled to myself as I crept up towards her. I was the bringer of jocularity! The clown prince and Fool of the royal Court! The man who laughs and the world laughs with him. The romantic comedy of the dorky prankster who of course eventually gets the girl.

She was reading a book that she held in her left hand, while her right hand rested on a brown leather bag with long tassels that hung from the same shoulder. A few of the tassels fluttered in the breeze that circled the piazza. Exterior. The bounty hunter arrives in the small town with the sun beating down. He takes out a neckerchief to mop his brow. Close up on his dirty face with several days' growth of stubble. He and his horse look sleep deprived and hypervigilant. There have been eyes on him from behind windows and the cracks in doors since he rode into town. He moves slightly in the saddle and pats the horse, whispering something in its ear (something just between the two of them). He checks the two guns on his belt and the shotgun in a holster on the side of the horse. The shotgun has been fired recently. As he reloads and flicks the empty cartridges onto the baking earth, we get a tracking shot to the roof of the saloon opposite where we can just about make out two armed figures crouched and ready for ambush. Close up on the eyes of the bounty hunter as they narrow. Before the two no-goods can get off a shot, the bounty hunter unloads both barrels of the shot gun. The men come rolling down from the roof amidst screams of pain. The bounty hunter says something else to his horse, pats it and dismounts. While walking slowly over to where the men are writhing in the bloodied earth, the bounty hunter lights a cigarette from a match struck against his beard and then pulls a roll of paper from the inside pocket of his fringed leather jacket. A close up reveals two wanted posters which he holds up and compares the likenesses with faces of the men before him. Satisfied that he has indeed got his men, the bounty hunter pulls out his two pistols and blows them away without a second thought. All in a day's work. The queue was moving quickly as usual and she was almost at the open bronze door. I made the briefest eye contact with the person standing behind her in the queue. He was a tall, brown haired, youthful looking chap. Even in the midst of my act, I couldn't help but notice the sad, faraway look in his eyes. His expression barely flickered as I mimed for him to stay quiet and not give me away. He and his horse need a drink and a comfortable place to sleep. Once I was close enough to her I tapped her twice on the shoulder very briskly and crouched down to her left. But first he needs to collect on the two lumps of dead meat lying before him. Her reaction was quicker, louder, and more forceful than I was expecting.

'Hey,' she shouted as the book fell to the floor.

I barely had time to register the alarm in her voice when she swung round to her right with such force that the bag flew out in a wide ark before crunching, with a dull thud and a slight crack, into the nose of the fellow standing behind her. Her eyes flitted quickly between pitied victim and me. In other circumstances, I might have just scurried off to avoid a scene. Not today, my friend. Today I was taking names and collecting on wanted posters.

'I'm so sorry,' I said, 'that was all my fault.' Blood spewed from his nose; tears streamed from his eyes. He was down on his knees like Elias from Platoon. I couldn't help playing the Adagio for Strings in my head. 'Should we get him to a hospital?' This last was addressed to the girl, Ali (her name had come to me), and she looked at me with shock and confusion in her rather nice brown eyes. I realized she was also trying to place me. Who was this idiot who had tapped her on the shoulder and caused all this carnage? I was slightly hurt by this. We'd spoken several times in class, and cordially too.

'I can't believe you did that,' she said.

'I'm so sorry,' I said, 'I was just coming to say hello and talk about George Eliot.' We both noticed her book on the ground at the same time. I bent down to pick it up and so did she, with the inevitable collision. 'Sorry.'

She took the book and placed it in her bag with a slight clanging noise. She looked close to tears.

'Are you okay?' I said.

She sniffed and turned away. 'I am all right. Please help him.'

'Does anyone have a towel?' I called. That sounded practical. I was still a little miffed that she hadn't recognized me, if truth be told. Someone in the line had produced a towel. She took it and knelt down to the injured and increasingly bloody victim. Give 'em over to the local law enforcement. I just want my money and I'll be on my way.

'Here, hold this against your nose. Keep pressure on it,' she said. I started to feel like a bit of a spare part. She seemed to know what she was doing. 'I am so sorry. We're going to take you to hospital. I think your nose is broken.' Her manner was calm and professional, like a nurse's.

'Keep moving past us please,' I called out. 'Nothing to see here!' I wanted to add.

'Let me take a look at your nose.' She removed the rolled-up towel gently to reveal a scholarly, handsome face (all things considered). Wrong guy, wrong place, wrong time. Like John McClane! Ha! Sorry. He got invited to the British Library by mistake, who knew! I sometimes wonder if I should say these things out loud more often.

'I'll call an ambulance,' I said to no one in particular.

'Mmmmnhses.' It was the first thing he'd said. She moved the towel away from his mouth. 'Glasses,' he mumbled.

'Can anyone see this man's glasses anywhere?' I called. 'They must've flown off.'

The bystanders had a look round and quickly located a pair of perfectly round spectacles. He took the glasses but seemed at a loss as to what to do with them. Clearly putting them on his very much out of joint nose was not a practical option. My gaze fell on the offending bag. I wondered what on earth could be in that brown leather bag that would break a man's nose. I swung my Star Wars rucksack from side to side on my back. I hopped from one foot to the other and rubbed my hands together. I imagined myself a ninja on a mission, under cover of daylight. Being a film student was simply a cover story. The ways of the ninja; silent, untraceable, hidden in plain sight until he strikes! I had been to see the barber the day before. My closely cropped hair still felt somewhat itchy. I suddenly felt like singing for some reason. As my hand reached out to Ali's bag, two paramedics arrived on the scene. She continued to speak comforting words to the victim as the paramedics assessed the damage.

'Yes, that's a broken nose you've got there, Mr...?'

Our new friend looked around, almost in mock-frustration, before pulling his British Library card from the pocket of his jeans.

'Mr Q Carter,' read the same paramedic.

'We're going to take you to hospital, Mr Carter,' said his colleague.

'Mmmmmmmmmmhhh.'

'I will come in the ambulance with him,' said Ali with absolute finality. My first ever prank couldn't really have gone much worse. Perhaps I am no Fool? I am nobody's fool. I shoot first and I ask questions later. I also smoke a great deal of cigarettes and sleep with several dames. It's all part of my job as a hardboiled gumshoe with a smart mouth and an even smarter line in sniffing out a conspiracy.

Our little troupe shuffled across the piazza to the Euston Road where the ambulance was parked. As the paramedics helped Quentin onto the ambulance, Ali and I stood next to each other (she was having a cigarette before going in the ambulance). There was more of a spring in her step and in her voice now. I offered to go by bus and meet them at the hospital.
'Thank you,' she said.
She exhaled the last stream of bright blue smoke (which I did my best to breathe in without her noticing; I just like the smell). She stubbed out her cigarette and without so much as a see you later, climbed into the ambulance passenger seat. I puffed out my cheeks and chuckled to myself. I'd better go and get the bus. Pick up all the bus driver's teeth, Jack. Every day is your movie if you look closely enough. He really has a hardon for this bus.

The day before

It's raining in my heart! We were promised rain and rain we indeed do have. Storm clouds are visible from my window. I hope we have thunder and lightning today. I love it. A juicy juice for breakfast for me. I have reading to do today for tomorrow's screenplay tutorial. And yet and yet and yet yet yet. Victorian literature really isn't my thing. It's too staid and traditional. I require a more stimulating stream of words and visuals. Morning in Manhattan. We can hear ships in the harbour and the growing hubbub of the fish market. But there's something stirring in the deeps. A pre-historic creature has come to town for a party, and the dinner is on us!

Porridge, nuts, oats, berries and honey for breakfast. And a nice cup of Earl Grey. The balcony is cool at six-thirty. There is a light fall of rain on the few people walking around Soho. People heading for work and opening up shops and cafes. I would like to work on my film ideas today, but I have all of that reading for tomorrow. A couple of cyclists go shooting past with helmets and rucksacks. Time for my morning exercises.

What is the cause of thunder?
What is the cause of rain?
What is the origin of all life?
What is it that causes our pain?

Ten more minutes on the bike for me. I look forward to a lovely sugar-free Red Bull with ice from the new refrigerator. I'm sweating heavily. I turn up the music and adjust my earphones. ACDC this morning. Our pain and gain and blame. Working away to make myself better. Starting the day as I mean to go on.

Is lightning a beacon
And thunder a warning
To us. My thoughts go wherever they want to during morning workout. I'm flying over London and then Manhattan and watching the monsters fight among the skyscrapers. Everyone else is petrified but I swoop in and out of the limbs and the fire as they clash and roar. I jab at them because I know they cannot hurt me.

Done. A lovely cold and fizzy drink. The dentist wouldn't thank me but I must motivate myself to exercise. I remove my cycling gloves and sit at the kitchen table. ACDC has turned to Led Zeppelin in my ears. I remove the buds and stretch my legs. I'm pleased with how this day has started. Who will I meet today? There are of course endless possibilities in a city this size. I wipe the sweat from my eyes. I tell myself to be bold every day. What have you got to lose. The sweat is making my eyes sting.

I select combat trousers, blue kangol polo shirt and my working cardigan (which used to belong to my Father). I normally only wear this in the flat but the guys at the uni cutting suite always comment on it when I wear it. I feel the urge to rub my hands together so I do it. My uncle's walk-in closet is vast. He is so rarely in contact with me that I sometimes forget this flat belongs to him and that I am not in fact an up and coming film director who has just purchased a prime piece of Soho real estate. I leave a note for the cleaner on my way out. I normally have a chat to her in the morning but I have to be getting along today.

The rain has pooled into some pretty substantial puddles which I hop in between. My legs ache from the workout. I like to feel that I've already accomplished something before I even step out of the front door to face the world. I have a few things I need to do today and I'm going to begin with a triple espresso at 39 Steps coffee on Berwick Street. I smell sweet perfume mingled with coffee and sugary products. They have very nice takeout cups here. I've kept a couple of them at home. There's a beautiful girl sitting at a table by herself. She has lovely blonde hair. She's listening to her i-pod and missing out on the atmosphere. Just singin' in the rain, what a...

'Hello,' says the girl behind the counter. Her name badge says 'Rita'. I've spoken to her several times before.

'Hello there,' I say, 'Good morning, tri...'

'Triple espresso, right?'

'You just read my mind,' I say.

'Ha ha, not quite. I have a good memory for regulars and what they like. You seem in a very good mood.'

myself am hell

I smile and I can feel myself blushing. I hate that feeling. I need to sit down and compose myself.

'Yes please, triple espresso and a slice of banana cake please.' I pay and she says to pick a table.

I sit along the side wall opposite a mirror. My face is still quite flushed. I wonder if Rita exercises before her shifts here. I could ask her. Does she work here all of the time? Everyday? Is she perhaps a student of anything? Both my legs are jiggling up and down on the stool. I put my hands on my knees to stop them. Staring at myself for too long makes me anxious so I swivel around on the stool. The blonde girl is sipping a cappuccino and moving her head to the beat. What is she listening to? What shall I put on when I leave? Bit of Oasis? The Morning Glory cover features this very street. I could have a browse in a few record shops if there's time. Mind you, I'll end up having to cram in a lot of stuff today at this rate. I'm already feeling physically shattered. My uncle has a cracking old record player that I should make better use of. I don't really know what he'd be happy for me to use while I'm staying there. I really don't know him at all well. Hang on, who's that? That's ... Yes, one of my classmates from Victorian Lit walking past the window. She always wears that same brown leather jacket and carries that bag. I could ask her if she wants to have a coffee with me. But she's already gone past and she looked a bit preoccupied to my discerning private eye. She always does when I come to think about it. Maybe I'll speak to her in Victorian Lit tomorrow. I always see her smoking by herself outside before the tutorial. Boldness. So difficult in the moment. What if people want to be left alone? But not everyone does, surely. I need to put aside some time for George Eliot today. The waitress brings over my drink and cake.

'Thanks,' I say. I polish off the espresso in a couple of gulps and fold up the cake in its napkin.

'See you,' I call out as I exit. I smell that perfume again. The blonde girl is tapping her finger and sipping her coffee. I'm fueled up now for the day. I'm Jack Bauer, never stopping to go to the toilet or even have a drink during the day. A man like me has no time for such practicalities. The audience can simply imagine that I

myself am hell

must have done such things at some point when they weren't watching.

The start of 'Hello' sounds just like the start of 'Wonderwall'. That must be deliberate? It soon kicks into its own gear though. It's just before nine and I think I'll pop into the comic book store down here just for a browse and maybe a bit of banter with the owner. Bit of an oddball but he usually comes out with some interesting stuff. I run down the street just because I feel like it. There aren't too many people about. I fly past the market stall holders setting up their food stands. Boom! A new world record. Whoever would have thought that I would be a picture of physical fitness?! Flying. Above the rooftops and seeing it all. Looking after the inhabitants of the city. I am a symbol to each and every one of them. I work alone. At night.

I'm reading a copy of Batman: Year One. Training. Training and discipline. He decided to do something and he just did it. An example to us all of what can be done by the strong-willed individual. He was an orphan too. He went away to re-form himself. Then he returned to Gotham to...

'This is a shop, not a library. You buyin' that or what?'

'Hello there,' I say, 'how are you? Do you remember me?'

'You been in 'ere before?'

Maybe it's a little early in the day for friendly banter. He's probably not a morning person.

'What are your thoughts on the Christopher Nolan movies? I'm looking forward to the third one. Apparently Bane is...'

'Shall I tell you the bane of my existence?'

'Okay,' I say.

He removes the graphic novel from my hand and returns it to the shelf.

'My own personal bane is college boys who think I've nothin' better to do than sit around all day talkin' about The Dark Knight and Heath Ledger and blah blah blah.'

'But culturally speaking, I mean...'

'Culturally bollocks.' He moves back behind the counter. 'Now, I've got Joker action figures over there if you want to buy one of them. Or you can pay for that graphic novel.'

I already have action figures of the joker, a big Batman and a copy of Year One in my room. I came here for...

'What you ain't gonna do is stand 'ere all day talkin' away and then fuck off without buyin' anything. This is a business, yeah?'

'This is Wayne Enterprises,' I say to him in full Christian Bale voice. 'I'm sure they'll call back.'

'You what?'

'I'm buying this place and implementing some new rules regarding browsing and bantering.'

He seems stuck between confusion and anger so I bolt out of the shop and into the street. I'm certainly not gonna be buying another copy of Year One, or another fantastic Bat Pod model just for a bit of friendly banter! Underworld is what I need to galvanise me now. That track, not the book. I mean, I love the book as well.

Angel boy in the doorway boy

The angel seeing signs and wonders.

People coming and going. Take your camera and follow them. Pick just one and they become the focus of the narrative no matter who they are or where they're going. Then you move on to someone else. Fly around and watch them all. The freedom to browse. Processing along Wardour Street with laser-like focus. Time for a haircut. The barber's being a place of guaranteed banter – it's part of the service. A cutthroat industry that takes no prisoners. A place to meet and talk and spin the yarn. My kind of place when I need a break from the office. I pick up my hat, grab the morning paper and tell Dolores that I'm taking a long liquid lunch. She raises an eyebrow and I flash her a smile. I make sure I'm packing because, well, you never know what's around the corner in this town.

Georgio's on Charlotte Street. Better take the earphones out. Couple of people before me in the queue. There's the paper here and a few magazines. They always seem to play terrible music in barber's shops. Maybe they don't want you to get too comfortable. In and out. I nod at the two guys sitting on Georgio's sofas. The effectiveness of the non-verbal gesture. The old "all right, mate, we're both heterosexual males in the year 2012, sitting in a barber's shop, no real need for any verbals, thanks gavnar." The place has a delightful smell of potions and powders and products. Georgio is putting the finishing touches to his latest creation with the cutthroat razor. I like that part of the process. Your life in the hands of a master surgeon. Keep very still. There may and possibly will be blood. There's a bird in a cage that sings and whistles. I must ask Georgio what kind it is. Why oh why does the caged bird sing? A young lad sweeps up the cuttings as Georgio works away and chats. He must be related as Georgio speaks to him in Italian.

The guy next to me is wearing a Chelsea shirt.

'Champions of Europe,' I say.

He looks at me. 'Oh yes, mate! Drogbaaaaaaaaa! Legendary, mate! You a fan?'

'I just like the game,' I say, 'from a tactical point of view. I don't follow any particular team.'

'Oh, right. Well, I guess that's better than supportin' Spurs,' he says with a snarl and turns back to The Sun.

'Yeah,' I say with my own attempt at a laugh, not really sure what I'm laughing at. The other guy waiting laughs as well.

'Would you like a drink, my friend?' says Georgio.

'Cappuccino please, Georgio,' I say. Saved by the bell, or at least the friendly old Italian barber.

Georgio has a collection of Italian football flags and pictures and mementos of the 2006 World Cup and Italia 90. I always enjoy talking football with him. He comes alive at the mention of Andrea Pirlo's passing. Football as art. There was a film that followed Zidane only for ninety minutes of a match for Real Madrid. It was quite mesmerizing.

'There you are, young sir,' says Georgio.

'An authentic Italian cappuccino,' I say. 'Grazi.'

'Of course. Yes please, sir,' he says to the Chelsea fan. Don't expect much conversation out of him, Georgio. I'll read the paper and drink my drink till it's my turn.

Mission accomplished in terms of a civilized haircut. Georgio has a terrific aroma of cigarettes and coffee. He always makes me want to try smoking. Not good for the old fitness though. I should speak to Ali from my class tomorrow; never mind just thinking about it. This is the moment in the movie when the hero decides to take action and become who he's meant to be. There's a Starbucks just up here near the tube station. I'll have a spot of lunch and then pop along to the library. I don't feel like any music at the moment. I need to keep my wits about me because enemy eyes are absolutely everywhere. Just follow my instructions if you value your life. My hair is close cropped and I can feel beads of sweat forming under the midday sun. It's harsh country out here near the Rio Grande. Nobody knows that I have a Star Wars backpack full of money here. This is that thing you've been dreaming about. Now what are gonna do?

A filter coffee and a sausage bap. I rub my hands together and look around me. Quite a few people packed in here for lunch. I'm starting to feel a little tired to be honest. I do find it an effort to keep talking to people during the day sometimes. Sometimes all I need is just to be near other people, not even to talk to them. In fact, sometimes too much conversation makes me feel like I want to run away as far and as fast as I can. I could just close my eyes right now. It's only midday and I have mountains of reading to do. I yawn.

'You're in need of oxygen,' says the girl sitting next to me.

'I am,' I say. 'Oxygen or something, for sure.' Is this the same girl from the coffee house this morning? Her hair looks the same. She has an i-pad on the table.

'I might catch the tiredness bug from you.'

'You might,' I say. 'Do you study?'

'I'm sorry?' she says.

'Absolutely no need to apologise.'

'What?'

'Nothing, um, are you a university student?' I say.

'No, no. I just have a day off today. I'm going to go and see a film later.'

'Which one?' I say.

'The Avengers?' Does she not know if she's going to see this, or does she just not know if this is the right title? People are so confusing.

'That new Marvel superhero film?'

'Yeah, it's meant to be fun.'

Ah! Let me seize the day and just try something here.

'Of course, you know, real filmmakers like myself tend to be a little skeptical about these big budget blockbusters with all their special effects and technical wizardry.'

I turn away as if the conversation is over. She leans in a little closer.

'You're a filmmaker!?'

'I wrote and directed a short feature that toured a lot of the film festivals a couple of years ago.'

'Wow! What was it about?'

'It was called Once Upon a Time in Little Italy.' Not a bad title. I go fully into character now.

'That sounds incredible,' she says. 'I'd love to see that. How long is it?'

'Forty minutes in its current version. Obviously I'd love to develop it into a full feature at some point. I just need some funding.'

She scribbles something in a notebook and tears the page out.

'Here's my name and contact details and the name of the production company I work for. Send me a copy of your film and I can maybe show it to my boss. We're always on the lookout for new talent.'

'Thank you,' I say. Wow!

'I'd better get going and see that awful film with all the special effects.'

We both laugh.

'Have a good day,' I say.

Of course, the slight drawback to this networking breakthrough is that I just made that story up in the barbers while

Georgio was chatting away to the guy in his chair and the young lad was sweeping up the hair. It could be a film one day. It's not really a lie if you fully intend to make films but just haven't quite got round to it yet. Anyway, the line between lying and creative licence is a very fine one. Maybe I'll have a go at writing up my Little Italy story as a screenplay. I rub my hands together.

I really do have a lot of reading to do for tomorrow. A bit of Kasabian to power me along to the British Library! I'm on the uni campus now and going by the big Waterstone's. The insistent beat of 'Days are Forgotten' powers me through the throng of students. I keep my eyes to the floor and dodge between the groups. On to Cavendish Square and the British Medical Association. You're not doing too badly at all, lad. This time next year you'll have a degree in film studies and the world at your feet. You just remember that. Keep on plugging away. No pain, no gain. You'll find yourself a job and a girlfriend and your life will be just fine. You deserve it. I'm sweating in my cardigan. Deserve's got nothin' to do with it. We haven't had the predicted rainstorms for today yet. I feel the urge to rub my hands together, so I do it as I walk along.

I'm at the library and I can't wait to settle down with my books and have some quiet time. I turn off the i-pod and join the long queue for the bag check. Please be quick. People are chatting away in groups in front of me. Please be quiet. The library will be quiet, that's the main thing. I'll probably need three hours on the main text and then an hour or so on some secondary reading, with a coffee break factored in. Then home for dinner. It's nice to know what you'll be doing for the rest of the day. Reading here and then home for dinner. I could watch a film tonight! Maybe The Dark Knight! Yes, something to look forward to. Library card at the ready and bag ready to be checked. They're still chatting. Please be quiet for me just now.

Part Four: The Japanese Garden

'Iris there with humid bow / Waters the odorous banks that blow / Flowers of more mingled hue / Than her purfled scarf can shew'

Milton, 'Comus'

London, 2012

    I'm standing at the front of the bus since there are no seats. I hold onto a cable and try to make sure my rucksack isn't in anyone's way. The bus stops at a red light. All of us standing passengers lurch forward. I look around at my fellow passengers - are any of them bound for adventure today? Is today an epoch-making day for any of them? Supporting players, with the camera firmly on me.
    University College Hospital is the closest to The British Library. I'm sorry about what happened to Quentin Carter. Was it my fault? Yes, but unintentionally. And what did she have in that bag? But he'll be okay, I'm sure of it. A broken nose can be fixed. As good as new. We'll have you fixed up in no time at all. No earphones in right now as I want to take everything in. I have been

singled out on this day for a purpose beyond my understanding. I must be alert and ready.

Are any of the people on this bus lonely? What about that girl over there reading a magazine? She doesn't look like the kind of girl who would ever be lonely. She's beautiful; she has a nice figure, accentuated by stylish jeans and top. Surely she's too popular to be lonely? But can't even the most popular person still be lonely late at night? Maybe I should go and talk to her? But in a flash, it's her stop and she's gone. She breezes past me without so much as a glance.

We're nearly at the hospital. I may get caught up in a John Woo shootout scene, with bullets, babies, and gurneys flying everywhere! Ha! I would have two guns and I'd save all of the babies and kill all the bad guys. I would barely break a sweat. It would all be in a day's work for a tough cop who shoots first and asks questions later. The protagonist is now on a different path altogether. The usual tracks of his life are no more. The future is now a voyage into the unknown. It is the test that the protagonist has been waiting for. Now, all bets are off.

The wheels on the bus go round and round.

I'm conflicted about hospitals in the sense that on the one hand they offer great people watching opportunities, while on the other they remind me of lots of...things. The air ambulance takes off from the roof as I walk towards the sliding doors. I shudder and rub my hands together and I suddenly need the toilet. I call Ali on the number she gave me before the ambulance arrived, and she tells me where they are. I walk the corridors as the head of neurosurgery who also just so happens to be a trained killer. Today is the day when terrorists decide to take over the hospital and kidnap a government official who's in for a routine procedure. Not on my watch!

I find the toilets and look at myself in the mirror while I'm washing my hands. Today is my day. The script focuses in on the man who will be the protagonist. I am the man apart. It makes sense that I am the one scheduled for change. I can make my own world; we all can if we have the bravery! Somebody comes in so I make my exit without bothering to dry my hands.

'Been a funny old morning, hasn't it?' I say to Ali and Quentin. They both agree and I sit with them for a little while. My mind cannot focus in on them. The supporting players. I have a leading lady on my mind now. Ali is fussing over Quentin. I didn't really need to come here, but I'm glad I did. I have an angel in the screenplay now. She will initiate the transformation in me. I simply must get back to her. I make some polite enquiries about Quentin's welfare, and with that I take my leave. Now where did I see her? Surely it was just around this corner?

Suddenly I'm blinded by white light. I fall to the floor, my hands shielding my eyes from the light. When I can feel the light and the heat begin to subside, I move my hands away and open my eyes. There in front of me once again, backlit magnificently, is the girl. Her white kimono is crisp and clean. Her tiny feet peek out from the cascading yet even hem of the garment, safely encased in their sandals and white socks. She reaches out a hand.

'Now I wonder what you're doing sitting there on the floor?' She smiles. She smiles and the light returns again, only this time it's no longer blinding. I take her hand and clamber to my feet, trying not to pull her over. Her hair is tied in a topknot in the traditional Japanese style, yet the few words I've heard her speak were delivered in an English accent. 'I'm Lucy,' she says with her hand still encased in mine. We adjust our grips slightly and shake hands in a sort of mock formal but nonetheless warm manner.

'Hi Lucy,' I say, 'I'm...'

'Shoooosh. Follow me.'

She leads and I follow. She leads me by the hand around a corner, and there in the middle of the quadrangle is her beautiful little white house. It positively shimmers, and so does she.

'But wh...' I begin.

'No questions now. We only have a little time together today,' she says.

She opens a door and we walk out into the quad. As we go up a pebbled path towards the house, I notice that the hospital has disappeared. The tall building I entered about half an hour ago, with its distinctive green glass, is nowhere to be seen. All that's visible now is the white house and the beautiful garden around it. No more people; no more air ambulance. It's nice. We walk the path, my hand in hers. She opens the door with its heavy knocker and shows me inside.

'I'll make tea,' she says, 'make yourself at home.'

The interior is the same bright white. We are in the kitchen, around which she glides like an apparition. She has a lovely old oak table, decorated with a vase of purple flowers, which she says are 'from the garden', as she turns for a moment from her very Japanese-looking teapot. I rub my hands together. Two ornate bonsai trees are housed in what look like specially designed arches on opposing walls. I look at the one closest to Lucy. There is an inscription on the pot reading simply, "Megan".

'Megan was my mother,' she says as she brings the teapot over to the table and places it on a metallic stand. 'Tea?'

'Yes. Please. That would be wonderful.'

'Have a seat.'

'Thank you.' We sit and look at one another. She has a knowing expression. She pours the tea into fine china cups that rest on saucers. 'You said "was my mother"?'

'Yes, I did indeed say that. My mother died in a car accident when I was a child.'

I take a sip of the tea, and its lovely steam fills my nostrils.

'I just have to ask...'

'Yes?'

'Well, how exactly does a person come to live in a beautiful little white cottage slap bang in the middle of a hospital on the Euston Road? I mean, this sort of set-up can't be all that common in the NHS...'

She smiles.

'More tea?'

'Yes please.'

'And would you care to hear some music, Tapper?'

'I would, Lucy.'

I reach instinctively for my i-pod but then remember that I'm in someone else's house. We stand up and I'm still holding her fingertips as we meet at the head of the table. This all seems a little bit too perfect, but then surely only a fool would question a perfect experience when it comes along. Perfection on the screen. Something that seems too good to be true.

'Come through to the living room,' she says, and leads me down a dimly lit corridor with white walls and another bright white light at the end of it. Lucy takes small, light steps; her feet hardly seem to touch the ground. Her little hand feels weightless in mine. We emerge into a large circular lounge area. She heads for a shelf in the alcove that's full of vinyl records. 'That sofa's very comfortable.'

I slump down into the white, two-seater sofa that is indeed extremely comfortable. My legs are jiggling up and down so I still them. This sofa is far from being brand new. It lacks the crisp, clean quality of the rest of the furniture and it's a little threadbare in places. I interlock my fingers behind my head and stretch out my weary legs. My workout this morning feels like a lifetime ago. I close my eyes. Was that this morning? When did I do my workout?

A distinctly threadbare theory of sofa-ology. I have no idea which record Lucy is going to play, it will come as a complete surprise. The swelling soundtrack of love. Telling the audience how to feel at a given moment. As I sit here, a vision of Lucy's garden fills my mind's eye. I glimpsed the patio area with its large wicker chairs and table through the double doors at the end of the lounge as I sat down, but there are only very small windows in this room. Very small windows. Tiny windows. Holes for light. Company. In somebody else's house. Not to be on your own for once for a day of your...life.

A magnificent vista of green, with water flowing through it. Piercing bright light. There are stone statues of samurai either side of twelve stone steps that lead down to what is in effect the crossroads of the garden. Two upon neatly cut grass. Behind each seat are four shrubs in boxes decorated with Japanese lettering.

'What do they say?' I ask.

'They are each dedicated to someone important to me. This one is my Mother, and the others are the staff who took care of me. I owe them a lot. Now, my soaring eagle, where to next?'

'Let's see some of your beloved bonsai trees.'

'After you, Mr director.'

I hover over the tops of the hedgerows and trees. I breathe in the sweet air of the garden and seem to frolic on its energy. Who needs triple espressos when you have this? I swing left before landing with a jolt within the garden's largest bonsai area. A world of sensation and jolting jolts to the system. Several cameras creating multiple aerial perspectives. When my foot touches the ground I hear the sound of a horn progressing on the air. Lucy emerges from an ornate summerhouse on an elevated plain.

'Careful with that landing, Mr.'

Before I can think of anything to say, she's talking passionately about her little trees and I'm taking in the fragrant aromas and sweet sounds surrounding me.

'These are Japanese maple.' Each tree grows in its own little pot. 'Here.'

She hands me a watering can and I get to work. She sprinkles something into each pot.

'Fairy dust,' she giggles. 'To make them grow.'

As I water the trees, I can hear birds chirping and twittering urgently in the hedgerows. If I wasn't already asleep this would be a lovely spot for a little pastoral snooze. I notice that the branches of the tree in front of me are bound with wire. Everything must surely be free to grow as it will in a dream landscape.

'I'm shaping them,' says Lucy. 'Sometimes nature needs to be pointed in the right direction.' She produces a pair of tweezers with which she removes a couple of tiny weeds and some pieces of moss from the tree's base. 'I love the root formations. Each tree is unique, travelling its own tangled path.'

I put down the watering can and rub my hands together.

'What does your Father do?' I say.

'Why do you ask?'

She frowns for the first time. Just had to ask, didn't I?

'No reason at all. It, it's just a thing people ask each other, isn't it? I'm sorry.'

'You're right, my dear. It's the sort of thing people ask each other just because. And for no other reason than that.'

It's almost like the dream me can't help but push and push people away.

'But it's fine,' she says, touching my arm tenderly. 'That subject is a little difficult for me, that's all.'

'Your Father's profession?'

'My Father in general,' she says with sadness welling in her eyes.

'Please just tell me to mind my own business in future. My parents are both in the film business, so I guess it's inevitable that I would follow suit. I guess you could say it's in my bl...'

'I know what happened to your parents,' she says this directly but without judgment.

Oh.

'He builds things.'

'Pardon?'

'That is what my Father does.'

I feel that the tears could come at any moment.

'Would you rather we change the subject?'

'He builds things. But more than that he owns things and controls them.'

The air fills with a sulfurous smell that conjures an image of an infernal furnace belching out fumes. Anything that grows can also rot and burn. I should not talk in this garden. I'm bringing emptiness and awkwardness into a scene that's supposed to flow back and forth with quick cuts and swooning romance with violins and flowers.

'Would you like to know why I needed this cottage in the first place?'

Thank God she's broken the silence. The stench again and a

myself am hell

black cloud hanging over this section of the garden. She doesn't seem to notice it.

'Was it something to do with your Mother's death?'

A single tear trickles down her cheek.

'Yes.'

'I'm sorry, I...'

'Don't be, I went through a terrible time but I'm well now. Look around, I no longer have a care team here. I'm back at my job and I have a little flat. I come here for the serenity, the peace. I also come to take care of my trees, to read and listen to music. Today I met you.'

'Yes.' I speak through my hand while it covers my face. 'I can see why you love this place. I wouldn't be able to leave either.'

She rushes towards me and kisses me on the lips.

'I love you,' she says.

'I love you too,' I say.

Yeah, yeah, I know. But it's my dream. We're hand-in-hand now. Taking flight, I experience the same mixture of nutritious air and foul by-product. I see the garden smashed and invaded, the trees sick and dying. This is the wrong film. We land in the opposite corner of the garden and the sound of the horn brings with it a pain that shoots into my hips and throbs within my skull. This part of the garden is dominated by a large tree with red leaves. Lucy's clean kimono makes a gentle sound as it brushes against the grass. We're still holding hands. Her hand is warm inside mine. We stand and look into the top of the tree. It's full of birds of many colours. The sun beats down on us. I can't maintain the perfection.

'Come and see my rose garden,' she says.

We float up together into the air; we laugh and sing; we spin around in the air but I feel myself within a cave and flying too close to the roof. Could I just wake up from this? I see an angel of destruction presiding over the garden. Everyone has departed and the horn of the apocalypse is rising from the depths of hell. No no no! Why?

We land with another bump amid a circle of yellow roses. They smell divine. We get up and dust ourselves down. The voice that won't be quiet. The voice. I rub my hands together. She said he controls. Like a director.

'Sorry for crushing your roses,' I say, 'I'm so clumsy and stupid.'

'Ordinarily I'd be very angry with you, but I just can't be angry with this face.'

She squishes my face between her palms in the way a mother might do to a naughty child. Normally this would annoy me. We sit down on the grass. It's warm and dry.

'Are you lonely, Tapper?'

Her look is serious.

'Yes. Yes I am, Lucy.'

'No girlfriend?' She smiles and turns away shyly.

'Not right now. There have been a few flings before but nothing too serious, I...'

'Tapper, no embellishments with me please.'

'Okay,' I say.

She looks me right in the eye. I notice she has little freckles on her nose. We kiss again. It's soft and warm and dreamlike (appropriately enough!). She appears utterly unaffected by the fact that she has introduced death and decay into her paradise along with me. Maybe death and decay were here all along? Her Father's forced presence in her earthly paradise? No, I feel pretty sure that everything wrong with this scene originates with the protagonist in chief.

There is a thin lake encircling the garden. It is full of carp, their scales catching the light and glinting and gleaming. They are large and look well-nourished.

'How did you get the fish in here?' I ask. 'They're magnificent.' We lie back on the grass together, still entwined in one another's arms. 'Do you still experience your symptoms at all these days?' I can hear a violin. It's very faint, but definitely there. Why do I ask so many questions? Which is itself another question.

'No, I don't. I work, I have a flat, I have friends. All that I've been lacking is someone to share my life with.' She holds me closer. 'And I think I've made some progress with that today.'

'Yes. Yes you have.' She leans on her elbow and plucks a tuft of grass. 'Can you hear music?'

'Of course I can, my love, I put the record on.'

'Aaah, yes. Of course you did.' I lie back and enjoy the increasingly soaring violin notes. 'Who is this?'

'It's Elgar's Violin Concerto in B Minor. It's a favourite of mine.'

'Mmmm, I like it.'

'I thought you would, Tapper.'

'You know that's not my real name, don't you?'

Tapper. Tapper. Tapper. Tapper. Tap. Tap…Tap

I wake up sitting on Lucy's sofa. I rub my eyes.
'You were dead to the world,' she laughs.
'I was floating and flying,' I say.
I yawn.
'You need some oxygen,' says Lucy.
'Yes,' I say.
They say yawning is contagious, I think.
'Come with me for some fresh air,' she says.
She takes my hand and we leave the cottage.

Part Five: Meet Cute

'He that has light within his own clear breast / May sit I' the centre and enjoy bright day; / But he that hides a dark soul and foul thoughts / Benighted walks under the mid-day Sun; / Himself is his own dungeon.'

Milton, 'Comus'

<u>London, 2012</u>

We sit next to each other on plastic chairs in a waiting area in University College Hospital. There are people coming and going around us. I feel something approaching joy and yet this feeling scares me. I am holding his hand and he doesn't seem to mind. With the other hand he is holding a towel to his shattered nose. He is still handsome despite the injury. I like his thick, light brown hair and even white teeth. I can't tell much about his speaking voice because it is obviously impaired. He has not tried to say much as I have been doing all of the talking. I can tell that he is listening closely to my every word. They have asked him if he would mind having a student observe his treatment, as this is a teaching hospital. They said that it will be a while before they can treat him.

myself am hell

'It was 2006 and we met during freshers week. We had what you might call a fairytale year together.'

He nods and I think he's smiling.

'I fell hard for him and I thought he had for me too. It could and should all have been so sweet. Perhaps it was. Perhaps I'm mistaken in questioning the past just because recent events have cast it in a new light. Is there any value in looking back and reconfiguring events and feelings from a position of experience? Maybe we do it so we can move on eventually.

At the end of that first year he announced out of the blue that he wanted to go and fight in Afghanistan. I thought it must have been some kind of joke. But no, he signed up and went off to complete thirty weeks of training to join the paras. By 2008 he was out there. Everyone else – his parents, my parents – seemed so happy about it all, as if they were waving him off for another term at uni. I had a terrible feeling from the beginning. That first tour he did, I was a complete wreck. I watched the news constantly and emailed him every day. If I didn't get an immediate reply I would call my Mother in a panic. Of course all of this affected my studies. I couldn't focus on anything. I almost begged him not to go out there again. If I asked him what it was like, he would say I could never understand. Isn't that just the perfect justification for keeping someone on the outside. The enthusiasm he'd had during his training had turned into something else after active service. I don't think it even crossed his mind not to go. I think it became a drug for him. Off he went for his second tour of duty. This time it was Helmand, fighting the Taliban, trying to win the hearts and minds of the locals...'

I realize that I've been talking for quite a while.

'I hope I'm not boring you, Quentin?' I smile at him.

'Gnup up ball. Beave cubby um.' He tries to smile but it causes him pain.

Quentin: This girl is so beautiful. I feel quite glad she hit me in the face. Extremely glad in fact. Yes, my nose hurts, but it's nice just to feel something, anything. Is this boyfriend still in the picture, I wonder? In a romantic sense, I mean.

I'm not going to hit anyone, I'm not going to touch anyone, I'm not going to go near anyone

Repeat

Shut up! My hand jerks. I want to hear her story. She asks if she's boring me. I try to speak through my towel: 'Not at all. Please carry on.' I love you.

Ali: 'Thank you. I haven't talked to anyone about this. Well, anyone except my friendly local priest.'

He looks at me. Is he smiling?

'Noor fweet?' – 'Your priest?'

'Yes, funny isn't it. I thought I had left all of that behind me at school. Perhaps you don't know how religious you are until you run into a crisis. Anyway, I don't think my friend the priest is going be too happy with me after this morning.' He looks at me questioningly.

I put my hand on his arm. An electric current shoots through me. I am about to resume when I notice our mutual friend come bouncing through the doors with a big grin on his face.

'Hi guys,' he says. 'Everything okay here? I see you've got a fresh compress on there, Quentin. I'm sure that will heal in no time.'

'Mmnhmmn,' Quentin nods.

'You look somehow...different.' He looks as though he is physically here but actually somewhere else entirely.

'I feel different,' he says slowly.

I look at Quentin but he is preoccupied with his nose and his towel.

'Well, thank you very much for coming but I think everything is okay here.'

'Great...er, I mean good. I'm glad you're okay, Quentin.' Quentin gives him the thumbs up. The prankster turns to me. 'Been a funny old morning, hasn't it?' This must be rhetorical because before I can answer he about turns and bounces out the way he came in. I turn back to Quentin.

'He was part of 16 Regiment and they had been back out there for around three months. I think he tried to keep anything too distressing out of his correspondence. He described the brigade doing their rounds in the community, trying to spread the good word of western-style democracy. I dropped out of university at the end of that first year. There didn't seem to be a whole lot of support available to me at the time. I remember he mentioned playing football with some of the local children on a dust bowl of a pitch. Can you imagine growing up somewhere like that? A war zone, a place under occupation from a foreign force? A place where the only way to make money is to grow opium poppies?'

Quentin: There's a story here. There's definitely a story here. I feel excited for the first time in ages. Is that inappropriate? I'm imagining this from all the different perspectives: the soldiers', the insurgents', those kids in the street, the adults who remember the Soviet invasion... She's looking at me. I realize I have a smile on my face. Pictures are appearing in my mind.

Ali: 'Are you all right? Shall I continue?'

Quentin: 'Yes. Yes, please do'. I feel like taking notes. Surely this is a positive sign? I'm engaged in something, interested.

Ali: 'He wrote about two walled villages where they were spending quite a lot of time: Khushhal Kalay and Shin Kalay. They got into a protracted firefight with insurgents in Shin Kalay. As they were advancing, am IED went off and killed one of his mates. Tom's legs were damaged in the blast. You can probably guess the rest.

Quentin: I can. The next section of the book takes place in the military hospital. Struggle, detail, triumph over adversity. 'And you had to take care of him, right?'

Ali: 'I felt it was my duty. I wanted to take care of him. I only heard once they had notified his parents. Mere girlfriends aren't important enough. I am no longer playing the devoted Mother Theresa now, though. Things have changed and the scales have fallen from my eyes.'

Quentin: She looks straight at me. Her voice is flat and has a slightly bitter tone. No wonder. Her suffering is of a different kind to mine. We're sitting very close to one another...

I'm not gonna touch anyone, I'm not gonna hurt anyone, I'm not gonna go near anyone...

Shut up!!! Leave me alone!!!
Ali: 'What was that? Are you okay?'
Quentin: 'I, I'm fine. What was what?'
Ali: 'That movement you just did with your arm.'
Quentin: 'Oh, that. Look, since we're being honest with each other can I tell you something?'
Ali: 'Of course you can.'
Quentin: 'Okay, here goes: I have OCD and depression. That's why I do that jerky thing sometimes – to get rid of unwanted thoughts. To try to anyway.'
Ali: 'What kind of thoughts?'
Quentin: 'Thoughts like, "you've just raped or beaten up that lovely girl next to you." I've been struggling a lot lately.' I can feel tears in my eyes. I look into hers. 'I was planning to kill myself this morning. I'd probably be dead if all this hadn't happened.' The tears are streaming down my cheeks. Is what I just said really true? Does it matter? She has her arms around me. Soon enough I have my arms around her too, and boy does it feel good. When we finally separate, I try to speak as best I can through tears and recently broken nose. 'I'm sorry for hijacking your story. My troubles must seem pretty pathetic compared to yours.'
Ali: 'Are you getting treatment?'
Quentin: 'Yeah, I guess.'
Ali: 'And medication?'
Quentin: 'I take medication, yes.'
Ali: Maybe we can help each other.
Quentin: I realize I'm squeezing her hand tightly and relax my grip a little. I wipe away a tear, careful to mind my nose. 'It feels good to talk to someone honestly. When you were telling your story, I was imagining it as a novel written by me.'
Ali: 'I also have a confession to make – it's nice to meet someone who has as many problems as I do.' We both laugh gently. I take his other hand. 'I have physically assaulted you, cried in front of you and learned your biggest secret in one morning. So do you write novels then?'
Quentin: 'I want to, yes.'

Ali: 'If I tell you my entire story, will you write it for me?' I offer him my hand. 'Do we have a deal?'

Quentin: I love her. 'Deal.' We shake hands.

Ali: 'And Quentin?'

Quentin: 'Yes.'

Ali: 'I'm glad I broke your nose.' We both laugh and cry, and then embrace again. I would kiss him but how does one go about kissing someone with a broken nose? 'Now if you will excuse me for a moment, I need to pop to the ladies then get us a drink. Make sure you keep that compress compressed, won't you.'

Quentin: 'Thanks, I will.'

Part Six: The Soldier

'Alas, good venturous youth, / I love thy courage yet, and bold Emprise; / But here thy sword can do thee little stead'

Milton, 'Comus'

A hospital ward somewhere in the UK, 2009

The soldier opens his eyes. There's a bright light above. He can smell something. What is it? Disinfectant. He's in a hospital. Of course. The last thing he remembers is a loud bang and a blinding flash. He remembers the sound of the casevac helicopter and the medics telling him to breathe deeply and slowly, then he remembers seeing but not really taking in the field hospital back at Bastion. How much time has passed since, he can't even guess. He pulls himself up to a sitting position. On patrol in Lashkar Gah. Leading his men. He knows something is wrong. On the bedside table are flowers and cards. There's a chair with a coat on the back, a leather jacket; Ali's brown leather jacket. He smiles to himself. He's back home in England.

He stretches his arms and yawns. Time for a quick check-up on the condition of his aching body. The top half seems fine. Arms, fingers, head, all present and correct. It's the bottom half that's worrying him. He's scared to pull back the sheets but he does it anyway.

Both of his legs are missing from somewhere just above the knee. He now has bandaged stumps. Before he can react to this, two things happen: firstly, he sees Ali in the doorway. He smiles and waves. She smiles and waves back. Secondly, he passes out.

Two weeks later the soldier is in his room at the Headley Court military hospital. It's pleasant and airy, made very homely indeed by the addition of paintings on the wall and family pictures on the mantelpiece, put there by Ali. Here she comes now with fresh flowers for the bedside table. She hums along to herself as she moves about the room tidying and keeping busy. The soldier is lying in the bed where he has spent the majority of his time since coming to Headley. The pushing gloves on his bedside table are the only evidence that he has left his bed at all since arriving here, wheeling himself to the dining room for meals. He has refused all encouragement to begin his physical therapy sessions.

The doctors had assured Ali on the first day that this was common. What gave her hope was the atmosphere of the place. More or less all of the patients here are from the military these days, with many of them victims of the horrors perpetrated by IEDs. Ali knows from her enquiries that he has been to see the psychologist on a couple of occasions. She wears her leather jacket, brown cords and converse as she busies herself about the room. She draws the curtains; she opens the windows; she even asks the soldier to move with a brisk 'excuse me, my love,' while she fluffs up his pillows. He sits up and says nothing.

'You will have to get up at some point this morning. I need to change those sheets.'

He stares, then laughs. 'So you get me up, take the sheets off, then make some excuse about there not being any clean sheets ready yet, so I might as well get dressed and go to my physical therapy, is that your plan of attack for this morning?'

She smiles. 'Will the plan work today? The longer you leave it, the harder it will be.'

He rolls over in bed, facing away from her.

'Up you get, come on. Time waits for no man.' She prods and pokes him until he has no choice but to sit up and reach for the pushing gloves. He presses the button behind his head on the wall to bring a member of staff to assist with getting dressed and into the wheelchair.

'Jesus! What gives with you?'

'I have tried the softly softly approach, and so...'

'And so, what's this, then, the tough love approach?'

'No, just love.'

Their eyes meet and hers are filled with tears. His seem like an armoured version of those that had once looked so lovingly into hers. She has a nagging feeling that her real, actual boyfriend is still out there somewhere in Helmand, sheltering from the rockets and the RPGs. How can anyone maintain their sanity amidst all of that carnage? Ali has read the newspaper reports of the massive air strikes that have destroyed towns and displaced entire communities. What do the soldiers think about the mission? Is it any different to the Soviets or to the Brits at Maiwand in 1880? Our lads don't have the luxury of sitting around reading newspapers saying how pointless the campaign is.

There had been an almost jovial atmosphere between Ali's and the soldier's parents on the day they had all arrived here with him. They were given a tour of the facilities and the vast garden. Ali had asked questions about recovery times and stumps and sockets, based on information she had gleaned from the internet. She felt useful, even though he had seemed embarrassed, wishing they would just leave him to face this new part of his life alone. She had tried to imagine how he must be feeling; like a student waiting for his parents to leave on his first day at university.

Three months later

Ali pulls her small car into a space in one of the several visitor car parks around the main house. As she turns off the engine, the sound of the Joni Mitchell cd that has accompanied her half hour journey is replaced with a deafening silence. She grabs her tasseled suede bag and brown leather jacket from the passenger seat and takes a deep breath of fresh air as she steps out of the car.

The air is clearly insufficiently stimulating as she then lights a cigarette and takes deep drags, consuming it as if it could be her last. Everything has been going relatively well for the past two weeks, so why this clear reluctance to go in and see her boyfriend? She drops what remains of the cigarette and grinds it underfoot, but instead of proceeding to reception to sign in, she leans against the car and lights another one, watching the blue smoke as it drifts away on the morning breeze.

She can still feel the weight of his treatment journal in her hand, standing alone and isolated in his room the previous day. Amidst the all-encompassing numbness, she recalls that she had encouraged him to keep the journal as an effort to improve his outlook. She sucks on the end of her cigarette for just a little too long and relishes the singed bitterness it inflicts on her lips.

Amanda and Jenna and somebody called Kimberley. The journal had been by the side of the bed, unguarded as if designed to test her resolve. After five minutes of lying to herself, she had opened the book to a random page. She was surprised to find an authentic voice inside. The tone was frank and filled with guilt at his treatment of her, his devoted girlfriend. She had begun to well up with feelings of self-loathing and renewed sympathy for him when her eyes fell upon a sudden confession of his unfaithfulness to her with Amanda and Jenna and somebody called Kimberley. Amanda and Jenna were friends of theirs from uni. They were friends she realized she had not heard from in probably two years. Who was Kimberley? She had closed the book carefully and placed it back in its place.

She is back in the car and smoking continuously. Joni sings of not giving peace a chance. Her knowledge of the hatred she feels for herself and for him has solidified into something small and hard that sits in her chest. She feels that it is letting her live for now, but not without the sure and certain promise that it will decide her fate. How long had this been going on? The radio silence from Amanda suddenly makes sense. How does one live with the guilt of cheating on a close friend? Perhaps more pertinently, how does one assuage said guilt by confessing and revealing that a war hero who gave both legs for his country is in fact a cheating rat? Better to avoid the issue altogether.

He has had his sockets designed and crafted for him by the master prosthetists at Headley. She was there for him if he had needed to talk about the pain of the blisters that the prosthetist team had told her about, but of course he never did. Stiff upper lip. He was back in uniform and back into a healthy routine. She had cried when he had walked on what they call the 'stubbies' here - the first stage, the first step.

She turns the volume up and allows Joni's swooping vocals to immerse her in distant places with other smells and feelings. A further cigarette is in her mouth and aflame with the automatic and unmemorable quality of changing gears on a quiet drive home.

She had been there one lunchtime when the soldier and some of his mates, all of them bilateral transfemoral amputees like him, called out to another soldier they knew. The latecomer's legs were intact up to points just below the knee on one leg, and it looked like straight through the knee of the other. The others all called him 'flesh wound' - a nickname to which he happily answered. Ali had asked one of them what this meant. She was informed that it referred to any amputation below the knee. What a place! She loved it here.

She likes to allow a cigarette to burn and smoke on its own for long periods before taking a drag and tapping the length of ash on the edge of the wound down window. What do matters of faithfulness count for against the loss of one's limbs? He is becoming a new person now and so is she. Perhaps now they are even. He has been punished sufficiently already. She hates herself for these thoughts. Do all of the soldiers cheat on their girlfriends?

The Soldier's competitive spirit has re-emerged. He has endured the pain and the falls, and the strain of those first few steps on the parallel walking bars that Ali felt she had seen before in films and tv programmes. He has a therapist called Chip, an ex-soldier who served in Iraq, with whom he has developed a special bond. Chip talks to him; he talks to Chip. As well as the physical work, he is having forty-five-minute sessions in a special oxygen chamber that help to enliven the dead cells in his stumps. His state of mind is being monitored by the dutiful psychologists. Ali had to find out about the oxygen chamber from Chip. She also found out about the positive work with the psychologists from Chip. Chip has a certain quality of entrenched sadness as if part of his role is to absorb this from others and preserve it.

    And so she stands outside the entrance to Headley smoking, watching the blue patterns as they swirl around themselves in the air. She does not wish to go in so she stands outside and smokes. She smokes with one hand while with the other she plays with a simple cross that hangs from a necklace she stole from a market stall. She holds its sharp points between finger and thumb as she stubs out the cigarette, wipes a tear on her sleeve, and heads for the reception.

    She arrives at his room to find hers and the soldier's parents looking at a range of possible prosthetic limbs. Ali recalls that she had asked one of the prosthetists to provide them with some sample designs yesterday. They welcome her warmly into the room while the soldier is having his physical therapy with Chip. The prosthetists have provided three prototypes from which he can choose. She finds that she no longer cares about this. She takes one of the prototypes in her hands. The soldier's mother says something to her about the prototype. She nods without comprehension. This is a wonderful piece of engineering. Is he deserving? Both sets of parents and Ali are holding, examining and discussing one of the prototype legs when the soldier and Chip return to the room. They come in laughing and joking, but the soldier's face freezes when he sees Ali.

    'What the fuck do you think you're doing?' He lunges at her and knocks the prosthesis from her hands. 'Get out!' he yells. 'Just fucking get out!'

She snatches the prosthesis and grips it tightly. She feels the urge to strike him about the face. Instead she tosses it in his lap and walks out in tears.

The staff at Headley had advised her that patience was the key, that once he has come to terms with his new life he will welcome her into it, but he just needs time. Patience and time are the key elements here. Patience. And time.

A further month later

Ali's hand hovers over the well-thumbed copy of The Old Curiosity Shop. Dickens is an old friend. It is a fresh March morning. Ali is not going to Headley Court today. In truth, she probably goes once a week these days. He has his new prosthesis and is working with his usual application, acclimatizing to walking on his new limbs. He has been working hard in the gym, strengthening not only his injured leg but his mind and spirit as well. He looks more like his old self. He looks good, much more like the physically imposing specimen he used to be. But now she finds herself attracted to other men and she gives her thoughts and desires free reign. She is trying to be in touch with her feelings as a human being and a woman. Not that she would have described it in such new age terms to anybody else. It is just that since what happened happened, she has felt emotionally compromised and limited. She feels sure that he would never have told her about his infidelity voluntarily. Never.

The books are laid on trestle tables with a reasonable crowd of book lovers milling around, picking up and looking, reading, occasionally buying. She has been doing various odd jobs: a bit of bar tending in her local pub; two or three shifts a week in a nearby family-run bookshop. She is not flush, but she is also not short of money. When she steals, the world is reduced to simple impulses and fears: can I get away with this? What happens if I get caught? She picks up the book. Its spine is lined and cracked.

I'm not gonna hurt anyone, I'm not gonna touch anyone, I'm not gonna go near anyone. Fuck off! Leave me alone!

Stealing the book is as easy as slipping it into her bag. She turns and breathes and there are bodies and distance between her and the book stand now. She feels something approaching happiness, however momentary.

She can smell coffee! The smell is coming from a specialist coffee stall. They are doing demonstrations on how to roast beans to perfection. There are four or five staff members. They are all passionately showing off their love for coffee to whoever approaches the stand. She likes enthusiastic people like this, people who care about a particular thing; be it coffee, books, knitting, whatever. Caring passionately is the important thing. It says something good about these people. They all wear black barista aprons that give them a look of professionalism – the coffee experts, the coffee scientists. The society re-built by the coffee scientists. Those with access to the coffee knowledge. The rise of Starbucks.

She orders a black coffee and chooses a mild Guatemalan roast. She does not engage her coffee scientist in conversation; she wishes only to stand and enjoy the aroma. Around her, she hears talk of arabica beans, brazilian blend, the best kind of coffee machine. There are coffee-themed pamphlets everywhere - a coffee lover's paradise. She reaches into a bowl of beans on the counter, letting them fall through her fingers before catching one and putting it in her mouth. It is bitter and pleasant as she crunches it. The sharp and fleeting joy of the compulsion performed. The relief of it all.

She takes her coffee and a croissant and sits at a table outside the coffee stand. There are people milling around in the emerging spring sunshine without a care in the world. Although, no, for who is really without a care? No one. We each have our cross to bear. One must learn to cope. She takes a sip of her coffee. Lovely. No need for any sugar. Just right. She takes out her book, holding it lovingly. She knows in her heart that she no longer wants him. What is so wrong with stealing the odd book or piece of jewelry? She sips and she smokes and she nibbles on the croissant while she drinks in the world and the people around her. Some crimes are victimless. Some are utterly selfish. Her mind drifts over the years and she remembers.

Arriving at Leeds University, Ali felt surrounded by pretty, popular girls with large breasts and bare navels. The thought occurred to her that nobody in her year at Catholic school had a pierced nose or belly button – or at least they hadn't then. Her roommate's name was Annette. She was short and a little overweight and she was studying Mechanical Engineering. Ali had instantly felt a little sorry for Annette. She also felt relieved not to be paired with a glowingly blonde member of the social elite. Partway through her first night at university, Ali realized that some of the boys in their halls were looking at her in ways that they were not looking at Annette.

She chatted to Annette that night about their lives and backgrounds, their likes and dislikes. Ali went to sleep thinking about boys. So many of them. Sequestered in her world of sin and guilt for so long with only other girls for company. And now university.

Waiting for Annette outside the Engineering building was when she saw him for the first time – tall, very tall, that rugby player's build. He was part of a group of loud lads bursting out of a lecture; his mop of gelled sandy hair sticking out in all directions and visible above the heads of his peers. For all of its anxiety-inducing social requirements, university afforded wonderful people watching opportunities. She sipped slowly on a takeout coffee. She also had one ready for Annette as a surprise. The weather was chilly and she was wearing her favourite old duffel coat that always reminded her of Christmas walks around the village with her Mum. She had two homemade broches on the lapels that she had produced during a productive summer of crafting. One depicted a bee while the other was a bright butterfly.

'Hey you!' Annette came bounding up to her with a big grin.
'Hey,' said Ali. 'I bought you a latte.'
'I love you,' said Annette as if she really meant it. 'I'm

parched.'

Did homemade broches matter once you left childhood behind and entered the real world? All that she loved now felt unstable. What should she keep of her old life and what discard? She worried constantly about her Mum. Ali found Annette's northern accent funny but also soothing. She put her arm around her new friend and they meandered along to lunch together.

They were on their third plastic cup of weak lager, standing together and moving self-consciously to the R and B music the DJ for the evening was pumping out. Ali had applied more makeup than usual that night and had encouraged Annette to do the same. Ali had bought what they had agreed would be their final round of drinks before returning to halls, when three boys staggered into them, nearly knocking them to the ground.

'Don't fancy yours much,' said the biggest of three as they continued on their way.

'Stay here a minute, Annette,' said Ali.

She marched over to them and tapped the big one on his broad shoulder. He turned around to reveal the very features she had been dreaming of for the last two nights. Her indignation turned to embarrassment in an instant and the colour rushed to her cheeks.

'Yes?' he said.

'You just knocked into us,' said Ali.

'Did I?' he said, as if genuinely unsure.

'Yes, and then I heard you insult her.'

He turned to his mates as if for support, but none was forthcoming.

'Please apologise to her for me,' he said with a drunken attempt at formality.

'You can do it yourself,' said Ali, pointing at Annette.

'I'm Tom, by the way.' He held out a hand which she wanted so much to ignore but found she could not.

'Ali.'

'Ali, how charming.' He gave her a little bow and she smiled against her better judgment. Her hand nestled perfectly in his and she gazed at their hands interlinked.

'Er, Tom?'

'Yes, Ali?'

'Your apology?'

'Oh, yes.' He lurched over to the bewildered Annette and offered her what appeared to be an extremely formal and fulsome apology that concluded with Annette's own hand encased in Tom's mighty mitt. He even brought his other hand into play for added emphasis. He strode back over to Ali, appearing to sober up with every passing moment.

'Now that was a textbook apology,' he said with a broad grin.

'Yes, it certainly looked it, I can't fault that,' said Ali.

'Can I buy you a drink?'

'No, you can buy both of us a drink,' said Ali, returning to stand with Annette while Tom barreled up to the bar. His mates looked on.

'How many's that so far this week?' said mate number one.

'I've lost count,' said mate number two. 'That's why they call him the shagmeister.'

'Too true.'

'Come on, let's get a kebab.'

One Friday, as she was leaving the School of English following a Strategies of Reading tutorial, a hulking presence in a rugby shirt came rushing in and crashed into her. She opened her eyes to see Tom gazing down at her with concern all over his face.

'You?' she said as he helped her to her feet. He began to rub her head gently.

'Sorry,' he said to the passersby trying to squeeze past, 'accident caused by me. Please go round us.'

She noticed that his voice was commanding. Probably the voice he used on the rugby field with his mates. She took a moment to summon her ire.

'You took quite a tumble, you know,' he said.

'Will you please get off and stop that,' she snapped.

He removed his hand from her thin hair.

'Sorry,' he said. 'It's what my Mum used to do when I bumped my head.'

She had not heard a dicky bird from him since they had slept together that night in freshers week. He had left for rugby training in the morning with only a vague promise to do something later in the day left hanging between them. So overwhelmed had she felt by the momentous nature of losing her virginity during freshers week, that it had taken a couple of days to register that the reality of this relationship was not keeping pace with her thoughts, in which she had already introduced Tom to her Mother over dinner. Perhaps she would have to brush this off as nothing more or less than a key developmental milestone ticked off the list. Was this not what people did during their first week of university, with no emotions or consequences involved? She could hear herself explaining to Annette in a deep and experienced voice that it was really no big deal. The two friends went for some lovely autumnal walks together and met up for lunch every day.

Her first instinct was to smile at such nonsense coming from this huge boy, but she could not allow herself to forget how angry she was with him, and doubly so now. She gathered her things and stepped unsteadily down to the pavement that ran along the row of houses that made up one half of the school of English. Tom followed her down.

'Do you even recognize me?' she said finally.

'Yes, Ali. Are you okay, not concussed or anything?'

'How would I know if I were concussed or anything? Doubtless it happens to you all of the time. You probably walk around in a concussed state half the time without even realizing it. You are probably concussed right now.'

He laughed loudly and she laughed with him despite every fiber willing herself not to.

'You're probably right,' he said. 'I was concussed the other day at rugby.'

'Has anyone noticed a difference?' she said.

'You're funny,' he said, as if he really meant it.

'You were quite funny the night that we...'

'Oh yeah. Look, um, I was gonna call you the next day...'

'I wonder how many other random girls you have had to say that to since the start of the term?' He was grinning as if this was all great fun. 'What are you even doing here?'

He took a book from his rather childlike knapsack and held it in front of her. She managed to focus sufficiently to see that it was 'Rabbit, Run' by John Updike.

'Have you read it?' he said.

She had not, but was not about to let him know that.

'Twentieth-Century American fiction elective.'

'And why on earth did you choose that?' In truth, she felt vaguely offended that Engineering students were permitted to do elective modules in twentieth-century fiction.

'It was all that was left by the time I got to the hall to choose,' he said with a slight chuckle.

'Well, are you not going to be late for the tutorial?' she said.

'I was already late,' he laughed. 'Look, can I call you?'

She willed herself to say no and walk away. Or to walk away without saying anything, her head held high in the air.

'Yes, if you must.'

'Great, I'll call you tonight. Nice to see you.' He ran up the steps two at a time, narrowly avoiding another unsuspecting victim as he clattered through the entrance. Ali swung her bag over her shoulder and left to meet Annette for lunch, an involuntary smile spreading all over her face.

There was a definite soundtrack to the event of those days. This was either the radio talk shows or the Joni Mitchell and Bob Dylan records Ali liked to play on the vintage record player her Mother had bought her to take to university. As 06 faded into 07, the subjects of terrorism and Afghanistan were back in the headlines. The girls shared an interest in keeping up to date with current affairs and liked to engage in one-sided arguments with irate callers to the phone-ins whenever they both happened to be studying in the room at the same time.

Ali would leave Tom with his head in a thick volume about the first Gulf War from which he was forever quoting. He may not have been reading much John Updike, or many of the engineering textbooks that Annette was forever offering to translate for him, but at least he was reading. Sometimes she simply had to escape from the room and the distractions offered by Tom's presence. She used the time spent walking to lectures to call her Mum.

'Hi, is that Graham? Hi Graham, it's...that's right, Ali. How is she? Mmm mmm, that is good. How is she on the new medication? Oh, good. Tell her to take her time, no rush. Does she want to call me back in a while? Oh great, okay, nice talking to you, Graham.'

'Hi love, I was just in the toilet. Did Graham tell you?'

'He did, Mum. No further detail required.'

'What? Oh, you're being funny. Always goes right over my head, love.'

'I know it does, but I love you anyway,' said Ali. She usually avoided talking to her Mum on the phone in public. Today, though, she appreciated the busy atmosphere and noise of the campus as a counterpoint to the almost imperceptible degeneration in her Mother's condition. 'You could have called me back later if you were indisposed.' Ali's Mum laughed.

'I wasn't indisposed, as you so delicately put it. I always want to talk to you when I can, love.' Ali felt a swell of emotion rising within her.

'I know you do, Mum. I always want to speak to you too. You and me against the world.'

'I don't want you worrying about me, though, love.'

'I know, but I still will,' said Ali.

Ali could feel the Spring heat prickling the hairs on her bare arms. She realized she had been in a good mood as it began to alter over the phone. Her orange and yellow summer dress had not only been influenced by the clement weather.

'How's that lovely boyfriend?'

'Fine, and please stop changing the subject. Shall I come home to go to the check up with you? What day is it next week?'

'Ali, that's precisely what I have the support staff for. It's what they get paid for.'

She had arrived at the Costa just off campus and could see Annette seated with her back to the window.

'I'm meeting my friend now, Mum.'
'Oh, lovely. Have a nice time, love. Which friend is that?'
'I only have one.'
'I'm sure that's not true.'
'I'll call you again later.'
'No need, love. I'm going to have a sleep and then perhaps do a bit of reading. You have fun.'
'Bye then.'
'Bye, love.'

In the Students Union canteen there was a TV broadcasting a 24-hour news channel. British troops were involved in heavy fighting in Helmand Province. The report mentioned a Green Zone along the Helmand River providing cover for attacks by insurgents. There had been a suicide bombing in Lashkar Gah. The reporter referred to the extreme force used by the British to clear the insurgents from an area referred to as 'the lozenge', between Lashkar Gah and Gereshk. The place where the reporter stood in his body armour looked like a smoking ruin.

'What a disaster,' said Ali, more to herself than Tom.

'We should always support our troops, no matter what,' said Tom with unusual solemnity.

'Oh, I agree, Tom.' She took a few bites of her salad. 'We can support the troops while still questioning the purpose of them being there.'

Tom shook his head and sipped one of the protein shakes that he had taken to drinking recently.

'It's easy to sit back though, isn't it. Until it actually hurts us, like those poor people on 7/7. It all became real for them and their families that day, didn't it.' There was something sombre in his manner that she had not seen before. 'I have a couple of mates serving out there. They signed up straight from school. They reckon it's a great life, the pay isn't too bad, and they think they're actually doing some good.'

Ali looked at her fingernails and noticed they were getting a little ratty and uncared for. A bubble of silence began to form around them.

'Are you serious?' she said finally.

'Maybe, I have to find what works for me,' he said.

She wanted so desperately to say something that would pierce this argument and defeat it utterly. She realized that all she could respond with were her own preconceptions and her opinions about war in general.

'What about the risks?' she mumbled.

'You take a risk every time you cross the road, or order the real ale in the Packhorse,' he said with a chuckle.

'That sounds like a pre-prepared answer,' she said.

'You know me, Ali, I never pre-prepare for anything.'

'That is true,' she said. 'But people are dying out there every day.'

'It's not something I would ever do lightly,' he said. 'I just want what you have. I want to do something I believe in and something that I'm good at.' He kissed her on the mouth and she felt that same thrill shoot through her body. The same thrill she had felt that night outside his halls when he had kissed her for the first time; the night that said everything she had ever felt or thought or read about love and physical desire.

'I have to hit the gym.' He placed his big hand on the side of her face and kissed the top of her head.

'So going to the gym is compulsory now, is it?' she smiled and raised an eyebrow. 'I had better start going myself.'

'You in the gym!' He chuckled again. She feigned offence and pretended to flex her muscles in a bodybuilder pose.

'Very sexy,' he said.

'I aim to please,' she said.

'Oh, you very much do,' he said, walking away from their table. 'This is where you say, "So do you, tiger, you rock my world!"' She nodded and said nothing, turning her eyes to the book that was already out of her bag. Tom was laughing loudly as he left, and Ali was grinning to herself when he called out over the noise of the student diners.

'Ali!' She could tell that her face had gone bright red.

'What?' she mouthed in utter embarrassment.

'I feel like I kind of won that debate we just had?' She laughed and indicated with her hands that he had done okay. He waved and turned and then left. She could never stay angry or upset with him for very long. That was one of his gifts. He was passionate and serious about serving his country in a way that he had never been about university. But what about all of the young men coming home maimed and disabled or not coming home at all? She tried to focus on her book.

The summer waves shimmered and crashed down upon a holiday shore while Ali and Tom walked slowly, hand-in-hand. A pebble beach in Kent, with swimmers and toddlers playing and yelping. Ali was thin and worried; Tom was muscular and bullish. Ali stopped and took away her hand. The tide caught hold of the pebbles and rotated them like pawns in an ancient game. They crackled and groaned at their lack of agency. Ali sat herself down as Tom walked on for a few steps, oblivious and gazing out to sea.

She held her knees close to her. He was skimming stones along the surface of the water. She counted five bounces from one of these efforts and she smiled at him in his trivial moment of success. He smiled back and attempted to outdo himself. The foam crashed loud but unthreatening on the shore. She closed her eyes and pretended she was alone. It could be anywhere. The liked to feel the sun on her skin. Their friends had left them alone to spend some time together but all of their conversations had stayed on the surface, plain and visible.

He flopped down beside her and kissed her cheek.

'I think you may have set some new records there,' she said.

'I think I might have done too, you know,' he agreed. 'You'll have to back me up when I phone the Guinness Book of Records.' He lay down.

'Sure,' she said.

'Do you want a coffee?' He gestured to a van serving takeout beverages.

'Sure,' she said, closing her eyes once again.

'This isn't the most comfortable beach to lie down on,' he said.

'You had better get used to that discomfort, soldier,' she said.

'Yeah,' he said with a big laugh. She heard him tramp away with the same vigour that had characterized his every move since the decision on his immediate future had been made. What would she do when he was away? Who would she be? But he was happy. The sea rumbled on in complete indifference.

'There you go,' he said after several minutes. 'There was a bit of a queue. I made sure you got some cinnamon on yours.'

'Thanks.' She opened her eyes and saw colours and shapes as they adjusted to the sunlight.

'Were you meditating?' he said.

'Just thinking,' she said.

'I've told you, you do far too much of that. I try and avoid it as much as I can.'

'Please do not pretend to be an idiot, my love.' She took him by the hand and drew him to her. 'You are smart and capable.'

'What if I'm not pretending? That would be more worrying,' he said. They both laughed, and she leaned her head on his shoulder. He put his gym-honed arm around her and they sat in silence for a moment. The sea was livening up and the white spray was ending itself like a suicidal flock of birds.

'Are you more excited or scared?' she said finally.

'Um, a bit of both in all honesty. Aren't they sort of the same? How did you feel when you left home for uni?'

'Going to uni is not the same as going to war.'

'I know, but I just mean everyone feels excited and a bit scared when they do something big, something new.' He did not seem scared, just ready to throw himself headfirst into whatever life had to offer. Was she in his future? Something big – that was exactly the thing with him. For some people, life wasn't worth living unless they were doing something big. How do you love someone like that? She closed her eyes again and held her knees. Everything felt smaller and more manageable in the dark, with the sound of the waves. Tom could not resist climbing to his feet and having a few more goes at breaking his own record. There was room for her in his big life for now, for now.

Helmand Province, Afghanistan, November 2008

A scorched dustbowl, an area hemmed in by mountains. Five army officers are taking part in a weekly game of football with a group of local teenagers. The field is a couple of miles outside the centre of the city of Lashkar Gah. The soldiers form one team, with however many of the kids show up for the game making up the opposition side. They are usually outnumbered at least two to one. The soldiers are also hampered by playing in their heavy military boots. Tom knows the members of this group pretty well. There is little Yusuf with his dribbles and talented left foot; then big Mustaffa, a good six inches taller and a lot brawnier than the others, and with a pretty full beard for a teenager; there is also Asif, the prankster and court jester who goes up behind his teammates and pulls down their shorts to hoots of laughter. The boys have been provided with a new football and pump by the allies. Their goals and nets have also been repaired. Younger people seem far more open to mixing with the British forces and talking to them than many of their parents, most of whom are living through their second occupation having already seen off the Soviets. What Tom takes away from meetings with tribal elders and young kids alike is that life in this country grinds people down.

When was Afghanistan ever peaceful? Surely it's better that they are the ones here with the guns rather than the Soviets, or the Taliban left to their own devices? These kids' Fathers all most likely make a living through opium poppies. It's the only game in town in Helmand. The soldiers at Camp Bastion don't tend to be judgmental or moralistic about things like this, leave that to the politicians. These people are surviving the only way they can. Will these boys have to do the same? The soldiers can't join in the game with automatic rifles over their shoulders. They keep their berets on during the games, that's their training coming out. The boys laugh at them for this and try to grab them off their heads whenever the chance presents itself. The boys play in the morning, at lunchtime and after school (when there is school). It's the evening matches that the soldiers feel free to take part in once a week. Tom always feels gladdened at how accepting the boys are of their presence; they even tell the officers off if they're late. Only Yusuf and Mustafa speak any English but that doesn't matter as football turns out to be a simple and effective common language. They shout at one another in Pashto and make dramatic gestures akin to coaches on the touchline. Long after the soldiers have to return to base for evening briefing, the boys play on into the dusk. Life as one long summer holiday, but with added bombs and mortars.

Crunch! Tom goes into a fifty-fifty challenge with big Mustaffa. No quarter asked, none given - that's the way the boys play the game. The ball squirts out and the game carries on with them tangled up together on the ground. Big Mustaffa gets up and extends a big hand to Tom, who gratefully accepts and clambers to his feet. They both laugh, and before Mustaffa lumbers off to rejoin the game they make the briefest eye contact. In Mustaffa's eyes, Tom can see acceptance and even affection. He thinks he can also see a kind of understanding of what's going on around him, certainly more so than with the other boys. He hopes that Mustaffa sees acceptance from him. Tom wonders what the future will hold for these boys once the allied military presence is gone. Will they still be able to play in relative safety? Relative safety meaning living with the rocket strikes aimed at the military base about fifteen miles from here. What do the boys think about the Allies being in Afghanistan? What's it like to be the country that always gets invaded? What will his own future be like after Afghanistan? He hasn't thought that far ahead.

Mustaffa and Yusuf spend as much time as they can with the Brits and the Americans. They are sponges, soaking up any little titbit of knowledge they can find. This generation are more open to outside influence and the culture of the 'Angrez' than their elders who were brought up on tales of Afghan heroism and British barbarism as the underdogs sent the invaders packing at the battle of Maiwand. Will there be much of a country left for these boys? Tom finds himself missing passages of the game in this way, just standing still and looking out over the mountains as the shouting and instructions go on around him. He's heard stories of opium brides, young farmers' daughters taken by / given to warlords when the farmer defaults on loan payments due to the US policy of eradicating poppy crops. What if one of these boys has a sister who has disappeared in this fashion? He's asked Mustaffa and Yusuf about their families and their past before but neither seems keen to share. The information sharing is definitely one-way with them. Tom has met their uncle, a friendly and funny old man who welcomes the allied forces as if he had personally invited them. The boys idolize him. They look different to the other locals Tom sees every day in Helmand. The boys told Tom that they are Hazaras from the North.

During one evening's game they hear the distant boom of a rocket attack on the base. The soldiers abandon the game and run to grab their helmets and body armour. Tom actually forgets about his rifle in all the commotion. When he realizes and turns back, he sees it in the hands of little Yusuf. The boy holds the rifle as if this is not a new experience for him. Yusuf holds the gun with both hands, then throws it to the soldier.

'Good luck guys,' he says.

In an armoured vehicle escorting trucks along route Cornwall. The dust is fucking unbelievable but smile, at least you're off the base and out for the day. He's riding shotgun in a Viking with Matty Phillips at the wheel – good man.

This was all part of Operation Eagle's Summit, with 16 Brigade providing the leadership and a fair amount of the manpower for the transportation of a turbine, in several parts, from Gereshk to Kajaki. Why they were involved in this travelling circus, Tom had experienced enough of Afghanistan by now to know you didn't ask questions like that.

The mission was pretty typical of his time out here so far – nothing connected with anything else; one day you were getting lectures on the Afghan poppy industry, the next you were completely destroying whole villages while freeing them from insurgents, and the day after that you were crawling along as part of a massive sitting duck of a convoy delivering this shipment just in from China to a fuck off sized dam. As long as everyone in the chain followed their orders, then the whole thing fucking functioned okay.

The crackle of the radio fired up and told him the convoy would be slowing down because the IED guys up front had found a mine. Great. The dust was just off the scale. Imagine living with this every day. It got in your hair, your mouth, your clothes, everywhere. He'd lost mates on his first tour and now on his second. He finally got what Ali had been so worried about. During training it had all been great fun. He'd never met such a good bunch of guys. It all felt like they were getting ready to go on a rugby tour, with the banter and the nights out and chatting up the local girls. Back in 08, on his first tour with the brigade, the mission statement and the brigadier said one thing but once you were out there and all hell broke loose, you felt like you were just on your own. On your own together with your mates. How do you win the heart or mind of someone who hates you for being in their country? Firefights with insurgents in the Snake's Head…

They had almost crawled to a complete stop. One of the guys was whistling in the back. Tom told the driver to scan the area and keep his eyes peeled – they were a fucking sitting duck out here. Fear just turns to adrenaline and you act on instinct, from your training too. When Ali wrote to him with her plans for where they might live and hinting about them getting married when he next came home. What was the future after all the dust and fighting? Ali. She wrote him all the time. Some of the guys found a picture she sent and stuck her head on a pornstar's body and blue tacked it to the wall behind his bed for a laugh. It was still there.

'Does she know what a massive shagger you are, Tommy?'

'Yeah, obviously, why do you think she's with me?'

How could anyone feel at home out here? But he actually did. What the fuck was wrong with him? His cousin Terri wrote to him too. The lads assumed her letters were from another girlfriend, and he never put them straight. He enjoyed Terri's letters as they didn't come with that horrible knot in his stomach and the pressure to grow up and plan for life after Helmand. Her assumptions about the relationship had caught him unawares. Marriage? Come on, none of the lads were faithful to their girlfriends. Or maybe one or two were. But you get enough real shit out here, no one needs it when they get home as well. She didn't know what he was really like with women. He should just break it off with her. Anything just to avoid confrontation. He grinned to himself at the stupidity of his own thoughts while the drones buzzed overhead and the convoy churned into gear again. What were their names? He couldn't even remember a lot of them. You just did it, girlfriend or no girlfriend. Amanda. She wrote to him as well sometimes. She was that same strong, smart type he seemed to go for. Maybe they could hook up when he got back. She'd sent him a pretty nice picture too.

His work, his life here, that's what kept Ali's fantasy world where it belonged. They might take fire today. Fire. That was it. The fucking buzz. They were rolling again. He could feel every nerve, every sensor was on alert. You just didn't think. What a fucking job! Blowing off the cobwebs and all those thoughts about settling down – bothering him on his relaxation time when he wanted to have a laugh with the boys and sink a few tins. The dust, man! You could only crawl along in this visibility. Not the sort of mission where you could get a bit of shut eye. Go to sleep and wake up in several pieces. He felt strong and alert – ready for whatever happened. Her letters were like attacks on his mind. He didn't even read most of them. Marrying some bird you shagged for a while at uni? The lads would fucking slaughter him. He smiled to himself. Look at that dust, man.

The boys walked through a pass in the mountains with the natural ease of a pair of born trackers. They could have made excellent tour guides for visitors eager to experience this barren landscape. But since Helmand had long ceased to be a destination of choice for hippies and spiritual adventurers, Mustaffa and Yusuf had no experience of meeting tourists, and they knew that these mountains were hiding places not just for them but for the Taliban and God knew who else. The boys experienced the stinging sense of fear that always accompanied their excursions to the hideout, because it was always possible that one of the many bands of Taliban fighters could have found the cave since the boys' last visit. The dust and heat of daily life in the region became oppressive in the spotlight of this particularly urgent form of anxiety. The boys had never voiced these fears to one another, but they had developed an unspoken system of taking it in turns to be the first to crawl through the narrow entrance passage.

'All clear, pal!'

This time it was Yusuf's turn to brave the unknown. He would doubtless be hiding in there somewhere, giggling to himself and waiting to leap out and surprise his friend. Mustaffa smiled at the thought. He emerged from the tunnel and raised himself up to full height. He stretched and called out:

'I'm through!'

Nothing. Mustaffa strolled over to the small clearing that showed the charred evidence of the last campfire the boys had built. He walked through the ashes to the seating area they had improvised with a few cushions and a rug, artfully stolen from their family home they shared with their uncle. He found what he was looking for straight away - a green military canvas bag that contained sweets, chocolates, used shell casings, and a couple of copies of Playboy that the boys had spent many a wide-eyed hour leafing through, all of which had been donated by the allied soldiers. He took a chunky mobile phone out of the pocket of his shorts, a Nokia, and placed it in the bag. One of the soldiers had recently given it to him, saying that it still worked. He and Yusuf could try it out some time.

One day he'd seen a group of them sitting round a campfire and smoking. He'd asked if he could join them. They said yes and offered him one of their special cigarettes. He'd tried it and it had burned his throat and shot straight to his head. The soldiers laughed but in a kindly way. They told him that this 'weed' was different to smoking a normal cigarette. They gave him one of their cigarettes to share with his friends, but told him not to tell his parents, which he swore he wouldn't. They didn't know, of course, that Mustaffa and Yusuf had no parents, or that Mustaffa knew very well what they were smoking as he had seen the hashish on sale in Kandahar. He and Yusuf had smoked the weed in this very hiding place. Mustaffa showed Yusuf how to inhale the smoke and hold it before breathing it out. The two of them had giggled the night away. Both of the boys knew very well that their Uncle Taleed would not approve of this one bit. He had warned them often of the dangers of narcotics, and of the harm the trade continued to do to the country. The boys had therefore agreed that this would be a one-off experiment. Something else that Mustaffa shared with Yusuf from his evening around the campfire was a story that one of the soldiers had told the others: this soldier had heard the story from one of his mates back at home, a two-tour veteran. The veteran was full of shocking stories of unreported things that had gone on in Afghanistan, such as the quality of the opium on sale in the bazar in the centre of Maiwand. This particular story came also came from Maiwand, not far from here, early on in the Allied invasion. The soldier's mate was part of a regiment tasked with going out at night and shooting rabid dogs in the area. One consequence of the invasion was that many once domesticated dogs were left to fend for themselves as locals fled their communities while the Allies and the Taliban clashed. When a British soldier was bitten on the arm by one such creature out on patrol one night, a crack team was dispatched to do some canine dispatching. The mate of the soldier apparently said that this had been the most unpleasant duty he'd had to perform during his military career.

All of the soldiers round the campfire seemed oddly (in Mustaffa's eyes) moved by the story. There were no laughs or wisecracks as was usually the case when someone came out with an anecdote. When Mustaffa told this story to Yusuf, the latter had said he wasn't surprised by this, that the invaders obviously cared more about mangy dogs than they did about people. Mustaffa said he didn't think that was the case. He tried to imagine how the small group of men tasked with this pretty unpleasant job felt as they trudged through abandoned villages, whole communities, in the hope or perhaps more likely the fear of coming across a rabid dog or two. How would they explain this to their loved ones when they spoke or wrote? Maybe you couldn't explain something like this to someone who hadn't been to war. The soldiers Mustaffa met thought they knew far more than some poor kid from the middle of nowhere. He told Yusuf to tell the allies nothing, but never miss an opportunity to learn from them. The words of Uncle Taleed. Mustaffa and Yusuf had learned of the Soviet occupation and other major events of Afghan history in Uncle Taleed's makeshift classroom.

'Look and learn,' said Taleed, and Mustaffa had taken this on board. He told the boys that the West saw Afghanistan as their personal plaything, to be manipulated and used as they saw fit. 'Look at the history of this country, boys,' — and this they most definitely did. Exiled from their home region and severely traumatized, Mustaffa knew instinctively that Uncle Taleed was giving them more than a dry history lesson and a replacement for regular school. Uncle Taleed's lessons were a pathway, a plan for a better life. He had taught them that nothing was ever clear-cut, and that while the Taliban were their sworn enemies, they were by no means the boys' only enemies in the country. Uncle Taleed's words were never far from Mustaffa's thoughts. Taleed was happy to use the West to overthrow the Taliban, but he had no illusions about the ultimate fate of this invasion, just like all the others. Taleed had taken the boys out into the mountains on camping trips.

'Look at this country, boys. Is this a place that will ever submit to occupation and colonial rule?' The boys had shaken their heads as they knew this was expected. Taleed had smiled at them.

'You will both understand one day. This is a singular country. It harms its own people but that is nothing compared to fury it hold in reserve for invaders. This country cares not who you are, where you come from, what your supposed ideals are, or what exactly you are doing here. Alexander the Great himself could not subdue this country for long. Afghanistan will release her white blood cells to fight anything that shouldn't be within her system. Biology, yes?' More nodding from the boys. More smiles from their uncle.

'Let the latest invaders take care of the Taliban.' Uncle Taleed spat in a rare display of the quiet force that rested behind his studious manner. 'I am convinced that our future lies away from here. We cannot allow ourselves to be swept up in the hurricane that Helmand will unleash on our American and British friends.' There was a cool breeze up in the hills near the village. Mustaffa liked camping out with Yusuf and Uncle as it reminded him of their escape from Mazar, and it made him feel safe and secure by comparison.

'You heard that they destroyed the Buddhas?' said Uncle quietly. The boys both nodded.

'I didn't know if you had heard, but I don't want either of you to worry about it. Those Buddhas live in your hearts and minds, they are more than mere sandstone. It will take far more than fools and their dynamite to wipe them away.'

'Are we safe now that the Taliban have been beaten?' said Mustaffa.

'I would say that we are safer, certainly,' said Uncle. 'I sometimes think that nobody is safe here for very long.'

'We should go to America, uncle – the three of us,' said Mustaffa.

Taleed smiled. 'All in good time, my child.'

As he leafed through one of the magazines for the thousandth time, a sound came from high up on the cave wall among the few chinks of light peeping through from the outside. A giggle. Mustaffa's plan of delay had worked and Yusuf had given away his position. He'd let him scrabble around up there a bit longer. As he munched on a handful of bonbons, he thought some more about the war and what it might mean for his country. Maybe the Americans could give himself and Yusuf a lift in one of their planes when they did eventually leave? And what about Uncle Taleed? He had been right about Helmand, as he was about most things. The foreigners acted like they'd stumbled into a region they knew little about. The country was too wild to accept their ideas of democracy and civilization. He wondered if Yusuf ever had thoughts like this, then smiled at the ridiculousness of his own question.

'The enemy of my enemy is my friend,' Uncle Taleed had said with a questioning tone. This was a good few years ago, early in 2002, when they had first come here from Pakistan. Uncle Taleed had been looking out at the small garden of the house where they stayed with distant relatives. Their family were Noorzai who had lived in the village of Shin Kalay for generations. Mustaffa was seated at the kitchen table with his books open.

'Is the enemy of my enemy actually my friend though, uncle?'

'We had better prepare for school.' said Taleed. 'Where is that brother of yours, still slumbering?' Taleed grinned and Mustaffa nodded and laughed.

Uncle Taleed's reputation as an inspiring school master had quickly spread. He taught sometimes thirty, sometimes forty or fifty lively young minds in the village's old schoolroom.

'What are they so afraid of?' Yusuf had said, to his uncle's great amusement.

'You will see what they are afraid of in a brief while, my boy. Now go and feed the goats before they start a protest.' Yusuf ran off into the garden, chuckling away to himself in that carefree manner of his. Mustaffa was helping Taleed set up the desks and chairs for that day's lesson. Nobody but Taleed knew what this would consist of. Sometimes Mustaffa suspected that his uncle made them up each day on the spot.

'In answer to your earlier question, my child, western enemies of the Taliban can be useful short-term allies to us. Do you recall that the three of us said a prayer of thanks when the Taliban fell? However, bear in mind that the Americans have no more idea about this country than the Soviets before them.' Taleed was whispering, as even a conversation in a deserted old school room in a tiny village in Helmand was not a free conversation.

The three of them had watched the TV news reports of September 11th in the cramped kitchen in an equally cramped apartment in Islamabad. It was here that Uncle Taleed had established a prototype version of his Helmand schoolroom with blackboard, two old school desks, and stacks of books. Since that day it felt like the whole world was focused on Afghanistan and the Taliban, and on the terrorist they had sheltered. As the events unfolded before them, Uncle Taleed called it 'a live history lesson'. Yusuf was confused and he protested that 'we're supposed to be doing story writing today.' Uncle Taleed told him that 'momentous events necessitate a change of timetable.'

Uncle Taleed lectured them that day on how Bin Laden was a rich Saudi who had come to Afghanistan to stir up trouble. He told them that there would be hell to pay for their country, for sheltering this man who had tried to blow up the towers once before and had now succeeded. There was a grim inevitability to it all. The Americans needed an easy target and the Taliban would provide them with it. The Americans never learned from history, you see, or the Brits either for that matter.

'Where do you think the Taliban will go when the invasion happens?' said Uncle Taleed. As with many of his questions, the boys were unsure of whether they were required to answer.

'Here?' said Mustaffa, his mind scrambling from the events of the day.

'That's right, boy,' said Uncle Taleed. 'The Taliban, the real Taliban that is, will retreat here to lick their wounds and see how it all plays out. They'll wait till the Americans get bored and tired of the heat and the dust.'

'If the Taliban falls, will we be able to go back?' said Yusuf. Mustaffa thought about this.

'Oh we'll go back,' said Uncle Taleed, 'all in good time, my boys.'

Yusuf plummeted from his hiding place onto the back of his friend, with both boys collapsing to the floor in fits of laughter.

'Nice landing,' said Mustaffa when he'd finally got his breath back.

'Thanks,' said Yusuf.

Mustaffa sat back against one of the cave's soft furnishings and leafed through the magazine a bit more. The boys always spoke in Persian when they were alone or with their uncle. Yusuf came over to join him and said:

'What you doing, big man?' Yusuf always asked questions to which he already knew the answer. Usually Mustaffa found this annoying, but today it just made him feel a surge of goodwill and affection.

'Going to the toilet,' he said, 'what does it look like, you nitwit?' The boys both laughed and Yusuf shadowboxed against Mustaffa's arm.

'You still in love with your favourite blonde?' asked Yusuf.

'Of course,' said Mustaffa.

'I wonder,' said the smaller boy, moving closer to look over his friend's shoulder, 'if you shouldn't be spending a little more time with your school books?' Yusuf's quizzical questioning was carried out in a perfect impression of one of their teachers who had finally taken over the village school and allowed Uncle Taleed to retire to his books and his long walks.

'Can I have a look now?' asked Yusuf.

'Enjoy,' said Mustaffa as he rolled up the magazine and pretended to swat Yusuf with it. Just about all the exposure to women that the boys had had came from the Playboys and Penthouses that they had been given by US and UK troops. It was hard to feel anything but warmth towards the occupiers who brought with them such exotic and forbidden treats. Yusuf studied the magazine as if it contained images of great works of art. Mustaffa continued to snack on sweets. 'We'd better not be too late tonight. Don't want uncle Taleed sending out a search party, do we?'

'Too right,' said Yusuf, 'I'd rather take on the Taliban than face one of uncle's lectures any day.' Both boys fell about laughing. Yusuf returned the magazine to the rucksack with due reverence.

The late evening light had nearly faded away when the boys emerged. There was always a wide variety of noises out here among the mountains at this time. The howls of wolves, the clatter of tumbling pieces of rock, the swirl of dust in the evening breeze, and the distant and ever-present sound of gunfire merged to create an eerie atmosphere. The boys stood side by side outside the cave for a moment. They both knew uncle would be disappointed if they missed dinner, then evening prayer. Neither of them could conceive of anything worse than disappointing their uncle.

'D'you think these hills are haunted?' A typical Yusuf question.

Mustaffa looked around and puffed out his cheeks, giving it due consideration. 'Yeah, I think so.'

'Why do you say that?'

'Well, just think about all the people: the soldiers, the Taliban, the Soviets, who've died out here.'

'Thanks a lot,' said Yusuf, 'now I'm even more terrified out here than usual. When I was hanging by my fingernails from the cave wall I was thinking about Bin Laden.'

'Oh yeah? What about him?'

'I was thinking what if we came here one day and found Bin Laden in the cave?' Yusuf seemed excited at this prospect.

Mustaffa burst out laughing and shook his head. 'We might crawl in their one day and see Bin Laden sitting on the floor filming one of his videos to send out to the world.'

Yusuf was silently laughing now. 'Yeah, we'd have to say "Excuse me, Mr Bin Laden, but this is our cave, now take your beard and all your video equipment and get out before we throw you out!"'

'Ha!' said Mustaffa. 'Do you think the Allies really know who it is they're fighting?'

'What do you mean?' said Yusuf.

'Well, the other day a bunch of men from the village were showing the Allies where some Taliban had their base. Remember?'

'Yeah.'

'The Allies blew them up! Booooooom!' Mustaffa clapped his hands. 'That's what I mean, though. Those guys weren't Taliban, they were just poppy growers.'

Yusuf shrugged. 'How do you get to know so much?'

'I use these,' said Mustaffa, pointing to his eyes. 'And these.' He wiggled his ears. 'We don't understand this country and we're from here.'

This was met with a further shrug. 'Uncle Taleed's the only guy who understands this country because he's studied it his whole life.'

'Agreed.' Mention of their uncle reminded them that they ought to be heading back.

Yusuf shivered and rubbed his arms. 'Let's get out of here,' he said.

'I thought you were a daring man of action? How can you be scared of the dark and a few ghosts?' said Mustaffa.

'I am a man of action,' said Yusuf with a cheeky smile, 'I'm just tired.'

'You ever think about the Buddhas?' asked Mustaffa.

Yusuf was quite as the insects clicked and chirped away in the evening air. Mustaffa turned to look at him. 'That's funny,' said Yusuf.

'What do you mean?'

'I see them all the time. I see them huge.' Yusuf widened his arms to show just how tall. 'Not scary, though.'

'I know,' said Mustaffa. 'I dream about them. Sometimes I see them when I just close my eyes. Do you know what they were called?'

'No.'

'Salsal was the bigger one and Shamama was the smaller one.'

'Salsal and Shamama.' Yusuf spoke the words as if weighing them up. 'How do you know their names?'

'Uncle Taleed told me, he knows everything.' They walked in silence for a little while.

'But they're gone now,' said Yusuf with a sudden note of sadness.

'They're not gone,' said Mustaffa. 'The Taliban blew them up, but they're not gone.'

As they approached town, Mustaffa broke the thickening silence.

'So you find it scary in the hills?'

'Yeah, a bit,' replied Yusuf, 'but everywhere's scary here. I know what you mean about ghosts. Promise you'll take me with you when you go to your fancy college in America?'

'Of course I will,' said Mustaffa, and he meant it. He picked Yusuf up and carried him on his back, doing a silly walk at the same time to make him laugh and forget about all of their ghosts for a while.

The city of Mazar-i-Sharif, 8th August 1998

Two boys were looking at each other from opposite sides of an elevated ridge that flanked the only road into their town. They were part of a group of six who had come from their homes in the still dark of the early morning. They had maintained a steady pace despite the meager breakfasts in their bellies, as they came from their different neighbourhoods - Saidebad, Kate Ariana, Ali Chopan - and met under the usual tree by the side of the road.

The boys were playing a game called 'Taliban', if "playing" and "game" were even applicable under the circumstances. In their six and seven-year-old minds, they were preparing for the ambush and capture of a Taliban supply truck that would provide much-needed food for their families. The only noise was the occasional emaciated bleat of sheep and goats awaking to another day of drudgery under the sun.

Yusuf was crouched in the dust. He brought to his eyes a pair of binoculars, removed from his Father's cupboard the night before. He scanned the road in the distance up to the point at which it emerged out of the clouds and disappeared into the mountains. Yusuf could made eye contact with his friend Mustaffa, directly opposite on the other side of the road. His was the important job of silently alerting the others with a fist in the air if he saw a vehicle approaching. The boys had gathered rocks to throw, and one of their number had a homemade slingshot. A couple of the boys had even taken sharp knives from the kitchen at home. Yusuf felt a chill run through him at the sight of the blades. All they had done thus far was throw the odd rock at a car and run for cover. Yusuf thought about encountering an actual Taliban car full of his people's sworn enemies. The boys had all seen dead bodies around the outskirts of the town when playing. Their Mothers told them to keep away from them, that it wasn't safe.

Yusuf and Mustaffa both had their usual thin porridge of oats and grains that morning, just about providing them with sufficient energy to run around. Yusuf hadn't seen his Father for several days. Mustaffa told him that his Dad was away as well. This would be some kind of planning meeting in anticipation of the next Taliban attack. The boys knew that their Fathers were commanders in the Hezbe Wahdat forces, but they were not encouraged to ask questions about their whereabouts. Yusuf's reverie was broken by a small stone that smacked into his forehead.

'Hey,' shouted Yusuf, 'we're supposed to be on the same side.'

'Quiet!' shouted one of the other boys further along the line.

'You were so surprised,' laughed Mustaffa. 'If I'd been a Taliban gunman, you'd have been dead for sure.'

'Shut up!' shouted another voice.

'I'm a far better soldier than you,' shouted Yusuf at his friend. 'And my Dad's killed way more Talibans than yours ever has.'

Mustaffa stood up.

'Sit down, you'll give us all away,' shouted another voice.

'My Dad was the bravest fighter in the battle and everyone knows it,' yelled Mustaffa. 'Your Dad pissed in his pants.'

There were a few giggles from the other boys.

'You take that back,' hissed Yusuf.

'I will not. Your Dad's a big cry baby who wet himself in the battle.'

Yusuf was clambering down the embankment and onto the road before anyone had a chance to stop him. Mustaffa climbed down to meet him halfway. Even at the age of six, Mustaffa had a considerable size advantage over Yusuf, so when the smaller boy ran at him and tried to knock him off his feet, Mustaffa was able to keep him at arm's length before applying a headlock and mussing the smaller boy's hair with the flat of his hand. When Mustaffa released him, Yusuf was enraged, with a bright red face. The other boys were cheering and laughing. Mustaffa edged closer to his friend and tied his arms up in a bear hug. He lifted him up and swung him round in the air.

'Wheeeeeeeee!' he shouted. He did this several times before Yusuf began to laugh. They were all laughing now, the seriousness of their mission momentarily forgotten. The boys climbed down from the embankment onto the road, their hardly full tummies bulging out from under their tunics. Most of them had sisters and since the intensifying of the fight against the Taliban, the elders considered it too dangerous to allow the girls to wander and play out in the open alongside the boys. When he thought about it, Mustaffa realized that when he was at home, his Father barely let Mustaffa's sister out of his sight. Most of the boys barely registered this change on a conscious level. One thing they certainly did notice was the food embargo placed on them and their families by the Taliban.

The boys took turns picking up Yusuf and swinging him around as he giggled madly. Eventually Mustaffa stepped in and brought this to a halt. They were about to return to their positions when they heard the distinct rumbling of a car engine. They turned to face the direction of the noise and saw a pickup truck full of armed men. There was no chance of returning to their hiding place because the car was too close. Besides, the boys could not remove their eyes from the machine gun mounted on the bed of the jeep. They stood still on one side of the road as the vehicle came to a halt with the engine still running. One of the men jumped down from the bed of the truck. He had a thin face with a long black beard and small eyes. Like his compatriots, he wore a black turban.

'What are you kids doing out here?'

'Nothing,' said Mustaffa.

'Nothing? Okay.' The armed man swung his rifle off his shoulder and cracked the stock into the side of Mustaffa's head. He sank to his knees but didn't make a sound. Yusuf had a rock in his hand that he wanted desperately to hurl at the Taliban before him, but the sight of the rifle and the dead look in the man's eyes frightened him to his core. The boys were all still and silent.

The man didn't seem to know what to do next, and the others in the truck were getting impatient. Yusuf pulled the other boys closer to him into a kind of huddle. Wordlessly they put their arms around one another and looked at the gunman.

'Come on,' shouted one of the men in the truck.

'I'm coming,' the man spat back at him. He walked up to the group of boys. He took his gun and mimed shooting them all. Then he laughed. 'Tell your Daddies we're on our way. And your Mothers and sisters.' The truck drove away. The boys helped Mustaffa to his feet. He had a cut on his head and said he felt dizzy. Yusuf noticed that one of the boys had wet himself. No one among them was laughing now.

'We need to get back and warn everyone that they're on their way,' said Mustaffa.

It was only when the boys had fallen into their typical running rhythm, and when the fear and adrenaline of the encounter with the Taliban had lessened a little, that the true gravity of the situation dawned on Yusuf. He hoped his Father and the other commanders were ready, and he felt a stabbing pain in the centre of him when he thought of his Mother and sisters.

Blood everywhere. Escape with your lives. Rockets exploding in the marketplace. Thousands dead. Kicking down doors and shooting the Hazaras. The bodies of men and women and infants. Numbness and noise. Cut their throats. Exterminate them all. Solid traffic fleeing the city. Cars fired upon. Uncle driving over bodies and asking for forgiveness. Those who weren't killed were loaded into giant containers and driven away. Hundreds of bodies were emptied into the unwitting desert. Bodies on the ground and bangs going off. A child's bedroom bombed. Traders in the market shot down while preparing their wares. The end of the world. Uncle didn't stop when a Taliban stood before him and tried to hold up the car. The car dragged the Taliban along for several feet.

Mustaffa's uncle drove and didn't stop until they reached the mountains in Bamiyan. He told the boys not to think about what had happened. He said there would be time for that later when they had settled in their new home, but not now please. He told them to get some sleep. He had some chocolate bars in the glove box that he gave to them. Yusuf slept; he wasn't sure if Mustaffa did. The boys and the sixty-year-old man had cried together in the car. He said when it was safe they would all cross the border into Pakistan; they would have a better life this way, he said. They would have food, shelter and safety from the Taliban. There was a map in the car and Uncle Taleed showed the boys exactly where they would cross the border, at a place called Spin Boldak. It looked like a long way to the border, but Uncle Taleed had been so calm since the attack that they both simply trusted him without question.

The boys huddled together on top of blankets on the floor of a cave and tried to sleep in the dry heat. There were insects floating in the faint light from the cave's entrance. The boys stared at them. As Mustaffa finally felt sleep enveloping him, he saw an image of his Father assaulting and robbing fleeing civilians, commandeering their vehicle, leaving them for dead. He couldn't tell if this was a memory or a dream, or both.

When they woke in the morning and walked out of the cave, they realized that they had slept next to one of the twin statues of the Buddha at Bamiyan, carved into the sandstone cliff face. The statue towered over them. Parts of its legs had worn away but the serene and welcoming quality of its face made the boys stand and take it in while the morning sun drenched the fields of the valley below.

'Did you know that these were here?' said Yusuf.

'No, I didn't,' said Mustaffa. He turned to Yusuf. The smaller boy was shielding his eyes. Mustaffa put his arm around his friend and hugged him. The boys looked around and saw images on the walls of the cave. Uncle Taleed must have slept in a different cave, or more likely in the car to stand guard. For a moment, the boys could almost have been tourists walking around a gallery, or foreign travellers taking in a cultural experience before getting back on their coach. The wind roused itself and buffeted a cloud of dust against the Buddha. Mustaffa pointed out an image of two birds with what looked to be a string of pearls between their beaks.

'Best friends forever?' said Yusuf.

'Brothers forever.' The boys performed the handshake that they practiced so often they could do it with their eyes closed and at blinding speed.

The walls of the cave were covered with colourful images of seated Buddhas as well as what appeared to be people meeting and trading goods in some far-off time. Mustaffa felt as though he were reading the walls and looking for a message within them; Yusuf quickly became bored and wanted to leave to find Uncle.

They were soon back in the car with Uncle Taleed. He had the radio on and the three of them sang along to pop songs on the BBC Persia service. It occurred to Yusuf that neither of them had prayed since early morning on the day of the attack. He told the others and, thinking back, they agreed that they should stop to pray when it was safe.

With a Taliban blockade visible in the distance, Uncle told the boys to hide under blankets in the back. He said it would be easier if they weren't seen; less questions for a frail old man driving by himself. With the boys hidden away, Uncle Taleed turned the volume down and switched to a local news channel. As he suspected, the Taliban had quickly taken over the broadcasts. Uncle Taleed understood a little Pashto so he could follow in general terms what the harsh voice on the radio was saying: the entire Hezbe Wahdat force had been killed by the Taliban at Qala Zaini, west of the city. So much for all of your speeches and your war mongering, brothers, he thought. The voice went on to deliver an ultimatum to the Hazaras remaining in the city: become Sunnis or leave Afghanistan. The only other option was death. This had been a broadcast by the Taliban Ministry for the Enforcement of Virtue and Suppression of Vice. Uncle Taleed shook his head and switched off the radio. As he approached the roadblock, he kept despair just about at bay with thoughts of the two boys who were depending on him. He felt the same nervous feeling in his gut that had come and gone since the Taliban attack and the cold realization of his worst fears. He covered his face with a handkerchief and said a silent prayer.

'Absolutely still now, boys,' he said.

Uncle Taleed knew that either their car would pass through the checkpoint, by the will of Allah, or he would crash through it. The starkness of the situation calmed his nerves and gave him clarity of thought. There were other cars in front and only a few Taliban manning the checkpoint. Thick dust swirled on the breeze as Taleed rolled down the window. He held the handkerchief in place and covered more of his face with his hand. The sun was blinding. Let us through. Two Taliban were looking in the boot of the car in front. The one who came to the window was no more than a boy. Another lost soul with nothing to live for but the barbaric doctrines of the Taliban, thought Uncle Taleed. Leave us to our journey, you pup. The young Taliban stared at Uncle Taleed with suspicious eyes. The others seemed to have found something of interest in the car in front. Taleed could feel the eyes of the boy soldier, but he wouldn't turn to look at him.

'What's in the back?' said the boy.

'Nothing,' said Taleed in his best Pashto.
'What?'
'There's nothing there.'
'What's under the blankets?'
'Nothing, I told you,' said Taleed.
'I can't hear you, take your hand away.'
Taleed's foot hovered over the accelerator.
'Hey!' shouted one of the soldiers in front. 'Come and look at this.'

The boy soldier hesitated, then waved the car through and ran to join his older mates. The car pulled gently away. By the will of Allah, thought Taleed.

Having stopped to pray, Yusuf sat in the back of the car with his eyes closed and he saw the Buddhas, huge and peaceful in his mind's eye. He didn't see the things he was afraid he would, and for this he was glad. The Buddhas seemed to glow and hum as he saw them. He hoped that one day he would see them up close again. How long had they been there? Thousands of years probably.

With the journey back underway, Yusuf was keen to share his vision.

'I see them too,' said Mustaffa, 'when my eyes are closed.' He smiled at Yusuf. As the car rattled along the bumpy road and the uncle continued to sing, Yusuf closed his eyes with his head resting on Mustaffa's shoulder. In his dreams, Yusuf saw the Buddhas.

'Your Fathers never thought much of me. They called me a coward and a weakling, only good for making jokes.'

The boys didn't know where to look as one of Uncle Taleed's rambling stories had taken an unexpectedly serious turn round the small fire they had made.

'No they didn't,' said Mustaffa, whilst in his heart he knew that Uncle Taleed was right.

'You're a good boy,' said Uncle Taleed, 'but you don't need to worry about my feelings. I know what people thought of me. But things have changed now. I will get you boys to the border if it costs me my life.' The boys both rushed to hug the old man. 'Look, I'm welling up now, crying like an old fool.'

'Would you like some more beans, uncle?' said Yusuf. Amidst the chaos, Taleed had instructed the boys to grab whatever supplies they could find.

'I would, thank you.' He wiped his eyes with an handkerchief. Yusuf removed their small pan from the fire and spooned some more of the very basic bean stew into his uncle's bowl. The three of them had made a comfortable enough campsite in a clearing on the road that would take them around Kabul and eventually to the border. They were all leaning on blankets and listening to the intermingling sounds of the woodland.

'Uncle?' said Mustaffa.

'Yes Mustaffa,' said Uncle Taleed with his usual smile restored.

'Will we see our home again, once we go to Pakistan?' Uncle Taleed finished his spoonful of stew.

'Yes, yes you will, my boy.' He set down his bowl. 'People should not be exiled from their homeland unless there is no other way, and unfortunately for the moment there is no other way. But my plan for you two definitely involves a return to this country, and hopefully to your home city one day.'

'Will we still celebrate Nauroz?' said Yusuf.

'We can adapt,' said Uncle Taleed, 'just as the Hazaras have always done. We will take our customs to a new land. They tried to wipe us all out back in the 1800s, boys. Did you know that? But it is just us three now. We just worry about each other, and we will be all right, by the will of Allah. What did you think of the Buddhas?'

'They were massive!' said Yusuf.

'And beautiful,' said Mustaffa.

'Good boys,' said Taleed. 'They date from a time when peace and prosperity reigned in the Bamiyan Valley. Life was filled with a sense of opportunity. The land was largely Buddhist, but it mattered not if you were a Hindu or later a Muslim. People came from all over to trade here or as religious pilgrims. Imagine what that must have been like, boys. Those paintings you saw are what happens when different cultures merge and mix with each other. That's what these barbarian Taliban will never understand.'

'Can we go to America one day, uncle?' said Mustaffa.

'I think that both of you will travel in the future. This country is too small to contain spirits like yours.'

'And what about you?' said Yusuf. 'We can't go without you.'

'By the time you two are grown up and ready to see the world, I will be a very tired old man. Now finish your stew and get some sleep.'

The boys smiled at each other and lay down on top of their blankets in the warm open air. Knowing that Uncle Taleed had a "plan" for their futures, that they even had futures, was enormously comforting for the boys as they drifted into a state of slumber before the flickering tongues.

'Uncle?' Said Yusuf.

'Yes, nephew.'

'Tell us a story about the Buddhas.'

Uncle Taleed stretched his arms before him. 'Are we all sitting comfortably? Because the tale I have to tell will take us all back to the year 629 AD, when...'

'What does AD mean?' said Yusuf.

'Ah! No questions till the teller of tales has spun his yarn. Now where was I? Oh yes, the year 629 AD. It was a warm night in Bamiyan, a lot like tonight...'

The boys settled in for the night.

Even as Yusuf closed his eyes and pictured himself as the avenging hero, killing Taliban in their hundreds with his sword of justice and leading an army of the wronged sons of Mazar, the fantasy was shadowed by something sour and insistent. He sat up and looked over at Mustaffa.

'Mustaffa,' he whispered in the darkness. The last embers of the fire crackled away to themselves.

'What?'

'Sit up, I need to talk to you.'

'I'm too tired,' said Mustaffa, but he rolled over to face his friend and leaned on an elbow.

'You know those things everyone was saying about our Fathers, that we said we'd never speak about again?'

'That we swore we'd never speak about, you mean?'

'Yeah, well I think today changes that and you and me can talk about anything now.'

'I guess you're right.' Mustaffa's expression had changed from sleepiness to apprehension.

'So we both heard that our Fathers hurt women during the war with the Taliban. Everyone heard it, right?'

'Raped,' said Mustaffa in a quiet voice.

'What?'

'Raped, that's the word, not hurt, hurt is different.' Mustaffa felt he knew what the word meant without ever having its meaning confirmed. He wasn't sure if Yusuf knew what this meant, but he supposed he must if he was asking about it.

'Well, we never thought it was true, did we? But my Dad used to take my sister away into a room, just them. She would come out in tears and she had bruises on her. I asked Dad what was wrong with her and he hit me.'

Mustaffa knew he had to share with Yusuf, even though to do so was to face up to something that he had been keeping at arms' length for several months. 'My Father was doing the same thing to my Mother. I heard it, but I didn't know what to do.' Mustaffa felt tears well up. Even though they had all cried openly earlier, he still tried to resist it.

'Cry if you want to. You can cry today,' said Yusuf. 'There's nothing you could've done, you know.'

'I know. And our families are gone now. Our Fathers were heroes to us - the mighty warriors. They weren't heroes, Yusuf, they were weak and cowardly. Uncle Taleed's right, they did laugh at him and call him runt. It turns out he's better than them.'

'Do you think they escaped?'

'No way.'

The silence hung between them like a thick fog.

'Sorry I upset you,' said Yusuf finally.

'It wasn't you who upset me, brother. Sleep well.'
'You sleep well too.'

In Yusuf's dreams, the Buddhas were brightly coloured and shining with jewels. Their heads were dressed with enormous wooden masks protecting the stone and the stucco from the elements. The Bamiyan valley was teeming with people of many nationalities: merchants and traders from here and there and everywhere. Many poor people were suffering and plague-ridden. The Buddhas had no immediate cure for their ills. They just stared on with wise disinterest. The Buddhas had no interest in commerce. They were present. They were there for everyone. The Buddhas were for everyone.

Part Seven: Tokyo 1975

'I'll speak to her, / And she shall be my Queen.'

Milton, 'Comus'

Shinjuku Koseinenkin Kaikan, February 7th

    The music blares out from the stage as Mrs Megan Hanzo makes her way back from the ladies' room to her husband's table, holding her five-year-old daughter by the hand. They are here for a performance by some famous American jazz musician who's currently on tour in Japan, not that this noise sounds much like music to Megan. The house is packed, but this music and the huge shades and nonchalant manner of the main performer are just too loud for her. Megan's small ears, in full view with her jet-black hair pulled back in an elegant bun, are ringing from the sheer volume of the performance, and she realises that the girl has stopped next to a speaker, holding her doll up against it.
    Megan holds her highball and her daughter's orange juice while she waits for her to finish whatever game it is she is playing.

She is such a strong-willed girl that it's often easier to let her do what she wants and avoid a scene. Megan hears her name being called and turns around to see her husband Toshiro beckoning her over whilst simultaneously beaming at three suited businessmen. Or are these ones politicians? It's hard to keep up with all of her husband's contacts. On occasions like this, she is expected to play the dutiful wife; nod, smile, look nice, and not much more.

Toshiro Hanzo is in his element. He is holding court before a gathering of movers and shakers. His smile is a mile wide and his repartee is in full swing. Megan takes a sip of her drink and assesses her husband from afar. He is a handsome, very well dressed forty-seven-year-old who still has that glint of youthful spirit and charm that so beguiled this visiting university lecturer from England fifteen years ago. His hair is a distinguished grey and there isn't an ounce of fat on him. Lucy is still leaning on the railing.

Megan and her daughter want for nothing. They have a vast penthouse apartment in one of the most sought-after areas of Shinjuku, and Toshiro has a fleet of black Mercedes cars and a team of drivers, assistants, analysts. She doesn't know for a fact he's ever done anything illegal, but she isn't stupid; Toshiro came from very humble beginnings in post-war Okinawa. No one rises so fast and so high in Tokyo without having a streak of ruthlessness. These thoughts ring as insistently in her mind as the wailing trumpet of the figure on stage.

'Lucy,' she touches her daughter's shoulder and gives her a slight shock. The surprised expression soon turns into a smile as the girl embraces her Mother around both legs.

'Shall we go and sit with Daddy and his important friends?'

Lucy grimaces. 'Mummy, they're boring.' Megan ruffles Lucy's hair and leans in closer over the railing. She surveys the packed house of enraptured jazz fans. Guitar and organ fill the void left by the trumpeter with the hair and the shades as he takes a slow and slightly limping walk around the stage. Megan feels an overwhelming urge to turn around and see what is going on between her husband and his associates.

'Edward Elgar used to suffer from migraines. They were

brought about by stress.' Megan has no idea why she's telling her daughter this.

'Yes I know,' says Lucy in a tired voice. Megan turns to see a slight figure in a long black coat enter the VIP area, flanked by two huge men in black zip-up leather jackets. She notices at this point that the men guarding the sanctity of the cordoned-off zone have the word "ATTENDANT" written in white on the back of their black t-shirts.

She entered the study with a swift turn of the old-fashioned key. She could count on one hand the number of times she had been in this room, even with Toshiro present. She had always known where he kept the key, but had never even felt the slightest urge to enter and look around until now.

Whenever Megan paused during her daily rounds of planning charity fundraisers with the other society wives and managing the staff throughout the three floors of their apartment, she thought about how her life with Toshiro was one of mutual secrecy. She saw unspoken boundaries and heavily guarded borders in every conversation they had.

Her contact with his money began and ended with looking glamorous in the jewelry and dresses he gave her, picking out new furnishings for the apartment, and planning luxurious holidays for the family. It was often only through the innocent questioning of her daughter, whom Toshiro found it far more difficult simply to ignore or dismiss, that Megan gained any insight into how her husband earned his money.

'Daddy?'

'Yes, Lucy.'

'What did you do today?'

'Today? Well, today I built a big new building.'

'Wow! All by yourself?'

'More or less, yes. I had a little help, but I did most of the work.'

'You must be very strong?'

'Oh yes, look at these muscles. I'm like Popeye the sailor man!'

He was good at making Lucy laugh, and this was one of the things that Megan still loved about him. Sometimes he would clown around and carry her on his back around the apartment to great whoops of laughter from all of them.

As the slight man makes his way towards Toshiro's table, he turns his head so that Megan can see his face in full view. He has a thin moustache and his mouth is down-turned, giving him a cruel expression. His hair is slick with some kind of oily product. Then something notable happens: all of the high-ranking politicians and executives get up as one and make their way over to the bar, leaving only Toshiro and his assistants and analysts, and the mystery man and his security detail. Megan sees the two men shake hands warmly and exchange pleasantries. She is used to seeing Toshiro meet with businessmen and politicians, but not men like this.

That happened much less frequently now. Megan took in the various gifts and trinkets from around the world, donated by foreign dignitaries. There was an enormous rhino's horn directly over the thick desk. Megan – an instinctive animal lover – winced at this. There was also a moose's head from some wealthy Canadian investors. Megan had asserted her primacy as manager of all household decisions and forced the ugly creature to be stored in the study. Who would want to own and display such a thing? A hunter of trophies, an apex predator.

Toshiro's files were stored in a black filing cabinet. Megan reached for the shelf above the desk and a small Faberge-style decorative egg. She flicked open the lid with one of her finely manicured nails and was not surprised to find two metal keys inside.

She turns back to the stage. Miles and the band are winding down, and there are now stretches of silence amidst all the jarring and swirling bursts of sound. Megan strokes Lucy's hair. She has always told herself that she would confront Toshiro if she suspected him of doing anything illegal. Has it always been easier for her to ignore this doubt in her mind and enjoy the luxuries?

Megan hears the scraping of chairs and she forces herself to turn around. Toshiro and the slight man shake hands and the latter puts on a pair of black leather gloves and has his trench coat placed around his shoulders by one of the heavies. This unwholesome band moves away from the table and there is the briefest moment of eye contact between the man and Megan before she looks away. One of the "ATTENDANTS" lifts the rope that separates the VIPs from everyone else and Megan breathes a quiet sigh of relief as he exits. Right on cue the politicians and executives begin to return to the table. Suddenly a final moment of silence from the stage fills with rapturous applause, and Miles and the band vacate the stage.

She unlocked the cabinet and began to leaf through the files. She sensed she would know what it was when she found it. There was a noise from outside the room as one of the maids went past with the vacuum. Megan had instructed them not to come into the study today, thus securing herself several hours of privacy. There was no risk of any of the staff informing Toshiro of this irregular behavior on her part. She had the complete trust of every member of her domestic staff. Besides which, none of them would ever voluntarily so much as look at the master of the house, such was the air of distant authority that Toshiro carried with him around the apartment.

Megan treats Toshiro's underlings with long-rehearsed indifference as she and Lucy approach the table. She sits down next to her husband with Lucy on her lap.

'I still don't see why you insisted on Lucy coming here. She's been bored out of her mind all evening.'

'Tut tut,' says Toshiro. 'It's not very gracious of either of you to complain about being invited to such a prestigious concert.' He places his hand on hers and a beam of light enters and dazzles her eyes from a large signet ring he wears on the little finger of his left hand. She removes her hand. 'Are you unwell, my love?' He reaches forward to place his hand on her forehead. Her instinct is to pull away and yet she remains motionless.

With the cabinet safely open, Megan paused her search and moved to Toshiro's globe drinks cabinet in the far corner. She looked out at the sheer drop below and the expansive terrace to her right. *In the early days after moving into the apartment, she had enjoyed long evenings out there with a glass of wine, taking in the view and absorbing the sounds of the city. Always alone.*

'You know that we, the three of us I mean, have witnessed the future taking place right here before our eyes this evening.'

Neither Lucy nor her Mother seem overly impressed by this revelation. Toshiro doesn't mind. He's used to being the only person in the room who can see the bigger picture. He looks out upon the stage where the mysterious sound of Miles Davis' wah wah attachment-boosted trumpet continues to reverberate. Lucy runs to him and takes his hand.

She used to marvel at how far and how high life had taken her. She had recently begun to think of the trappings of her life in Tokyo as geography, merely that. The intoxication of the oxygen at this elevation had worn off completely. She had friends without a tenth of the wealth and social status but with love and fulfilment in their lives, and with children who weren't banished in a chauffeur-driven car every day to some ridiculously expensive private school for the rude offspring of the extremely wealthy.

'Can we go for milkshakes now?' she says.

'Milkshakes?' says Toshiro. 'I suppose you have been good this evening, hasn't she Mummy?'

Megan would like to tell him not to communicate with her through their daughter. 'She's always good.' Megan pushes a strand of hair from Lucy's face.

She selected a laphroaig from the globe and poured a healthy measure into a tumbler with plenty of ice. She thought of herself as a secret agent taking reckless chances on enemy territory in the midst of a covert mission. She laughed to herself at this characterization.

'Milkshakes for three it is then,' says Toshiro with a clap of his hands. He picks Lucy up and hands her to her Mother. His staff busy themselves for their departure from the venue.

'I think an early night would be better, don't you, Daddy?'

She raises her voice above the murmur of scraping chairs and tables.

He turns his head and looks at Lucy.

'I happen to think good little girls deserve a special treat from time to time.'

It took Megan no more than an hour to find her smoking gun. Substantial payments into an offshore account by someone with the codename 'Comus'. These were personal accounts in Toshiro's name of which his wife had no knowledge. Clearly Toshiro had income streams that were strictly off the books.

Megan says nothing but walks past her husband with her hand holding the back of Lucy's head.

'Who was that man you were talking to?' She doesn't turn around completely but moves back and forth rapidly with Lucy like she used to when the girl was a crying baby who refused to go to sleep.

There were several payments of between forty and fifty million yen every two weeks or so and going back at least three years according to these records. She didn't know what this all meant, but she knew that she had succeeded in her mission.

Toshiro doesn't answer; he flashes her a look that takes away her breath and sends her rushing for the exit with her daughter.

She washed up her glass in Toshiro's sink and shut the globe. She turned and faced the signed poster of Miles Davis' Kind of Blue that was framed and hung above the door. She felt quite light on her feet as she tripped away to instruct the staff on the preparations for dinner. She didn't forget to lock the door and leave the key in as she had found it.

May 7th - The Imperial Hotel

Toshiro Hanzo, looking every inch the prominent Tokyo

citizen in a brand new grey suit and Armani shoes, raises his champagne glass and prepares a toast: 'To new Japan.'

'New Japan,' reply his two associates, one of whom we have already encountered: the slight gentleman with the thin moustache from the Miles Davis concert. The other gentleman sitting with them in the hotel's upper lounge area is new to us, but just like Toshiro and his sour-faced friend he is expensively attired. Unlike them, his taste for the finer things in life clearly extends to the copious consumption of food and drink, as a thick roll of fat bulges at the neck of his extra large shirt and suit jacket. He is sweating and uncomfortable and repeatedly tries to loosen his tie.

The restaurant was full and the background chatter at a constant level as the young couple finished their meal. They shared quick looks and quiet laughs as their second date progressed well. The spark of attraction had been present from the first awkward kiss on the cheek. For this second meal, they had once again kept the conversation to fairly safe and neutral topics such as her impression of the Japanese university system and his excitement at his breakthrough success in the property business.

'More wine?' said Toshiro.

'I couldn't, I have work in the morning,' said Megan. 'Thank you. I'll have a coffee, though.' *Toshiro topped up his own glass and waved to gain the attention of the waiter. He found her foreignness intoxicating and freeing even as it grated against his own Japanese sense of tradition and propriety. Toshiro clicked his fingers in a brusque manner that made her look down at her menu but also sent a tingle down the back of her neck and her arms.*

'Coffee,' said Toshiro to the scuttling waiter. 'And another scotch here.'

'Yes, sir.' *The waiter was about to move away at a rapid pace when Megan felt the urge to stop him.*

'Sorry,' she said.

'Madam?' *He cast a wary glance towards Toshiro. Here was a man who seemed habituated to occupying several spaces at once.*

'Can we make mine a cappuccino please.' *She realized she had her hand on the waiter's arm. She removed her hand.* 'If it isn't too much trouble?'

'Of course, madam.' He bowed to both of them.

'Why would it be too much trouble?' said Toshiro.

'Hmm?' said Megan.

'Let the man get on with his job. Italian coffee is on the menu, yes?' He looked at the hovering waiter.

'Yes, sir.'

'Go on then.' He waved the waiter away and he left as rapidly as he had come. There was a moment of silence that allowed Megan to appraise him once again. His suit was crisp and it fitted him well. His hair was neat, with just the right amount of gel sweeping it over to the side. He gave off an air of comfortable affluence with perhaps more than a touch of arrogance. Within two dates, Megan had realized that her eyes were always on him.

'He was enjoying your attention. They feed on the sympathy of the customer.' His measured tone had returned.

'Maybe you were jealous when I touched his arm.' She surprised herself sometimes when her emotions were engaged.

'Of course I was. Here was I thinking that we were getting close. I thought a third date might be on the cards.'

She smiled. 'A third date, sir? How presumptuous of you.'

'I know, and for that I can only apologise and offer my resignation.' She laughed. 'After I've had my scotch.'

'Naturally.' The drinks followed and the atmosphere lightened further. As they stood up from the table, Megan observed that Toshiro had left a more than generous tip. Something else caught her eye underneath one of the adjoining tables: it was a wallet.

When Toshiro had her coat ready to place around her shoulders, Megan was down on all fours under the table. Toshiro seemed on the verge of complete exasperation at this latest breach of protocol. During their dates, he found himself alternately swelling with indignation and pricked into a state of exhausted but happy deflation.

'Hand that in to this man,' said Toshiro. 'I have a taxi waiting for us.' Megan looked around and tapped the stuffed wallet against her free hand.

'They must have only just left,' she said. 'Do you remember who was sitting there?'

She addressed this to their waiter, who looked at Toshiro as if for assistance before answering. 'Yes, madam. It was Mr and Mrs Tamahaka.'

'White hair? Elderly?' said Megan.

Toshiro looked at his watch and puffed out his cheeks.

'Well, yes,' said the waiter. 'They are two of our oldest and most regular customers.' He was holding out his hand for the wallet. Toshiro nodded at him in encouragement. The waiter extended his hand, pleased to be in Toshiro's good books. Megan moved the wallet away. The two men shared a concerned glance.

'Did they come in their own car?' said Megan.

'Yes, but...' said the waiter.

'What kind?' said Megan.

'A Mercedes, madam.'

'Let's go,' said Megan. She grabbed her coat and dashed from the dining area, leaving waiter and wannabe business tycoon in a shared state of bafflement.

Megan was climbing into a taxi and calling to him when he managed to make his way past a throng of late evening diners and out of the restaurant.

'Over here!'

He hurried over to the car and she shuffled over to make room on the back seat. He looked at her and then at the driver who had turned around.

'Where to?' said the driver.

Megan grinned at Toshiro. 'Follow that Mercedes, sir.' She pointed at the sleek German automobile that was just that moment pulling away from the valet parking service. The driver laughed. Megan laughed. Toshiro couldn't help but laugh himself.

'Okey doke,' said the driver. 'James Bond,' he said to himself upon turning back to the wheel.

'Quick, quick!' said Megan. She could barely contain her excitement.

'It's okay,' said the driver, 'I can see where they're going.'

Megan took Toshiro's hand in hers and jiggled up and down in her seat.

'How much fun is this?' she said.

'I...' began Toshiro.

Megan leaned over and placed her head on his shoulder. He hated the feeling of losing control of a situation as the taxi bobbed and weaved as best it could through the busy city streets.

The neon lights whizzed past the taxi windows and the driver seemed to be enjoying the experience as he whistled tunes to himself.

'Don't you lose them now, Mr,' called Megan in an attempt at an American accent from the movies.

'I got 'em right in my sights, lady,' said the driver in his own approximation of a hard boiled film character. Megan squeezed Toshiro's hand and her eyes beamed with glee.

'There'll be a pretty tip in it for you if you do your job right, buddy.'

The driver laughed. 'You just sit back and enjoy the ride, missy.' A gap appeared in the traffic ahead and the driver filled it eagerly.

Toshiro looked from one window to the other as the colours of the city produced a dazzling kaleidoscope in his brain. It was quite beautiful. He didn't usually allow himself the indulgence of reflections on matters of aesthetics. He found thoughts and feelings flashing through his mind with the unfiltered clarity and insistence of the neon rainbow outside. On a couple of occasions during the journey, Toshiro had felt like telling the driver to mind his manners in front a lady. However, Megan's level of excitement and the risk of appearing foolish in front of her had restrained him.

'All this just to return a wallet?' said Toshiro. 'I don't get it.'

'I know you don't.' She put her arm around him and smiled.

The journey took half an hour of stops and starts and rapid accelerations before the taxi came to a halt in a parking area lined with trees. Megan was still nestled next to Toshiro and he sensed that she might be falling asleep. He kissed her on the head and she sat up.

'Where are we?' she said.

'Tokyo zoo,' said the driver. 'What the hell they're doing here at this time of night, I'm sure I don't know.'

Megan pulled a handful of notes from her clutch bag.

'Here's your reward, cowboy,' she said, handing them to the driver.

'Thank you kindly, ma'am.' The driver tipped an imaginary hat to her. 'They've already gone in.' He motioned with his head to the Mercedes parked ahead of them.

'Would you be so hind as to wait for us while we go in?' Megan had returned to her normal voice.

'No worries,' said the driver as he lit a cigarette.

'Come on,' said Megan.

There must have been some kind of fundraising event happening at the zoo. Toshiro and Megan wandered amongst venerable patrons in eveningwear who were sipping champagne from flutes and making small talk as the baboons and gorillas in the enclosures looked on with expressions of vague interest. Megan took a champagne flute from a waiter. Toshiro declined with a tired wave of the hand. There were curious nocturnal noises coming from the animals. Megan quickly located the elderly couple seated at a table and receiving the fastidious attentions of what seemed to Toshiro to be just the latest in the evening's apparently endless parade of waiters. She held the wallet high in the air and shouted.

'Yoo-hoo! Excuse me! Coming through!'

She dragged Toshiro by the hand in her wake. By this point in the evening, he felt powerless to resist the force of her personality. There was no longer sufficient room in his mind for the very important meetings he had in the morning.

Megan was already deep in conversation with the elderly couple as Toshiro hung back. He heard snatches of their conversation and he saw Megan handing over the wallet with great ceremony. The gentleman's expression changed from confusion to relief as he realized that yes, indeed, his wallet had been missing.

Megan seemed to have made two new friends.

He felt numb but in touch with all of his extremities. It was a feeling akin to drunkenness. He was not in any way in control of events. How had this happened in the space of one evening? He heard the animals and the small talk. He was a vacuum at the function, a nonentity and a black hole. The waiters walked around him. It felt as though they walked through him, continuing with the work without paying him the least attention.

He tried to focus on his feet on the floor; he wanted to feel in touch with who he was, who he had been before this evening. He rocked back and forth on his heels and wondered what the people at the function saw when they looked his way. He needed to be taken aside and comforted. He hugged himself. It looked as if Megan was exchanging contact details with the couple now.

All at once she had completed her mission and she sprung over and was hugging him. He put his arms around her.

'You have big strong arms, Mr,' she said into his chest. He felt an instant stirring in his loins that snapped him back to the present. He held her more tightly in order to prevent her moving away. She seemed happy with this, snuggling further into him.

'Wallet successfully returned?'

She smiled and he could feel her nodding slowly. 'A very successful evening, I'd say,' she murmured somewhere in the darkness of his chest.

He picked her up and plonked her down on his lap as he slumped into a wicker chair next to a wicker table. She giggled.

Megan hung her legs over the side of the chair. His erection was now beyond denial or concealment. He knew that she felt its presence. Intercourse prior to marriage was not part of Japanese culture. But the young body in his arms was not Japanese. He kissed her on the mouth and she thrust her tongue up against his. She held his face in her hands for what seemed like an age as they explored the interiors of each other's mouths. Finally, they broke for air amid the animals and the function attendees.

'You always do the right thing, don't you? That's you, isn't it? You have to do what your instinct tells you is correct. Right?'

'Stop talking.' She forced his head back with the force of her forward motion and the thrusting and desperate searching of her tongue.

'And what's your thing, Mr Hanzo?' She thrust her hand between his legs and held his head with her other hand.

'Come with me.' She giggled with delight as he carried her out of the function, leaving the animals to their curious looks and nocturnal noises.

Toshiro barked his address at the driver, who seemed a little surprised at the turn events had taken. He had been looking forward to some more chat with the pretty foreigner, if truth be told. Ah well, c'est las vie. He drove on as the couple went at each other on the back seat. He caught as much of this as he could in the mirror.

'Are you going to show me your fancy place?' said Megan.

'That's not all I'm going to show you,' said Toshiro, breathing heavily.

After a beat, they both burst into laughter.

'That was a terrible line.'

'I know, sorry.' He winced and she kissed him.

'Wish I could take this thing off,' he says. 'When are our esteemed visitors getting here?'

Toshiro pulls back his sleeve to reveal an impressively chunky Rolex. 'The royal party should be here in half an hour. Don't worry, gentlemen, I have mints. Can't very well meet the Queen of England with booze and cigars on our breath, now can we?' With that, Toshiro pulls three individually packaged cigars from his inside pocket. 'They're Cuban, my friends, the best.' Toshiro is looking forward to his introduction to the British monarch. He's also relishing the prospect of taking his seat in the hotel's auditorium with its artful stone supports and balconies.

The large gentleman nods in approval at the taste of the cigar. All three appear to be enjoying themselves in their distinct ways. The lounge is open and elegantly lit. Toshiro always feels that the space in this building is somehow more beautiful, more crafted than the space outside. This is not the sort of thought he would ever voice in this company, but he has enjoyed many a long conversation about buildings and architecture with Megan, and Lucy loves looking at the photographs of the buildings he has put up all over Tokyo. He has enjoyed cigars and scotch here many times and he always makes sure to arrive early in order to have a good look around and enjoy the building that the American Frank Lloyd Wright designed and bequeathed to the city. Toshiro has a theory that the higher you rise in Japanese society, the more bizarre and remote your experience of the country becomes. He used to think he knew exactly what being Japanese meant, but these days he's not quite so sure. At such moments, he comforts himself in the knowledge that whatever Japan is, he's at the top of the food chain.

Before the meeting, he asked his driver to drop him outside the hotel gates so that he could enjoy the walk up to the entrance, with the compact, neat building emerging before him. The ornamental pool you passed on your way in was a nice touch, so ordered and yet so natural.

'Did you know, gentleman,' Toshiro is feeling expansive all of a sudden. 'This very building survived an earthquake some years ago, when all of its neighbours crumbled?'

The large man makes no response. The sour-faced man seems a little displeased by this departure from practical matters of business.

'Does that impress you?' he says.

'Well, yes. I mean it was because of a unique design feature in the foundations. Quite incredible really.' Toshiro sips his drink and regrets his attempt to broaden the scope of the conversation.

'I have to say, Hanzo-san, that you are a man who knows how to celebrate a successful deal.' The large man pats Toshiro on the leg and laughs a loud belly laugh.

'Well, Tanaka-san, we're not celebrating just yet. Remember we still have a few little kinks to iron out.'

Mr Tanaka scoffs and waves a dismissive hand. 'What are such kinks to men like us?' he almost shouts. 'Anyway, I'm sure our friend here is taking care of any such potential setbacks. Right?' Tanaka gestures in the direction of Mr sour-face. He pointedly does not make eye contact with the man.

'Mr Kichi's efficiency is beyond question, Tanaka-san,' he says. 'Did this morning go as planned, Mr Kichi?'

'Like clockwork, Hanzo-san,' says Mr Kichi. 'My men called to confirm that the job was done before you gentlemen arrived.'

Mr Kichi almost smiles, but not quite. Toshiro wonders what he was doing when that call came through. Perhaps he had been looking at the hotel garden - part of the hotel yet still somehow organic. He had taken a stroll on the wooden decking. It was nice to remind himself occasionally that inside his business suit beats the heart of a true innovator.

Toshiro notices that Kichi hasn't lit his cigar or touched his drink. Sometimes he wonders if Kichi is human at all. In many ways, this yakuza crime lord is more like a myth than an actual flesh and blood person. Yet Toshiro knows that in the 'construction state' that he more than anyone is shaping, you must work with men like Kichi. Toshiro sips his single malt and savours its complexity.

Toshiro was never naïve about how construction works in Japan. It was simply a matter of getting things done. He had known Mr Kichi for many years. He recalls their first meeting at the pachinko parlour. The rising mobster and the rising construction magnate having a meeting of minds next to a desk stacked with wads of notes. With a snap of his leather-gloved fingers, Kichi could subdue any union and secure any permit. People sometimes said no to Mr Hanzo and Mr Tanaka; no one says no to Mr Kichi. There are consequences to saying no to Mr Kichi.

When strolling around the garden earlier he had slipped into a reverie concerning Lucy. What would she think of him? What would she come to learn of him? He saw carp in the pond and his mind switched to hunters and predators. Lucy would only have to look up wherever she was in Tokyo to know all about her Father. Frank Lloyd Wright would doubtless have hated the sleek, anonymous high rises that Toshiro and Tanaka plant in the garden of Tokyo, but there wasn't a lot of money these days in hotels that looked like ancient temples, earthquake-resistant or not.

Kichi's quiet but piercing voice brings Toshiro out of his reverie: 'We have one further obstacle to our success, gentlemen. You both know very well that I specialize in sweeping away such obstacles with these hands of mine.' He jolts his gloved hands forwards in a choking motion at which Toshiro and Tanaka both recoil. Kichi sinks back into his chair and seems to be on the verge of a fit of laughter at their reaction that never quite forces its way from his throat. Such exchanges must be routine to this man.

Toshiro entered the study and locked the door behind him. His usual feeling of calmness and control was absent. Toshiro did not jump to conclusions as he looked up at Miles Davis. He needed a drink before getting to work this evening. Having nudged the needle on the record player to the opening track of Kind of Blue, he found himself by the globe and unscrewing the laphroaig bottle. He sipped his drink in the leather chair and processed three simultaneous pieces of information: Firstly, the level of fluid in the bottle was lower than he could account for; secondly, there was just the slightest whiff of his wife's perfume as he had opened the globe; thirdly, there was a purple nail with a trace of adhesive on the back that did not belong in his drinks cabinet.

She must have known that her presence would be easy to detect and yet still she had chosen to invade his privacy. He knew what she had found without needing to check the filing cabinet. Had this outcome been inevitable? And if so, from what point in their relationship? It thrilled him to think of the turmoil that the misplaced nail must have caused her. He thought about her boldness and fierce integrity as he picked up the old-fashioned telephone with its earpiece and microphone, the telephone that she had called ostentatious when he had purchased it. He dialed a number and looked out upon a rainy Tokyo evening.

'Mr Kichi? I'm so sorry to disturb you this evening but, well, we have a slight problem.'

'Now, if you will excuse me, gentlemen, my invitation to the visit of her royal highness Queen Elizabeth II appears to have been lost in the post.' Kichi clicks his fingers and two of his men scuttle over with his long coat and fedora hat which he tips to his two associates before marching from the room. Tanaka and Toshiro remain in silence. In the end love and loyalty fade but his legacy is forever. Let the hordes of salary-men cram themselves into trains every morning and work their fingers to the bone, taking their little power naps at desks or on elevators. Let them grab flowers for their wives amidst the rush for the train station on the way home. Let them fall asleep on the sofa after their dutiful wives have cooked dinner and put the little ones to bed. For the men who are making modern Japan around them, the oxygen is of a far more rarefied kind.

Merely look up, Lucy. Just for me. He drains the single malt and takes a deep drag on his cigar. He thinks he'll take another stroll in the garden to listen to the music of birds and become a part of that lovely space again even if only for a little while.

She hadn't come to Tokyo with the expectation of finding love. She had only come to the city on a couple of trips with her friend/boyfriend Ken. They had met at university in England and would sleep together when they were both lonely. He was at once too soft and cuddly and too absorbed in his work to be a true love match for her. On those trips she had fallen in love with Japan. He had fallen into the role of facilitator of her permanent move, finding her the appropriate forms to complete and sourcing potential apartments. Megan accepted all of this as her due in the way that beautiful young women do. They maintained regular contact, meeting up every so often to discuss work or terrible dates they'd been on, but in introducing her to his country, Ken had also set in motion the process of her outgrowing him. Whatever hopes he had once had of a long-term relationship were quietly extinguished by her unyielding pursuit of independence.

She worked long hours lecturing in English literature and taking Japanese lessons every other evening. She had been on one or two dates with colleagues just to escape another solitary evening of preparing lectures and brushing up on her Japanese. Of course, all they talked about was work and this made her feel even more alone. She seemed to see loneliness all around her in Tokyo. She hadn't made any female friends here. She had always found other women to be guarded and suspicious around her, due to her looks first and then her brains. She didn't want to tell family in England about this as it would only worry them. Ken remained her friend, but it didn't seem fair to burden someone who so obviously loved her with her terrible feelings of isolation. Much as she loved her new country and the electric sense of striving and vital life it gave her every day, she had begun to second-guess her big move. And then, at a dinner held by the Business School of the University, she met and talked to a man.

Earlier the same day, Hibiya-Koen park

Megan Hanzo looks at her elegant gold watch for the fifth time in the space of a couple of minutes. She is dressed in preparation for the arrival of the British royals at the nearby Imperial Hotel. She will be accompanying her husband as part of the greeting party for Queen Elizabeth and Prince Phillip. She feels conspicuously overdressed for the park.

'Somewhere you need to be?' asks a man in his mid-forties who is walking beside Megan through a long avenue of maidenhair trees. Ken Nishikori is Megan's oldest friend. His somewhat shaggy appearance belies a keen mind. All Megan knows about Ken's work is that he does something for the security services. 'I don't get you, Megan,' he says. 'You're meeting the Queen of England in an hour. And yet you seem set on making trouble for yourself.' He shakes his head of unkempt hair in disbelief.

''Twas ever thus,' she replies, looking at the path.

'Indeed,' he says.

'Surely you know me too well to try and warn me off, Ken?' says Megan.

'I do know you too well for that, Megan. But I'm gonna try to warn you off anyway. Please don't go down this road.'

Ken lights a cigarette from a pack of Lucky Strike as they

walk along. The park is busy but relaxed on this spring morning. The sun is out and the tall trees are providing some pleasant shade. In the distance, the two of them can see the bright white mirage of the daffodil garden.

'If I do nothing, I'm an accessory,' she says in a questioning tone. Ken laughs in a manner that suggests a deep weariness.

'You and the wife of every tycoon in Tokyo, and the wife of the Emperor himself. Are you trying to tell me that you actually needed concrete proof that your husband has been and is involved with organized criminals?' His delivery is so straight that she can't help smiling. She reaches out for his hand and he takes it somewhat hesitantly.

'Have you never heard it said that love is blind?' she says.

'I've heard it said and I've also lived it.' It's Ken's turn to look at the floor now.

'Well, love is also blinding. It comes down to what you can live with. Did you do some digging for me?'

Ken takes a quick look around them and edges closer to Megan.

'Keep walking and look straight ahead,' says Ken, his voice now a whisper. 'I performed the most basic, surface-level check of the accounts that you found.'

He marches on apace.

'And?' Her hand takes hold of his sleeve as they come to a halt at the end of the avenue of trees.

'And... what do you want me to say, Megan?' Ken stops and turns to Megan. His eyes dart all around and almost imperceptibly he draws a line with his index finger from his ear to his chin. Just as swiftly, he sets off again with a walk that is almost a run. 'Am I telling you anything you didn't know or feel already?' His voice falters and he discards the half-smoked cigarette and lights another.

Megan's hands are over her mouth and Ken's heart sinks as he realizes that she is crying. He puts his arm around her and she settles for a moment into the old familiar embrace.

'Is this worse than you thought?'

She can't help but laugh again. 'Yes and no. Who else would he be involved with? He won't settle for second best in anything.' She has heard of the gesture that Ken made but she has never seen it performed in the flesh.

'Here.' He hands her a handkerchief. Ken walks around and stretches his arms. 'You know you could just do nothing?'

She shakes her head and dabs her eyes again.

'That's not who I am, Ken. I always thought of myself as a person of integrity. Maybe I lost sight of that somewhere amidst all the receptions with the Queen. Looking the other way seems to be a national pastime in this country these days. And I know I shouldn't say that as a gaijin.'

Ken smiles. 'You're as entitled to say that as anyone, because it's true. What if looking the other way is all that keeps you alive? Besides, you're too far down this road. Look, I'm not the sort of chap to say I told you so, but I did warn you about guys in the property business. Admittedly I wasn't exactly the most impartial witness, but...'

'I know you told me. I remember. I thought you were just being jealous and protective.'

'I was.'

Her tearstains have left a mark on his shirt that they both look at for a moment.

'Please think carefully about what happens next. Once I pass this information up the food chain, it's out of my control.'

'I know that, Ken.'

'These people don't play by the rules, Megan.'

'Are you scared?'

'Yes, aren't you?'

'Yes.'

'Good.'

He strokes the fine material of the gown that covers the top of her shoulder like a second skin. His hand moves up and then down almost as a reflex.

'Talk to no one and don't do anything out of the ordinary that might arouse suspicion.'

'Okay.'

'Well, you'd better be running along to your royal reception.'

'What are you going to do?'

'Me? I need a drink.' And with that he heads off in the direction of the Matsumotoro restaurant.

She stands alone among the sightseers and the running and playing children.

'Thank you!' she calls after him.

'Don't thank me yet, Megan. I'll see you in a week.'

One week later, Barnaby's love hotel, East Shinjuku

Megan sits in a café in the pleasure district. She can see the entrance to the love hotel and is waiting for Ken to arrive. She takes a sip of black coffee and thinks about Lucy, safely tucked away at her private school in the hills. She knows that one day her daughter will understand why she's doing this. She doesn't know why Ken has chosen a love hotel as their rendezvous. In many ways it's the perfect place for two people to conduct private business. During her first year in the city she explored many and various aspects of Japanese culture. She smiles to herself as she thinks back over some of the adventures she and Ken had together as he showed her around his home city. She realises now that that time was an awakening for him as well as her. Perhaps even more so for him.

She looks up and sees him pacing around outside Barnaby's, looking extremely conspicuous with his long brown coat and uncontrollable hair. Despite her nervousness, she can't help smiling at this member of the intelligence community who stands out like a sore thumb wherever he goes.

The entrance hall of the love hotel is an attempt to imitate the style and layout of an English country house. It has two large, ornate armchairs that are more like thrones. There are paintings of Tudor kings of England on the walls, which Megan finds somehow comforting. The process of booking in is completely anonymous, with a voice panel to speak into and a gap through which cash and keys can be exchanged. Ken asks for "kyuukei" - the "rest" option as opposed to the "stay" option.

Their room is spacious. It amazes Megan that they are in the midst of hundreds of such establishments here in Shinjuku. She takes off her coat and lays it on the room's four-poster bed (presumably a continuation of the Tudor theme).

She walks around the room. The wallpaper is an underwater scene with starfish and dolphins swimming around. The lighting is blue neon. Despite her better judgment, Megan quite likes the room. She picks up and examines several of the ornaments on the bureau: a glass dolphin, a ceramic shark. There are condoms in a bowl by the side of the bed.

'Fancy a drink?' asks Megan.

'Yes, most definitely,' says Ken.

Megan unlocks the mini bar with the room key and pours them both a healthy measure of Suntori whiskey. She places the glasses down on the bedside table. She then removes a copy of the Tokyo Times from two days ago and places it on the tabletop. He takes the newspaper and reads a front-page article describing the murder of one of the paper's own reporters on the evening of the parade through Tokyo to welcome the British royal family. The report states that the journalist attended the parade on his day off before meeting his girlfriend for a few drinks in a Shinjuku bar and then going on to a nightclub. Just before two in the morning, with the club nearly full to capacity and the door security conspicuous by their absence, an unidentified perpetrator entered the premises and threw several explosive devices (later identified by the police as grenades) into the crowd. Thirty people were killed in the blast and nearly a hundred injured. Among the dead were sadly the journalist, his girlfriend, and several of the friends they met at the nightclub.

'Why are you showing me this?' Ken asks.

'It goes into much more detail inside, look.' Her long nails make a noise as she turns the pages that Ken cannot ignore. He watches her turn the pages.

'It says this man was an investigative journalist who had previously gained national recognition for exposing widespread corruption in the commissioning of major construction projects.' Her nail becomes a jabbing pointer as she spears the picture of the shell of the nightclub.

Ken sits down on the bed. 'So?'

'So?' The paper is still open on her lap.

'I mean, it's tragic and everything. But, Megan, these things happen every day in Tokyo. It's a message: pay up every week or there will be consequences. This poor guy was just in the wrong place at the wrong time like the other innocent people who died.'

'Or it was a hit on him made to look like one of the usual protection money issues?' She is folding and unfolding the paper and squeezing it into a thin tube.

'A hit? Megan, your nerves are so far on edge that you're seeing conspiracies everywhere.' Tiredness seeps out of Ken's every gesture.

'Ken, it's all in the article. They mention "boryokudan" and the violent tactics these groups use. They say this man was deliberately targeted because he was a crusader against organized crime in the city. They say some of these groups are led by people who came from Korea after the war and faced discrimination in Japan.'

'Megan, how is any of this relevant to your situation?' He reaches for her hands in order to bring her some stillness if only for a moment.

'This man Toshiro is involved with, well he's not pure Japanese, is he? He's clearly one of these people. One of the people who do things like this.' She makes a limp gesture with the rolled-up newspaper and then lets it fall to the floor.

Megan gets up and fetches Ken's drink from the bar. She places it on the bedside table and sits down beside him. They both look around at the neon and the fish.

'Well,' says Ken after an interminable silence, 'what are your thoughts?'

Megan looks at him. 'My thoughts are that you should pass

on my suspicions to your colleagues and then we wait and see what happens.'

She stares straight ahead.

'You really think that's the way to go?'

'You mean you don't?' says Megan with fire in her eyes.

'Well, if your husband is mixed up with the kind of people who throw grenades into nightclubs full of people – which it looks very much like he is – you won't just be a threat to him but to them too. Think about that.'

'Well, it just so happens that Lucy and I have a flight booked to London in a week.'

'Ah,' says Ken.

'We're staying with my Mum for a week.' Megan's voice has dropped to near whisper.

'And you're thinking of making it a more permanent stay?'

'She's all that matters to me now, Ken. Seriously, what's keeping me here?'

He seems on the verge of saying something but suppresses it.

'And don't think he can get to you there? He's not just gonna let you take Lucy.'

'He will if it's better for business. Toshiro is a pragmatist and a businessman before anything else. He won't want to be getting involved in illegal activity on foreign soil that could start shedding unwelcome light on what he's getting up to here.'

Ken removes his glasses and massages his temples. He digs out a ten-pack of Lucky Strike cigarettes from his coat.

'Could I have one of those please?' she says.

'I thought you quit years ago.'

'I did,' says Megan, with cigarette now dangling from her lips. 'But under the circumstances, my long-term health doesn't seem like such a concern anymore.' She lights the cigarette with a silver lighter which she fishes from her coat pocket.

'You sound like you've given this some thought?' The blue smoke swirls into the neon and the underwater world to create what Megan considers to be an appropriate atmosphere of a polluted fantasy.

Ken exhales loudly and puffs out his cheeks.

'If you're going through with this England plan, I should hold fire on alerting my colleagues.'

'Why?'

'Because there's no surer way alert Toshiro that he's being investigated, and who the source was.'

'You're more than just as pretty face, aren't you?'

He smiles and blushes slightly.

'I'm just a speccy technician with funny hair. But I'll do anything I can to help you.'

'I know you will.' She takes Ken's hand. 'So?'

'So, I have a contact in the Japanese Embassy in London.' He takes out his fountain pen and writes down a name in his notebook. He tears it out and hands it to her. 'Once you're in the air, I'll make you an appointment with this man. Tell him everything you know.' Megan reads the name on the paper then rolls it up and places it in her purse.

'You always did underestimate yourself, Mr Nishikori.' She takes his glasses off and places them on the table, then rearranges his fringe a little. She takes a step back as if to see the effect of her cosmetic alterations. 'No, no difference at all. You're a lost cause.'

'Tell me about it, my fashion sense is ...' Ken is interrupted by a light kiss on the lips. 'Whoa, what was that?'

'I'd have thought that was obvious,' says Megan as she moves in for another kiss. This one is longer and lingering. Megan moves over to the bed and begins to undress. 'Go and lock the door.'

Ken does as he's told. He fumbles with the lock, and by the time he returns to the bed Megan is out of her very chic dress and standing before him in some very silky and frilly underwear. They kiss once more and Megan loosens his tie.

'Megan, what is this? Don't think I'm not very excited about this turn of events because I am, but...' Megan sets about removing his suit jacket.

'If this is our last time together, let's make it a time to

remember.'

'Whatever you say,' says Ken.

'We have one hour, Nishikori-San, will that be sufficient time?'

'You obviously don't remember sex with me very well,' laughs Ken.

'Oh, I remember it very well,' says Megan.

'I never stopped loving you, you know,' says Ken.

'I know,' says Megan as she gets into bed.

Ken is up and dressed, with a smile on his face. He and Megan had not slept together for fifteen years before this, but there she is now, back in his arms if only fleetingly. As she doses, he looks at himself in the full-length mirror. He can't see his features too clearly in the dull neon. What he sees in the eyes looking back at him is the same spark he had as an idealistic and occasionally wild student, leaving Japan for the first time to study in London. He picks up his bag and walks over to the slumbering Megan. He kisses her sweet-smelling hair and she stirs briefly.

'Don't go,' she says.

'I have to, darling,' he replies. 'I have to get back to work.'

She props herself up on an elbow.

'I guess I'd better get going too,' she murmurs. 'They'll come and turf me out in a minute.'

'Thank you.'

'You don't have to thank me, Ken.'

'I know that, but thank you anyway. We probably shouldn't have any more contact before you leave.'

She nods.

'Be safe, Ken.'

'You too.'

He opens the door and is about to leave.

'Oh and Ken?'

'Yes?'

'I love you too.'

'I know.'

As Ken walks out of one of the love hotel's various discrete side exits, he notices the shadows of two figures falling across the doorway. Before he can turn his head, he hears a "pop"... and then nothing.

Kichi's No 1 and No 2 henchmen carry Ken's body the short distance to the black Mercedes. No1 unlocks the boot and they carefully lift the body and place it inside as if it were a bag full of precious and breakable ornaments. As No 1 lights a cigarette, No 2 ensures that all limbs are safely stowed inside. The boot closes on Ken. No1 is now making a phone call from a nearby pay phone while No2 lights a cigarette of his own.

'Boss?' says No 1. 'It's done...No no, we know. Your instructions were very clear... Thank you, boss.'

'Your instructions were very clear, boss,' mimics No2.

'Fuck you,' says No1, 'You need to learn to kiss ass a bit if you wanna stay alive.'

'I've stayed alive till now,' says No2.

'Till now,' says No1, dropping his cigarette and crushing it underfoot. 'We'd better get on.'

'I hear you, brother,' says No2, dropping his own cigarette to the floor and crushing it underfoot.

The Mercedes speeds along the highway. No 1 is driving while No 2 smokes and talks in the passenger seat.

'Don't go too fast, pal, we don't want to have an accident with this cargo on board.' He sucks on his cigarette.

'You don't say, genius,' says No 1 with both hands on the wheel. 'Where did you learn that, the Penguin book of corpse disposal?' No 1's irritation has turned to amusement at his own witticism.

'Yeah, it was actually. Have you got a copy?' says No2.

'Oh yeah,' replies No1, 'all hitmen are awarded that book the day we graduate from hitman college.' No1 guides the car expertly through the early evening traffic. 'Shall I put on the radio?'

No 2 gestures with his hand to indicate his total indifference. 'It's all corporate these days,' he says, 'no sport at all.'

'Don't think about it, pal, it's just a job. We provide a service, that's all. If we weren't doing it, someone else would be,' says No1. He thinks for a moment while overtaking a dawdling Mazda. 'Wouldn't it be fun to be one of those types you see in films? Y'know, the man with no name who punishes the wicked.'

'Yeah,' says No 2, 'that would be cool.'

They drive on in silence and No 1 once again considers putting the radio on.

'What are we doing with him?' asks No2 after a mile or so.

'We're not doing anything. We just leave the car where they tell us with the keys in the ignition and someone else takes care of it,' says No1. Darkness is beginning to descend on the city.

'What'll happen to him then?' asks No2.

'He's gonna be strung up in a public place to send a message,' says No1.

'A message to who?' asks No2.

'Whom,' says No1.

'Whatever,' says No 2.

'To anyone who feels like sticking their noses into the boss' business,' says No1.

'Funny old world, isn't it,' says No2.

'You can say that again, brother,' says No1.

'Funny old world, isn't it,' obliges No2. The slightest trace of a grin appears on No1's face.

They drive on for a few more miles in silence except for a Tokyo jazz station humming in the background.

'Listen,' says No1, 'we haven't changed anyone's life. We're no more morally responsible for that guy's death than a hammer is morally responsible for whacking in a nail.'

'You have a real way with words,' says No 2.

'People like the boss, someone's in the way they get trampled. Could be the Queen of England. Doesn't matter. You and me, we do our job, we go home to our wives or girlfriends. They're the ones who make things happen, and they're the ones who have to live with it, not us.'

No 2 nods slowly and smokes his cigarette.

'I have to say, my dear, that I'm not altogether sure you should be going on this trip to England.' Toshiro delivers this in nonchalant fashion three days prior to Megan and Lucy flying to London.

'I'm sorry?' says Megan.

'There's no need to apologise, darling,' he smiles.

The evening sky is clear and some late shards of sunlight hit the penthouse glass and disintegrate into many colours. Lucy is helping her nanny to pack away the painting things from the kitchen table. Toshiro continues to chew and then dabs at the corners of his mouth.

'Why is she leaving so early?' he says.

The plates are cleared away and the staff prepare the dessert settings.

'Why do you let her get down from the table between courses?'

Megan pours herself another cup of coffee and offers the pot to Toshiro.

'Why don't you let the staff do that?'

'My word, somebody is full of questions today. Usually at dinner we can't get more than the odd grunt out of you.'

'He usually grunts,' says Lucy with a big smile as she throws her arms around Megan. Toshiro taps Lucy on the arm with two fingers.

'The grunty, grunty bear wants you to sit at the table for your dessert, missy.'

'I don't like dessert,' says the girl.

'Little girls like dessert,' says Toshiro. He unfolds himself from his seat and tickles Lucy under the arms. The girl unfolds in a fit of giggles and she runs around the oak dining table to take her seat. They are served their crème brulee and Lucy requests a coke for which Megan gives her assent with the slightest of nods.

'A small glass, thank you,' says Megan.

'Too much sugar,' says Toshiro.

'Does Daddy not have any urgent work to do this evening?' Megan takes the glass and can and pours a measure of the bubbling liquid that hums to itself in Lucy's eager hands. Toshiro stretches and pours himself some coffee.

'It just so happens that Daddy has plenty of time to catch up on family business this evening.'

'How nice for us all,' says Megan.

'How nice,' says Lucy. 'Would you like to play a game of hide and seek with me, Daddy?'

Toshiro grins that grin of his.

'I would love to, sweetie. I must warn you, though, Daddy is extrmely good at both sides of the game.' He never once takes his gaze from Megan's. She tries to return it but is forced to look away.

'Just half an hour, all right? Then bedtime,' says Megan.

'Okay Mummy.'

Lucy kisses Megan on the cheek and scurries off into the vastness of the penthouse. Toshiro rolls up his sleeves.

'A lot of space in which to hide,' says Megan.

'She knows I'll find her,' says Toshiro. 'I will always find her.'

He calls out his countdown from thirty and the two parents hear their daughter's giggles from some shadowy corner.

The three men clamber out of the car and immediately Toshiro can hear barking dogs, arguing couples from the apartment buildings, and shouting kids. He pauses and inhales. He avoids plunging his expensive shoes into several muddy puddles, in one of which he catches the most fleeting of reflections, obscured by shadow and dirt. His two security men for the evening seem rather tense. Toshiro has never bothered to learn their names. He refers to them in his head as Grunt and Shunt. Two of Kichi's usual heavies are standing at the rear of the pachinko parlour.

'Evening gentlemen,' he says.

'Evening, sir,' says henchman No 1.

'I need to see Mr Kichi on a rather...delicate matter,' says Toshiro.

'Assuming we know who you're talking about, sir, would he be expecting your visit tonight?' says henchman No 2.

'You can drop the pretense,' says Toshiro. 'You know me, I know you. I know who you work for.' Toshiro can't feel his own security detail looming with their usual closeness.

No 2 steps forward from the doorway to reveal a slight but athletic-looking build and a neat crew-cut that displays a long scar on the top of his head.

'Your security detail will need to be patted down I'm afraid, sir,' says No 2.

'You can try,' says Grunt unconvincingly.

No 1 – larger, more heavy set and more openly carrying a weapon – steps down from the door.

'We don't want no trouble,' says Shunt. Toshiro shakes his head.

'Go and tell your boss I'm here please,' says Toshiro.

'Take your big old hand off that pistol, friend' says No 2 to Grunt.

Toshiro can see that his Grunt does indeed have his hand on the handle of the gun in his belt. He indicates with his eyes that the bodyguard should do as instructed by No 1.

'Okay, that's better,' says No 1.

'Now, one of you Macbeth gravediggers go and tell your boss Mr Hanzo is here to see him, okay?' says Shunt.

'We don't take orders from the likes of you,' says No 2. He looks to No 1 who gestures with his head. No 2 flashes a glare at Shunt before opening the door and entering the building.

Toshiro checks his chunky watch.

'You're brave sporting that round here, Mr Hanzo,' says No 1.

'So you do know who I am then?' says Toshiro.

'Of course, I've seen you with the boss before,' says No 1.

'So what was all that performance in aid of?'

'My apologies, Mr Hanzo. I'm training the kid there in the art of extreme diligence.'

'How admirable.'

'Thank you, sir,' says No 1. ' Now, shall we get the onerous but necessary formalities out of the way while he's gone?'

'Yes.'

No 1 pats them all down with the minimum of fuss.

'I'm afraid I must also ask for your handguns before I can let you gentlemen into the building.'

'Give them up,' says Toshiro without turning round.

No 1 extracts the guns from Grunt and Shunt's shoulder holster and belt respectively with no little ceremony.

'Don't worry, gentlemen, I shall guard them with my life,' says No 1, conscious of the fragile egos of people in his line of work. 'And by the way, Macbeth gravediggers?' He tuts and wags his finger at Shunt who shares a confused look with Grunt as No 2 opens the door.

'We need your guns before you can go up,' says No 2.

'Good boy,' says No 1, 'but all taken care of.' He hands No 1 the heavy lumps of metal. 'Look after those please. This way, gentlemen, and thank you for your patience and co-operation.'

'At long last,' says Toshiro.

Lucy is in bed and Megan heard Toshiro leave in the elevator an hour ago. She checks the plane tickets in her locked desk draw in the library. She tapped her leg and straightened her skirt for the umpteenth time in the last hour.

When does lying become like breathing? She stands on the terrace in the growing evening darkness. The sky over Tokyo is not black; it is blue and red and purple, and neon. The passports and Lucy's birth certificate and the return tickets for show, and the contact at the Foreign Office.

She had heard nothing from Ken, but then that had been their agreement. Planes are flying overhead. How do you pack for a one-way trip? To start again with a clean slate. She would find work as a lecturer. But her PhD was so old it was practically prehistoric. Perhaps private tutoring for stupid rich kids then? Whatever, she would earn honest, clean money for Lucy. There are weight limits on these flights. She'll have to leave some of her toys behind. Toys can be replaced. She looked around at the pot plants and bonsai trees that she and Lucy had so lovingly tended over the last few years. She placed her hand on one of the little trees and felt a kind of warmth and vitality that was so lacking in her own life.

What if Lucy would be better off staying here with her Father?

Shut up.

'Kichi-san,' says Toshiro, shaking the smaller man's hand. 'Thank you for seeing me at this hour.' Kichi's hand feels slightly damp and the room is airless and stale-smelling.

'Of course, my friend,' says Kichi. He pats Toshiro on the arm and clasps his shoulder again and again. 'You seem a little...flustered, my friend.' Kichi picks up a dishcloth and scrubs at something on his shirt cuff. He then checks his nails. 'Have a seat, have a seat.'

From his seated position opposite Kichi's desk, Toshiro can see that Kichi's dark trousers are covered in something thick and shiny. As Kichi sits down, Toshiro can see that his usually immaculate gelled hair is looking bedraggled. Kichi stares at Toshiro as if suddenly surprised by the other's presence in his office.

'A drink?' Kichi doesn't wait for Toshiro's answer. 'A drink.'

'Scotch if you have it,' says Toshiro.

'Scotch if you have it,' mumbles Kichi to himself. He has no shoes on and his small feet make a pitter-patter as he moves through the office. 'Cigar to go with that scotch?' He calls loudly.

'No, no thank you,' says Toshiro.

'Jumpy, jumpy,' mumbles Kichi with a cigar of his own jammed between his thin lips. 'I will be one moment, my friend.' He pads over to the door. 'Make yourself at home.'

The day of the flight and Toshiro has already left when Megan wakes up in their vast bed. The alarm clock says 6 am.

Check-in is at 9:30. As she showers, she wonders what her next shower will feel like. Will the water feel different back in England? Her tears merge with the water as she laments her life in Japan. What happens to a dream deferred? A dream destroyed.

'Lucy.' She touches the girl lightly on the shoulder. Lucy rubs her eyes and performs a dramatic stretch. She is warm and snug in her pyjamas.

'Morning Mummy.'

'Morning angel, did you sleep well?'

'Have you been crying, Mummy?'

'No, baby.' Lucy sits up in bed.

'Are you sure, Mummy?' Megan sits on the bed and strokes Lucy's hair.

'Why would I be crying when we're going on a lovely holiday?'

'I don't know, Mummy,' says Lucy.

'Exactly, now you get yourself up and we'll get you dressed, okay?'

Lucy leaps from the bed and takes her toy bunny rabbit to the bathroom with her. Megan looks around the room.

'You did remember to pack your very favourite toys and other things to show Granny?'

'I did!' calls Lucy with a toothbrush in her mouth.

Down on the street, the bags are loaded into one of Toshiro's black Mercedes. Megan holds Lucy by the shoulders and the girl tries to wriggle free to speak to the driver. These people have been like family to her all her young life. She doesn't even know she's leaving them behind. She had hugged and kissed all of the staff upstairs, as if they were kindly aunts and uncles and treasured friends. Megan can feel herself welling up again. She will miss them all as well. What will happen to them? She can't think about that now.

Megan feels a little better once they are in the car and crawling in the heavy morning traffic.

'Don't worry at all, Mrs Hanzo,' says the familiar driver. 'We'll make the airport in plenty of time. Should be just right for you both to check in.'

'Have you spoken to my husband this morning?' says Megan.

'No, madam,' he says. 'Not a word. He gave me all the instructions for today last week.'

'Last week,' says Megan.

'Yes,' says the driver. He looks in the mirror.

'Is there anything wrong, madam?'

'No, nothing at all,' says Megan.

Lucy is playing a game that involves spotting different coloured cars and awarding herself points for each of them.

'Two red cars so far,' she says, 'that's twenty points for me. Mummy, why aren't you playing?'

Megan gazes out of the window at the city passing her by. So anonymous and vast and yet every piece of it treasured by her in different ways.

'Black car! yells Lucy. 'It's just like this one, Mummy.'

Megan doesn't respond.

'Mummy!'

'What? Lucy, could you be a little quieter please.'

'Sorry, Mummy. But look, it could be Daddy coming to wave us off at the airport. Or maybe we forgot something and he's bringing it to us?'

Megan moves across the leather seats and sees the Mercedes about a car length behind them. She checks the number plate. Not one of theirs.

'It isn't Daddy,' she says. 'It isn't.'

'Oh well,' says Lucy. 'Oh! Orange car. Thirty points to me. You're way behind me, Mummy.'

'I am,' says Megan with a smile. 'Ooh, motorbike. Fifty points to me!'

'That's cheating!' says Lucy.

Toshiro looks at his watch. He notices his foot tapping so he stops it. There is a painting hanging on the wall of a mountain scene covered with snow. Toshiro rises to examine it more closely. Up close, the snow has a bluish hue that almost seems to emit its own coldness into the room. There are figures in the painting that are dwarfed by the vastness of the landscape; they might as well be insects.

'Look but don't touch,' says Kichi as he re-enters with a clean suit and freshly slicked hair, and shoes on.

'Apologies,' says Toshiro. He can never seem to stop apologizing in this man's presence. He has never heard Kichi apologise – not for anything. 'This is quite a piece.'

'I suppose,' says Kichi, limping over to the desk. 'I always face the other way.' He seats himself and his eyes bore into his guest behind dark glasses. 'Fix yourself that drink, would you.'

'I'm fine thank you,' says Toshiro.

'That's not like you at all,' says Kichi.

'I should really be getting home. The domestic situation is ... I won't bore you with all the details.'

'Please don't, I've already had a trying day,' says Kichi with the faintest flicker of a smile at the corners of his mouth. 'Give me the essentials only.' Toshiro shifts in his chair and feels that involuntarily tapping foot again.

'Well,' he says, 'my wife is leaving for London at the weekend and taking my...'

'Our staff are clucking away like mother hens down there, Hanzo-san. What a life they have, eh? No responsibility, no crown of authority weighting them down. But they gripe and they moan, and they want this and that.' Kichi seems vaguely amused by his interruption. His face then slips into some frozen reverie.

'She's taking my daughter with her,' continues Toshiro loudly.

'Mmm,' says Kichi. 'Wife takes daughter.'

'Yes, to visit her Mother. They go every year, but...'

'But this time you think they might not come back?' Toshiro nods grimly.

'You were right to bring this to me.' Kichi walks to the drinks cabinet and fixes them both a scotch with ice. Toshiro, facing the painting, hears the clinking in the glass.

'Neat for me please,' he calls out. After a moment Kichi places a scotch with ice down in front of him.

'We don't do it here,' says Kichi, suddenly all business. 'Not here.' Toshiro nods his understanding.

'You understand me?' says Kichi.

'Yes.'

'Good, good. You still love her?'

'With all my heart.'

'But more pressing concerns win the day, yes?' This sick bonhomie is more than Toshiro can stomach, but he finds he cannot look away from the dead eyes of this career criminal. Their blankness is at one with the wintery landscape behind him.

'Yes,' says Toshiro.

'I have an associate who will work with people in London to take care of this.' He brushes his gloved fingers together to indicate the simple conclusion of this transaction.

'We let her go then?' says Toshiro.

'What did I say? Let her fly away to England.' He mimes this flight with his hand.

'And what about my daughter?'

'You want her to be part of the deal?' says Kichi matter-of-factly.

'For God's sake, she's my daughter!' Toshiro bangs on the table with something like desperation.

'A joke in poor taste, Hanzo-san,' says Kichi.

'My apologies, Kichi-san,' says Toshiro carefully.

'Your daughter will think it was a car accident, as will everybody else.'

'A car accident, you say?' says Toshiro.

'Yes,' says Kichi, 'or some such. Now, I need my rest.' They shake hands. The dead eyes in the snow. Dead. Snow. 'Gather up your clucking hens and take them on home.'

Yes. Take them on home, thinks Toshiro.

At the airport, Megan is sweating. Her eyes feel heavy and her head aches. It is 9:30. She wants to shout at the driver to hurry up with the bags and get them inside. Megan looks up and down the dropping off and picking up area. Her hand shakes as she buttons up Lucy's coat.

'It's too hot, Mummy.'

'Just please do as you're told, Lucy.' Megan feels her heart thump with every car that pulls up and just as swiftly departs. The bags are loaded onto a trolley and a spotty young porter wheels them into the terminal. There are people rushing everywhere; security people with guns standing around in groups. She holds on tightly to Lucy's hand and after a moment decides to pick her up.

'Hey,' says Lucy, 'I was looking in my bag for blue teddy.'

'He's in there,' says Megan, 'I checked yesterday.'

'But I can't see him, Mummy.'

Megan looks around her and checks the entrance doors. She scans the numbers and the destinations flicking away on the huge boards above them. There it is: London Heathrow, Gate 15, checking in now.

'Shall we run to the gate and see if we can get to the front of the queue?' she says to Lucy.

'If you want to, Mummy,' says Lucy, sounding sleepy all of an instant.

A man in a tweed suit and polished shoes steps through the automatic entrance doors and seats himself at an empty café table. He catches the eye of a server and requests a black coffee. He has a black leather briefcase which might contain books or papers. There are patches on the elbows of his suit jacket. As his coffee arrives, he shifts in his seat to ensure a clear view of Megan lifting Lucy into her arms. He removes polaroid images he has of both of them from his inside pocket and compares them against the real thing. He knows the gate they will take off from. He knows when they will arrive. He places the pictures facedown on the round table before him. He sips the coffee and replaces the cup on its saucer with the merest clink. The man is of middle-age with a full head of still-black hair that is parted at the side. His sharp eyes dart from side to side and then he takes a gulped breath in through his mouth.

'Hhhhhhhhuuuuuuuuuuuuuuuuuurrrrrrrrrrrrrrrrrrrrrggg gggggggffffffffffffffffffffffff.'

One fellow customer looks up but the implacable expression and respectable appearance of the man convince the potential inquisitor that further attention is not warranted. The man finishes his coffee without rushing. He extends himself to the height of his average build, picks up his case and leaves the café area. He cleans his glasses and takes a last look at Megan and her daughter as the former breaks into a run with the latter in her arms.

'Come on then.' Megan sets off at a run to the escalator and jumps onto the moving steps. Lucy laughs and so does Megan. The escalator fills up around them. Megan thinks that she will be able to breathe once they are seated on the plane and Lucy is snuggled in the seat beside her with blue teddy and bunny. She thinks of the Embassy contact in her bag. And Ken. What if this contact can't do anything to help them? They reach the top of the escalator and Megan starts to run again. Lucy wakes up and groans. They bump into people, but Megan doesn't stop or turn around to apologise. Rushing. Legs aching. The same place where she came in. She sees her younger self arriving in Tokyo for the first time and looking around for Ken. What would she say to that girl now? Two selves. They are on a travelator now. She is breathing heavily. She uses the gentle forward motion as an excuse to stand and rest for a moment.

The Chameleon checks into an airport hotel and hangs a spare suit in the closet. He places his briefcase on the single bed and from it removes a very discreet handgun which he proceeds to dismantle and wrap up in one of the hotel towels. He lifts the receiver on the receiver on the room's telephone and dials a number, letting it ring three times before replacing the set. He is engaged and in a pattern of awaiting further instructions, a state in which the Chameleon allows himself to rest without ever relaxing his readiness for rapid response. He tips three red capsules into his hand from a bottle he carries in his jacket pocket. He swallows them with water from a glass. He sits motionless with his palms on the room's desk. He feels the familiar tickle in his throat that quickly erupts into a

'Hhhhhhhhuuuuuuuuuuuuuuuuuuurrrrrrrrrrrrrrrrrrrrggggggggggffffffffffffffffffffffff.'

Here in private he allows himself a profound grimace just as the phone rings.

'Yes? ... This is he, yes ... You can depend on that, Mr Kichi,' he writes notes on the hotel's stationary as he speaks. 'A contact within the Embassy in London, indeed ... I will call you upon arrival ... Thank you.'

The Chameleon rises and removes his suit jacket which he folds and places on the chair. He draws the blinds and turns off the light. He lies down on his back without removing his shoes. He places his hands on his chest and he waits. In one hour, the familiar tickle will erupt from his insides:

'Hhhhhhhhuuuuuuuuuuuuuuuuuuurrrrrrrrrrrrrrrrrrrrggggggggggffffffffffffffffffffffff.'

London

The Embassy member of staff they had sent to interview her looked like he was only just out of short trousers. He was diligently writing down everything Megan said. He had asked for permission to record the interview and she had assented despite a growing feeling in the pit of her stomach that this was all a waste of time. What was her life, or Lucy's for that matter, to these people?

'What will you do now?' she said as the junior official put the lid back on his fountain pen and pressed stop on the tape recorder. He seemed somewhat at a loss how to answer this question.

'I will report everything you have told me to my superiors,' he said in a matter-of-fact tone as if hearing such stories was

myself am hell

merely a part of his daily routine.

'And can the Embassy help in terms of mine and my daughter's safety?' This question really did defeat the youngster.

'I, I may be speaking out of turn, madam, but that would be a matter for the police rather than for the embassy.' Megan nodded in resignation and that feeling returned in a spot slightly further up in her stomach. Tiredness washed over her like an ever-rolling wave. All of this had to be over now. There must be peace for them here. As the junior official bade her an extremely formal farewell and continued about his duties, Megan realized that she had no more fight left in her. And yet, as a uniformed guard escorted her through the rear gates of the property, the prospect of finding them both a permanent place to live, and of Lucy going to school and making new friends, brought a broad smile to her face. It was a lovely, sunny day in prettiest Mayfair and the very idea of conspiracy and danger felt like something out of a cheap novel. There were one or two clouds overhead, but no rain was forecast. Megan's feet hurt in her smart heels. She needed to see Lucy. She hailed a taxi.

The Chameleon wakes and switches on the hotel room's overhead lamp. He is fully clothed and he rises and stretches. The clock on the wall reads 6am exactly. He selects a city trader's pinstripe suit, tie, shirt and braces from the room's closet. He opens the main door slightly and notes the pair of overtly stylish Italian shoes that have been polished overnight in accordance with his requirements. He showers and shaves and dresses for the day. He applies a dollop of brylcream and slicks back his hair. He takes his Filofax and a smart-looking briefcase and is about to leave for breakfast when the phone rings.

'Chameleon?'

'This is he – loud, proud and ready to take on the world at just after 6:25 in the AM.'

'The subject has an appointment today at the Embassy, two o'clock. Might be a good time to...'

'I'm gonna cut you off right there, my good man. You stick to your business and I'll stick to mine. No offence of course.'

'Er, no, of course, I was merely...'

'You were merely about to attempt to tell me my business, sir. And I'm merely saying that there's absolutely no need. You just leave it all to me. I do this sort of thing for a living, you know.'

'Of course, er, quite.'

'Please don't try to contact me on this number again. You'll know when the job is done.'

'Thank you, I ...'

The Chameleon hangs up and looks at himself in the mirror. He practices his grin and his wink and his finger point. Satisfied, he heads downstairs to a breakfast of champions followed by an emergence into a fine Mayfair day.

He peers over the top of his Financial Times to see her, elegant and attractive in her late forties, making for her car laden with shopping bags. He almost feels an urge to offer to help her lift them into the boot. The Chameleon is no gambler, though, and he knows that to allow her to see one of his many faces is to increase the risk of something going wrong. Instead, he hails a passing taxi and instructs the driver to follow the blue Rover pulling out of the car park. The driver seems on the verge of some kind of protest when he is silenced by a wad of notes shoved into his hand.

They follow Megan is silence as she picks Lucy up from school and drives them both to her Mother's house. At one point the driver begins to whistle, but is cut short by The Chameleon's swiftly delivered, 'Could you not do that please,' accompanied by a flashing smile. The Chameleon decides to get out on the quiet, rather pleasant street where Lucy and Megan are staying. He walks along on the opposite side of the road. The Chameleon has long since accepted the whimsy with which he enjoys these moments spent imagining the everyday lives of the people whose lives he is about to alter forever. That they have no idea their lives are already in the palm of his hand allows him to approach them with something akin to tenderness. He could view their last few moments of life in a way that they, of course, could not. He smiles to himself and observes the course of his late afternoon shadow along the road. Some people are more shadow than substance, he thinks. He can almost see his reflection in his shiny shoes. He crosses the road to stand before the little blue Rover, his hands clasped against his filofax and newspaper. A light breeze whips against his carefully pinned red tie. His braces feel tight against his shoulders underneath the pinstripe jacket that also conceals a holstered pistol. It occurs to him that he could walk up the steps to the front door, rap politely three times, and when Megan or the grandmother opens the door to answer – possibly in the middle of a sweet, everyday conversation about something Lucy did on her first day at school – bang! One in the head, then the body folds in on itself. He marches past and into the lounge where little Lucy is playing. He tells her to keep quiet with a gesture and a big smile … The girl looks at her Mother in the kitchen before she screams. He moves into the kitchen and sees that Megan has the knife draw open and is withdrawing a substantial blade. Pop! Down goes Megan. The child is screaming far too loudly now. A blow to the head? No, a cloth soaked in chloroform should do it.

All of this flashes through The Chameleon's mind and is dismissed in a matter of seconds. The job must be clean and untraceable. It must not look like a gangland hit, like a hit of any sort. The Financial Times crinkles in his hands and he finds himself on Megan's Mother's drive. This flaunting of his own rules sends a curious thrill through The Chameleon. He can hear Lucy playing in the garden. The garage door is open and he can see the back wheel of a vesper from the previous decade. This job requires some further days of reconnaissance. The Chameleon smiles to himself and taps his filofax. He will provide a progress report after dinner this evening.

The ending, when it comes, is quick and quiet. Quick because The Chameleon nudges his land rover into the oncoming vesper and sends it and its rider careering into a tree. Quiet because The Chameleon has chosen this spot as one lacking in traffic and surrounded by thick forest on both sides. There is no need to check the condition of the body. There is smoke billowing from the smashed scooter and blood dribbling from the helmet. This is the culmination of two weeks of diligent and quite satisfying work for the Chameleon during which time he has provided regular pay phone updates to the contact at the Embassy who has in turn updated Mr Kichi. He has enjoyed following Megan on her scooter rides through London and the surrounding countryside. He was nearby and overheard her discussing a proposed solo weekend trip with the Grandmother in the garage. He found that he was comfortable being close to her, safe in the knowledge of his professional prowess. He had assumed the persona of a traveller, a Sunday gentleman driver with leather gloves and corduroy trousers, and a body warmer over an unassuming shirt. The weekend away was full of pleasant cruising and equally pleasant stops at countryside eateries where The Chameleon would observe Megan from a distance, eating a ploughman's while enjoying a coffee or even a half pint of warm ale.

    Sitting here now, he almost feels sorrow at the state of this woman he feels he has come to know. Almost, but of course not quite. He realizes as he drives away that his sorrow is for the end of an enjoyable job. Back to Japan now for him. And what of the child? He takes a last look at Megan's obscenely arranged limbs on the tree and drives off. The child still has a grandmother. And a Father. He will report to his employer via a payphone this evening.

Part Eight: Comings Togethers
'Be wise, and taste.'
                                  Milton, 'Comus'

<u>Ali, at the hospital, 2012</u>

The double doors close behind me and I feel like skipping down the corridor. I pat my inside pocket for cigarettes and a lighter. I realize that for once I don't feel the guilt that usually goes with this habit and the thought of all the objects on my desk at home. Doctors and nurses move past and around me. I will need to know the name of his psychiatrist. I walk past the doors to the canteen and something catches my eye. I stop and look through the canteen doors: it is our resident prankster. He is sitting at a table with a coke and a burger. His lips are moving and it seems like he's muttering or singing to himself. I would like to light a cigarette here and observe him for a while, but the law being the law and I need to get back to Quentin as soon as I can. I order coffee for both us. It feels nice to order for two again. Does this mean I'm no longer alone? I smile to myself and then I hear violins in the background, somewhere behind the general noise of the canteen. Mr Tapper looks like he's trying to name that tune. The coffee does not look great here. Shall I get us something to eat as well? Is it too soon to be eating in front of one another? Mr Tapper now looks like he is having a full-blown conversation with himself. I look at him as I finger the lighter in my hand. Two coffees to go. The violins are still going strong as I exit the canteen.

Two weeks later

    I spend most of my time at his flat as it is a little awkward having him stay round at mine. I feel bad about what happened with Andrew. But not that bad. It was simply a case of poor timing. It has only been a couple of weeks but I've already seen a marked improvement in Quentin's mental state. I am contributing towards rent and bills whenever I stay over here. I have no idea how he manages to pay his rent as he is not working. Some of us have two jobs while studying for a degree. I tell him he drinks too much coffee and he says a life without fine coffee is not worth living. I cook him healthy meals and we talk all the time. I make time for him in my life. We talk and talk.

    'I am so proud of you and your recovery, you know?'

    'Thank you,' he says.

    We are in bed together with the radio on and drinking coffee. I have lectures in the morning and I know I should not drink coffee this late but this is part of our routine. The lovemaking and the coffee and the talking into the night.

    'Dr Kimberley says that it's small steps to a normal life again. A couple of weeks ago I was going to kill myself. I don't want to rush myself back to that.'

    I am stroking his sandy hair.

    'One of those steps could be a haircut tomorrow, Mr Carter.'

    'Don't you like the wild man look?'

    His head is resting against my thigh.

    'Oh, I like it very well, as you know.'

    'But?' He looks up with a cheeky grin.

'Well, it might not be a bad idea to, you know, smarten yourself up a little bit?'

'Why would I want to do that? I'm a writer, this is what writers look like.'

'I know that, baby, and I think it is so great that you are writing and creating.'

'But?' He smiles that smile again. I wonder if her has the energy for another bout? Where am I getting all of my energy from?

'If you were to go for job interviews, for instance, you might want to be a little bit more presentable and bit less bohemian? Just something to think about, no pressure.'

Quentin, 2011

I finished Cambridge then took my MA. I was okay but I wasn't completely back to my old self. Can anyone choose to be their old self? Is that even desirable? In the wake of a period of mental illness, I found the draw of romanticizing my former existence and dwelling upon the monument of my former self quite irresistible. To be one's old self. I had a BA and an MA, all very nice and proper, now start a lovely and neat career as…something. The only thing I've ever really wanted to be is a writer? No, you misheard me, I said a career. I spent a few months at home annoying my parents. I'd spend my days running with the family dog, shopping for second-hand books on the Charing Cross Road, and drinking espressos in lovely little coffee bars. It was an enjoyable fug; I bothered no one and no one bothered me. It couldn't last, though, and an aunt suggested that I could set myself up as a tutor to eager young minds while I figured out what I wanted to do. Why not, I thought, despite my utter hatred of the very idea of being a teacher of any sort. My aunt, of course, had the ideal first tutee for me in the form of her less than academically promising son, my cousin Jack. Suitably enthused by my sudden turn to honest labours, my parents very kindly subsidized the deposit and first month's rent on some shared lodgings on Aldersgate Street. I supplemented my income with a curious job producing revolutionary pamphlets for an independent outfit called The Shepherd Press, with a small office in Soho. It was owned by an eccentric and wealthy former theatrical agent who never appeared at the office.

My aunt and uncle live in a big house with a large garden in leafy suburbia. The place is set in a paradisaically quiet little village with a straight road running through it. Jack is tall and heavily built. He is suited to playing number 8 for his sixth form rugby team, but not at all suited to the requisite amount of reading and analysis to pass his English Lit A-level. Jack has a sweet nature and I enjoyed getting to know him. My only previous memories of him were as a baby. Jack always has some kind of rugby shirt on when we meet at the dining table for our thrice-weekly study sessions. He tries to engage me in conversation about anything other than his core texts (Macbeth, Seamus Heaney poetry, A Room With a View and The Catcher in the Rye). I tell him how fortunate he is to be studying Salinger at his age. He doesn't seem to agree with me. Sometimes I get up to go to the toilet or make a drink and return to find that cousin Jack has slipped out to meet up with friends. On these occasions I just laugh. My aunt is paying me a considerable hourly rate for these sessions.

Jack ended up with in D in his English Literature A-Level, with which he seemed quite delighted. He says he could never have written an exam essay on Catcher without my help. I told him it was my pleasure. I would certainly miss the cheques from auntie. While I was mentally comparing my idea of what Jack's essay might have been like with Holden Caulfield's questionable treatise on 'The Egyptians', my cousin informed me of some potential new clients among the lower sixth formers in his rugby team.

The members of the new flock were Kenneth, Marco and Herbie.

I knew then that I wanted to write, to produce ... something. Not to teach or to study but to write.

The pamphleteering job I found through the Times Literary

Supplement. It was mainly just transcribing and writing a little copy. The money was negligible, but the people were an interesting assortment of venerable one-time revolutionaries and ageing members of the anarchist party.

I never touched him. Never. Don't look at the evidence, just ... Talk to Dr Kimberley. It's not why he left to meet his mates. Shut up. Just.

Typing radicalpamphlets to be mailed to a select number of subscribers. I corrected punctuation and spelling. I tidied up phrases and polished vocab. I also got into the habit of adding my own contributions here and there and nobody ever seemed to notice. Many of the contributors were volunteers who I suspect came in mainly for the conversation. We drank strong coffee from an ancient machine and chatted away, and people brought in muffins and donuts. I didn't really have any friends but at that time I didn't really want any. I had a massive store of books along with a rather decent coffee machine and a growing collection of old VHS tapes that I watched on a VCR given to me by one of the grey anarchists. I made reasonably healthy meals and enjoyed the odd cold beer with them. I joined a gym not far from the flat and started putting in some serious miles on the treadmill. I wasn't joyously happy, but then who is? I was just okay and that was fine with me. Most days, if I wasn't on tutoring duties in the evening, I would have a little sleep when I got back from work before hitting the gym. I would then sit and read in my favourite armchair, which had once belonged to my grandmother, until my eyes began to feel heavy.

One of the old anarchists is called O'Shaunessy. He is one of those people with an apparently friendly manner that quickly becomes all-too friendly and, in my mind, creates suspicion of his motives. He likes to bring up my time at Cambridge despite, or perhaps because of, my clear reticence in discussing it with him. I feel he can sense my desire to live in the moment and free myself from the past, and he revels in making me uncomfortable. He clearly gets some kick out of these very passive attempts to unnerve me. He asks what I will do with my future and says what a shame it would be to waste my qualifications. Everyone else sees him as a harmless old man, but I see something in those little pinprick eyes of his that I don't like one bit. My heart always sinks when he bumbles his way over with some lame pretext of talking to me about work. Soon enough he'll be lurking over my shoulder and reminiscing about his own student days while slurping his tea. I try to think of a strategy for dealing with him; he's there every day as he has little else to fill his time. The man gives me the creeps, though, and I just seem to freeze whenever he's around.

 I have five (count them!) keen students now. I don't see myself as a teacher, more as a mentor. I hate talking about this stuff. I do like being able to pay my bills with only occasional help from my parents. My running regime is picking up nicely. I love the mental clarity of foot in front of foot. A run can change my mood from low to medium high without any conscious effort on my part.

 Sometimes when I'm studying Shakespeare with one of the guys over coffee and biscuits, I flash back to that thought about my cousin – that I had done something to make him leave the study session. Sometimes the creeping feeling of unease begins before I even arrive at their houses for the sessions. This becomes an acute fatigue of mind and body. I have a fear of these flashes happening during one of the sessions. Gleams like the flashings of a shield. I wander home and collapse into bed following a session on Wordsworth. I collapse into bed and one morning I cannot get up. I go to the GP and get myself the required sick notes. The GP also gives me a letter of referral and a contact number for a private psychiatrist he knows. When I tell my parents about this, they agree to pay for the sessions immediately. I see Dr Susan Kimberley every Tuesday morning. She has increased my medication and recommended a full programme of physical exercise, writing exercises, planning for the future and seeing friends as frequently as I can. I'm unsure how many of these I will be able to fulfil; I'm keeping up with my exercise for the moment but anything that involves talking to other people, I'm not so sure.

 I have joined the British Library at Dr Kimberley's suggestion. It's a lovely building but my mind isn't feeling receptive to new learning. The more I focus on getting rid of the thought, the more permanent it feels. Dr Kimberley has advised me that going back to work may be the best way forward, but how can I? Nothing has been resolved. I have learned nothing about myself. I know that Milton attended Christ's and Cromwell Sidney Sussex, and that they may have met and conversed on March 20th 1649. I know, I know I know I know. I still exercise at Dr Kimberley's instruction. One of Mum or Dad will usually visit me each day. I watch films and I read. I send off my council tax cheques. Some days I eat, while some days I just stay in bed. Not gonna touch anyone. But you did, didn't you. When I don't shower for a few days I notice that old university smell; the smell of university and the smell of decay. Decaying flesh and humanity. Nothing is ever over and done, over and finished with.

On the days when I feel a bit better, I make coffee for myself and I think about writing. I go to cafes with Mum and Dad. Dr Kimberley tries to prevent me from engaging in compulsive behaviours, but I can't help asking her for reassurance. She knows that this will only bind the thoughts more tightly to my mind. Sometimes she cuts the sessions short because I'm in an especially obsessive and compulsive frame of mind. What else does she expect? I maintain the barest connection with reality by continuing to pay bills and shop for groceries. My parents still talk about me going back to work. I stay in bed or lie on the sofa with the TV on. I don't want to carry on living like this. Dr Kimberley tells me that I should keep going to The British Library and reading. About what? About anything. Strike up a conversation or two with other readers. I can't. Why? What's the worst that can happen? Record your thoughts and feelings. Record any intrusive thoughts that come. This is a positive step that I can take. Do some writing while you're there. I think of Milton's endurance through blindness. He knew there was no cure.

I start a new routine of running in the morning, then library in the afternoon, then home for a cooked meal in the evening followed by thought diary and attempts at writing. I manage to keep this up for a week. Every morning I wake up hoping for a

change; every morning the disappointment crushes me anew. The library sessions morph into research on OCD and depression. I pore over dense medical articles. This is, as you can probably imagine, utterly exhausting. Milton saw through the darkness inflicted upon him. Why can I not do the same? Because myself am fucking hell
I'm not going to, I'm never going to...so...

April 2014

It's an Easter Sunday celebration with our respective parents. Ali's Mum won't stop talking about Tom and how he's doing now. Ali is working hard on her Masters in Victorian Literature. She works all the hours God sends. I think she's one of those people who loves to feel that everyone else thinks she's working too hard and suffering! I refuse to indulge her in this and I know that annoys her. Perhaps I'm being unfair. I can be unfair sometimes. I tell her that she can't use studying as I crutch and she tells me I don't know what I'm talking about. Maybe she's right. I'm back at work now after weeks of her nagging me, and I have to admit that I'm really enjoying it. It's like I have my old life back. I still see Dr Kimberley once a week. The old anarchists are still somehow going strong in Soho; I've just slipped back in like nothing ever happened. I don't think a lot of them even noticed I'd gone anywhere to be honest. The structure of work (loose as it is) is so good for my mind. It's more like membership of a social club than a job. I still have plenty of energy for my writing, mainly in the evenings. Ali broke up with Tom but he's still here in our flat and in my words. It's strange but I grow closer to him while Ali has removed him from her life.

'What that man has been through is like a resurrection, begging everybody's pardon,' says Ali's Mum. She crosses herself and seems mortified that she may have committed some form of blasphemy.

'Mum, can we please talk about something else?' says Ali.

'But your Mum is right, Ali,' I say. She flashes me a look. I shouldn't wind her up but it's just too easy.

'I am not denying that,' she says. 'I know what those guys go through and how tough it is, mentally and physically, to recover. But we are not a couple anymore, so...'

She looks unbearably sad all of an instant so I take her hand. We frequently veer between calculated attempts to get a reaction from the other and utter horror at the form that inevitable reaction takes. This seems to be a pattern we fall back into again and again despite, I think, neither of us really liking it.

'That's not so easy for some of us,' says Mrs Cooper to me. 'As a Christian, when I see somebody suffering like that, I have to go towards them. Ali will tell you, Quentin.'

'I know that, Mum. You are a good Christian and a good person.'

There are tears in Ali's eyes. I reach out to hug her but she is hugging her Mum so I sit back. Mrs Cooper kisses Ali's head and strokes her hair. I never really know how to react when the subject of religion rears its head. I suppose if she finds it comforting, where's the harm?

'You would keep in touch with them, of course. Of course you would because you do the right thing,' says Ali.

'Look at the way you cared for him,' says Mrs Cooper. 'You're right, you did more than your fair share for him.'

'I know, I know,' says Ali and she sits back in her chair and dabs at her moist eyes. I give her a smile, which she returns, and I pat her hand.

'It must be wonderful to still see the religious significance of holidays like Easter and Christmas,' says Mum. A split infinitive from Mother. I notice and I know Ali does too. Why do things like that matter to some people?

'You two must come on a trip back to Wicklow with me one day. Father Conlan delights in visitors. He's ninety and still serving the parish. Can you believe it?'

I have my arm around Ali and I'm relieved the conversation seems to have washed her up on the shore and left her to me. Ali's religion seems to me to be a stick with which she beats herself. I have enough feelings of guilt with the OCD.

'He's never been caught up in any, er, scandal, has he?' says Dad with a mischievous twinkle. I shake my head and try to will the comment back into his big mouth.

'I'm sure I don't know what you could mean,' says Mrs Cooper.

'He was making a bad joke,' says Mum with a swift elbow to Dad's ribs.

'Ooff! Apologies, Mary. Just my attempt at humour. I can never resist a Catholic priest joke!' He chuckles to himself and then becomes engrossed in polishing his glasses, utterly oblivious of any offence caused.

'Well, I fail to see that a person's faith is a laughing matter at all,' says Mrs Cooper with a wag of the finger.

'He's sorry, aren't you,' says Mum. Dad carries on with his glasses till he realizes he's supposed to be saying something.

'What? Yes, of course,' he says.

'He was only teasing, Mum,' says Ali.

'Was he?' says Mrs Cooper. 'You naughty scamp! Fancy teasing a devoted Catholic on Easter Sunday?' She's smiling and laughing now.

'I did fancy it,' says Dad with an enormous guffaw.

'I shall have to watch you, Mr,' says Mrs Cooper.

Ali and I share a look and a grin.

'Anyone for dessert?' I say.

My parents are making polite conversation with Mrs Cooper while Ali and I chat and laugh over the washing-up. All of an instant the calm of a Sunday afternoon is shattered by a shout from Mrs Cooper.

'Good lord!' she says. Ali and I share another look before returning to the lounge. Mrs Cooper has her hand over her mouth and is staring at the shelf above the TV. I turn to look. Of course. How had I failed to move it?

'Holy Mary,' she says. 'What are you doing with that on your mantelpiece?'

I have nothing to say.

'I bought it from a charity shop, Mum. Please don't be so dramatic. I think you need to sit down and take it easy. You know you are not supposed to get over-excited.'

Ali guides her Mother to the sofa and quickly has a table and a cup of tea in front of her.

'How did such a thing end up in a charity shop of all places?' she says.

'Drink your tea and try not to worry about it, Mum,' says Ali. 'Would you like a biscuit?'

'What? Oh, yes. Yes please,' says Mrs Cooper.

She is still involuntarily crossing herself. I stare at the holy relic in my home. The purloined totem that places a curse upon she who stole it and the unholy place in which it rests. Strike the poet down with blindness. Fire Cromwell to the point of murderous passion, then cool him to the point where such an object would cut him to the quick with remorse of conscience. I must speak to Ali about this object.

Two days before Christmas, 2016

Two days till Christmas and the Tottenham Court Road is packed with shoppers; families and tots with bright and red faces. Don't avoid anybody in the crowd, there is absolutely no need to do that. Don't worry so. Ali is cooking a full turkey dinner for my parents and her Mother this year. This is beginning to feel very official. An invitation to Christmas with Ali and Quentin.

'Try not to drink too much today, baby. I know what you're like when you get together with him.'

This feels like one of those gently delivered knives to the belly, the kind that I discuss with Dr Kimberley at our fortnightly sessions. I know she's only trying to look out for me but I still get that dead feeling inside that makes me want to run screaming away from here to solitude and quiet. I know she wishes to be my sanctuary.

'You should not really be drinking at all with your meds.'
Grab her and punch her in the fucking face
No
Stop it
Please

I was busy thinking about The Adventure of the Blue Carbuncle. Found at the corner of Goodge Street and the Tottenham Court Road. A fucking Christmas goose – but no longer. A mind turning on itself and not for the first time. We're on Oxford Street now.

I simply will not
I wouldn't

'Can we just sit down and get a drink somewhere please?' I say.

'What is up with you, baby?'

She reaches out to feel my forehead but I jerk my arm away.

'Oh God, baby, are you having one of your episodes?' She stops on the Oxford Street pavement and people walk around us and make faces.

'I don't have episodes, Ali.'

The shopping bags in my arms are suddenly heavy. I'm starting to sweat despite the cold. There's a Starbucks behind Ali and I motion with my eyes.

I'm sitting with my Christmassy coffee and a large muffin and starting to feel a bit better. I think about my sessions with Dr Kimberley. My feet connected to the ground. Focus on that muffin and this coffee. Take the heat out of all those hot thoughts, Quentin.

'This Christmas shopping lark is pretty intense, isn't it?' I say.

'Are you okay?' she says. 'Shall I call Dr Kimberley?'

Her phone is in her hand.

'You can't call her on the weekend, Ali.' I reach out and take her hand. She puts down the phone.

'Please talk to me then,' she says.

Her eyes are bright and moist.

'I was a little flustered back there but I'm fine now, baby, honestly.' I rub her hand. 'You look beautiful today.' She smiles and brushes the strands of chestnut hair from her face, looking bashful all of a sudden.

'Do I not look beautiful every day?'

'That's a given,' I say, taking a large gulp of syrupy sweet eggnog-infused coffee. 'But especially so today with the warmth coming to your cheeks and all your warm wintery clothes on.'

She rubs her hands together as if to emphasise my point.

'I always find Christmas so stressful. Why can it never just be enjoyable?'

'Christmas places a burden on people like you who want everyone else to be happy,' I say.

'People talk about selflessness as if it were something to change about myself.' She rests her head on her crossed arms on the table and smiles up at me.

'Yes,' I say, 'society seems to prize putting oneself first these days. Most people aren't selfless, they're quite the opposite.'

'I don't want to believe that, Quentin,' she says with her head resting on her left elbow.

'You don't want to believe it, but you do,' I say with a smile.

She sits up and she looks tired. There's a long strand of hair hanging down over her face. I don't know if she's ever looked more beautiful.

'My beliefs are my beliefs and my faith is my faith, Quentin. I can't take this view that everyone is selfish and horrible.'

'I know that,' I say, 'and I know your faith has helped you through many dark times, but do you really...'

'Really what?'

'Nothing, forget it. We're both just stressed out from Christmas shopping.'

The Starbucks is filling up with shoppers taking a break from the seventh circle of hell that is central London at Christmas. Thankfully we're only getting last minute bits and bobs today. We're meeting Tapper in one of his Soho haunts in a bit. She sips her tea and looks away to indicate that as far as she is concerned the matter is closed. Drink your drink and enjoy the quiet. Rest your legs and feel grounded.

When I come back from the toilet, I can see she's been crying. I move around the table and enfold her in a hug. She feels frail and warm. I feel her tears against my chest. I hold her in my arms and we squeeze each other. She lifts her head and dabs at her eyes with a couple of napkins.

'Do you love me?' she says.

'More than anything.'

'Let's promise to have a lovely Christmas with no arguments,' she says with a laugh.

I laugh too.

'Pinky promise?'

'Pinky promise.'

She goes to the bathroom before we leave for the pub. Maybe I shouldn't drink today. I look down and see damp stains on my t-shirt. Marks of woe. If Tapper were here, he'd make a Fight Club reference. Here she comes. I take her hand and we head for the pub, back into the throng.

Here comes Tapper with the drinks and some packets of crisps. He's on the cider tonight. He distributes the crisps.

'Thanks,' I say.

'None for me thank you,' says Ali.

'Don't tell us she's given up crisps as well as booze?' he says to me.

'I have not given up alcohol, I simply drink it in moderation. To me, five pints of cider and some crisps does not constitute a meal,' she says.

'What does then?' says Tapper, munching on his salt and vinegar.

'Six pints,' I say.

'And two packets of crisps,' he adds. We both laugh and she shakes her head with a smile.

'Are you spending Christmas with Lucy?' says Ali.

myself am hell

'I certainly shall be,' says Tapper. 'Lucy is gonna do some fancy Japanese cuisine for us.'

'While you sit there with your feet up, no doubt?' I say.

He looks momentarily offended by this before nodding in agreement. The pub is filling with customers, presumably relieved that a day of Christmas shopping has reached its end.

'Do you ever cook for her?' says Ali.

'I do sometimes. She works late at the gallery a lot so we don't see each other at dinner time that often.' He takes another sip of cider. I look over at Ali and she raises an eyebrow at me.

'What?' says Tapper.

'Quentin and I just wonder when we're going to meet Lucy?'

'I'm not sure I'm quite ready to inflict you two on my beloved,' he says. 'It's all going so perfectly that I think I'll just keep her to myself at the moment, if you don't mind. Our relationship is a bit like that film where the guy falls in love with the Mannequin who's come to life, but she's only real to him. What was that one called, Quentin?'

'Mannequin?' I offer.

'That's it,' he says. 'Our life together is on a different level entirely. I have my friends, she has hers and we're happy like that.'

'So we won't ever get to meet her? Says Ali.

'I'm not saying that, it's just that if something's working, why make changes? You know, like when directors start tinkering around with their old films and end up ruining them. Your film no longer belongs to you once it has been released for public consumption. A filmmaker should no more be making changes to an already-released film than a parent send their children in for plastic surgery...'

'Fine, let's change the subject,' says Ali. 'What religion is Lucy?'

'That's not really changing the subject,' says Tapper.

'And how do you know she has a religion?' I add.

'Does she?' says Ali.

'No, not that I know of,' says Tapper. 'I feel like she's almost developed her own religion based on her experiences. She's had a tough life, you know. She's had to fend for herself for a long time.'

'Like you did,' says Ali.

'Yeah,' he says, 'but I never really had to fend for myself. I always had people to take care of me.'

'But you don't see them anymore?'

'Let's not get too heavy this evening,' I say.

'I'm just interested in other people's lives, that's all,' she says.

'What you mean by that is you're interested in how anyone can live without family telling them what to do and a heavy dose of religious indoctrination.'

'That's quite harsh,' she says.

'I know, I'm sorry.' I take her hand but she looks pissed off with me now. Sometimes I go into argument mode and forget that I'm talking to someone I love.

'Let's just forget it,' says Tapper. He never likes talking about his past. I respect his right to reveal as much or as little information as he wants to.

'You should show more interest in the lives of other people if you want to be a writer, Quentin,' says Ali. 'I'm interested to know what other people believe and the things that help them get through the day.'

'But you have no right to keep interrogating him,' I say.

'I'm not interrogating, just interested. You don't think I'm interrogating you, do you?'

'Not at all,' says Tapper. 'If you could turn down that spotlight a tad, though.'

They both laugh. She puts her hand on mine but I pull it away.

'Please don't "should" me,' I say. 'You know I hate that.'

'What do you mean?' she says.

'I would ban the word "should". Who can impose that word on another person?'

'I think someone is being a little sensitive,' she says to Tapper.

'Yeah, she didn't mean anything, mate,' he says. 'It's just

something people say. It's not actually a command, like a command to a secret agent through his earpiece.'

'What if I mocked your religion?'

'Everyone just chill please,' says Tapper.

'You do laugh at my religion,' she says. 'Anyway, let's change the subject please.'

'And what's this "if you want to be a writer"?'

'This is why I wish you wouldn't drink with your meds,' she says.

Push her and she will fall and hit her fucking head.

There it is. A flash. I look at Tapper but he is unreadable. I want so to move my arm in that herky jerky way but I mustn't.

'I think I might call it a night and get a taxi,' she says more to Tapper than to me.

I will absolutely never. Ever. Push her.

She tries to kiss me on the cheek but I won't let her.

She says goodbye to Tapper and says she will see me at home.

You just punched her.

'Ali?' She has her hand on a black cab's rear door handle. 'You should take that candle-holder back to the church.'

'What?'

'It's a curse on us. Take it back and atone.'

'We need to talk,' she says.

'Okay,' I say.

'When you're sober.'

She climbs in and the car pulls away.

I'm not going to…Ever…

Easter Sunday, 2018

Mum is getting worse. I always knew there would be a managed descent, with the eventual need for care in a home or hospital. I never imagined it would happen this soon. It is with immense pride that I am about to submit my PhD thesis. Mum is very pleased and the last time we spoke she asked when Quentin and I will be getting married (as if this were an inevitability). I feel I never quite know how Quentin is doing. I don't know if he does either. Mum couldn't make it over for Easter this year and he didn't want to invite his parents. I will have to go over and see her soon and probably staff for a while, but I don't know if I can leave him right now. I don't know if I should. He gets trapped in his own head sometimes and he needs me to bring him back.

'How is your writing going?' I say.

'Very slow,' says Quentin, very slowly. The TV is on but I am not sure if he is watching it. His eyes are looking into the distance.

'Are you still enjoying it?' I say.

He is silent. Has he heard me? He has been taking days off work lately. I go to prepare the dinner and he picks a book from the shelf and returns to his seat. I prep away in the kitchen with Radio Four humming along in the background. I wish I could plan for the future with him. Sharing your life with someone. Sharing one's life with another.

'Shall we eat in front of the TV?' I call from the kitchen.

'Yes,' he says.

I hand him his plate. 'Would you like a black coffee with dinner?'

'Yes please,' he says. He turns to face me and smiles; the piercing clarity of his eyes hidden behind something else, something dark that is not really him at all.

'I shall be right back,' I say. I know his eyes are still on me. I am only wearing track bottoms and a t-shirt. The thought occurs to me that I am in good shape through pilates and yoga. Perhaps tonight the art of seduction will bring him out of himself? I cringe at my own phrasing. To bring him out. Carry him out of himself. He told me that Dr Kimberley talks about getting out of your own way.

'There you are.'

'Thanks,' he says. I seat myself next to him as The one Show theme rings out its familiar tune. We eat in silence for a few moments. His silences drive me mad sometimes. They are not moods as such; I can just tell that his mind is somewhere else, somewhere I am not. I have spent so much of my time by myself reading and studying. When I get home I want to open up, to talk and to let out my emotions. Lately I feel that the real him, the person I love, is hidden away somewhere. It seems to be my job to correct him and regulate him. What is his job for me?

'Do you remember the episode of The Royle Family when they watch The One Show through the window of somebody else's caravan?' I say.

He laughs.

'In the pearl of pissing Prestatyn,' he says with a grin.

'I loved that show,' I say. 'So did Mum.'

'Great writing,' he says. That word seems to hang between us. I don't like talking about her in the past tense.

'Please never think that I am trying to pry into your writing, Quentin,' I say. He puts his plate down on the coffee table and leans his head on my shoulder. I stroke his hair. 'Are you okay?'

He puts his arm around me. We sit like this for ten minutes or so. His hair is all uneven when he lifts his head and sits back. He takes off his round glasses and lays them on the coffee table. He tries in vain to flatten down his hair and we share a smile.

'Did I upset you?' he says suddenly with panic in his eyes.

'No, of course not.' The One Show is coming to an end. 'They do fill these shows with some utter rubbish.' He appears immobilized. 'Wait, upset me when?' People upset people all the time.

'I...any time...recently, like in the last few days?' He rubs his temples.

'No, love.' I take his hands in mine and kiss them. 'Hold on, is this one of your episodes?'

Oh God. Remember what to do and how to be of help. The pent-up tiredness of the last few weeks of work on the thesis rises to the surface and settles there.

He sighs heavily. 'Yes, you could call it that.'

'This must be bad because you are looking to me for reassurance, right?' I say.

'Mmhmm.' His head is once again pressed into my arm.

'But then, that is the compulsion part of the condition, right? If I give you reassurance, that feeds right into the condition, right?'

I remember the things he told me about it as well as my own research.

'Yeah.' He sits back and then puts his head in his hands. 'But please just do it for me this once. Forget what the manual says and just help me out, please.' His voice is cracking.

'I would not feel right doing that, baby. I want to help you, I do.'

'This will help me. Dr Kimberley won't see me when I'm like this. She says I have all the answers and I don't need reassurance.'

'Then she is correct,' I say.

'But sometimes I can't resist it,' he says. 'I can't endure even though I know I should. Please, did I upset you and hurt you?'

I shake my head. 'I will do anything to help you except that.'

'Like the Meatloaf song,' he says with a faint smile.

'Exactly,' I say. I get up. 'Chocolate pudd for dessert?'

'Yes please.'

I heat up the little puddings in bowls in the microwave. I have work in the bookshop tomorrow. How long should I keep my two jobs? Everything has to move on and change. Such is the nature of progress. What is progress if you're on your own, though? I don't want a solitary journey.

The pudding is nice.

'Is that why you took time off work?' I say.

'Yeah.'

He is eating and watching the TV. Eastenders.

'Please know that I am here for you. If Kimberley said what you should avoid, did she also say what you should do, to be proactive?'

He rubs his eyes and crosses his legs beneath him. 'The usual – she said I should keep a thought diary and live with the thought. That I should live with the discomfort. When you think about it, all of the OCD rules are quite negative and prohibitive:

don't do this; don't do that; resist this and that.'

'Yes,' I say, 'they are. They almost leave you hanging and waiting for your mind to return to normal. Is that how it feels to you?'

He nods slowly.

'And you can't just wait for it to happen,' he says.

'The onus is on you to make it happen?' I say.

'But I don't have the energy,' he says, staring at the TV.

'I know,' I say. 'What does Kimberley think you should do if you are unable to work?'

'Write, spend time with you,' he says.

'We could go away somewhere?' I say.

'Really?'

'Why not? I have plenty of leave I can take. We could go somewhere and lounge around and get some sun?'

'That actually sounds fantastic,' he says.

We fall into an agreeable silence and cuddle on the sofa. I begin to wonder if my seduction plan from earlier might still work. Probably the last thing on his mind.

'Ali?' he says.

'Yes, baby.' There is a dumb action film on now that I am quite enjoying in a mostly ironic way.

'We should take the candleholder back.'

'Not this again. It's been too long now. I never go to that church anymore. I avoid it if truth be told. Why not keep it as a reminder of being lost and finding each other?'

'Because I'm still lost,' he says with a frankness that takes the breath out of me for a moment. 'And seeing that thing every day – just knowing it's here in the flat, well it gives me a bad feeling, like I'll never get better.'

'But you will, you have made massive progress. This is a setback only, you will see, my love.'

'It would feel like something positive to take it back and make it right, that's all.' He sounds tired.

'To atone for my sin?' I say.

'To begin to atone for both of our sins,' he says. My

discomfort rises and brings with it the naming of its source: a person other than my priest talking about my sins. We are all sinners, but we don't talk about this in our daily lives.

'How about later today then? I will do anything if you think it will help you to feel better, Quentin.'

'On Easter Sunday,' he says. He nestles into me again and I kiss his head and stroke his hair.

'Yes.' Silence settles around us again. Facing up to my sins for him. Forced attrition.

'Did I hurt you?' He says this after several minutes. I rub his arm and kiss him again.

'It's okay,' I say for want of anything more meaningful to contribute.

'Please answer me,' he continues.

'Rest, Quentin. We have both had a long day.'

'You won't answer me, will you? It's a simple question.' He is sitting up and there is panic in his eyes.

'We will take the candleholder back later,' I say. 'What shall we do after that? We should do something nice.' I always notice the word "should" now, but he doesn't today. I can't reach him, and he's using me like on of his compulsions.

'Did I hurt you? Please tell me, I can't fucking take this.' He tears at his hair and face.

Oh no

Later the same day

Make your burnt offering.
Make your sin offering.
Submit all of your sinful thoughts for assessment.

A single offering to God from a single man on the way to the place of worship in the evening sunshine of a Spring day. Tramp along the streets and carry your joint offering in a bag. Make use of the holy water and all hail to Mary, Mother of God. She smells clean and fresh. The offering to God. She has it. I won't touch, I won't go,

I won't make an offering to them, to the priests The life of the Church and the life of the Mind and you can't go back to the time before this when I Censor myself and count my blessings and prayers at once. Truth revealed through a process of rigorous thought by An ascetic in the desert who counts out his prayers. He covers his face with cloth and closes his eyes to the stormy sands. God is with him. He dies and the desert birds feed on his carrion. They make of him a sacrifice to their god.

    I will not, I will not. I will not, I will not
    I will not
    In the rose garden in the garden with Rose
    The poets all perish. We breathe our last.
    Father, Son and Holy Spirit.
    I will not steal, I will not steal
    I will
    Look at all of the evidence and just lay it out to reveal God's mystery. People of faith need God while the rest of us need only our eyes and ears and our minds.

    We have something to return: an object. To make things right. I feel her hand on my arm. To make everything whole again. The organ plays while the Priest and his Sheep talk in hushed and urgent tones. Should not the shepherds feed the flocks and the hungry sheep rot inwardly upon itself? While the grim wolf grim wolf grim wolf and the evil beasts sit in judgement upon my head and tell me unequivocally that I have sinned My head fills up with thoughts relentless that will not leave me to be

    The Church is no sanctuary for me or for her. Make it whole? I came here to understand God's ways to men and to fill my head with the Holy Spirit through thoughts thought and word and deed and holy water and sacred oils. I need His reassurance and the weight taken from my mind but instead the beast with six wings flaps in my peripheral vision. My mind is a scriptorium filled with impurities in thought and fucking word and deed –

    Thought –

    Impure thoughts in the house of God that cross yourself as muchasyouwant and count your prayers out and fuck it I don't want to go near any one and I won't I my ambitions and pride and this and that

    In the Church
    'I will help you'
    Help me to escape me to go back to to
    The object returned to
    Here is where we come to know God Give me the sacraments reveal to me and tell me everything give me the evidence to know that I will never go never go near to Ultimate reassurance
    Word –
    Never never never my thirst for the words of the words of Henry Lawes my sensual folly with no truth at all to it just thinking
    Where is my notebook to write my dogmas? Give me the breath of the Holy Spirit and I shall write my the poet's commonplace book to
    'Calm yourself, everything is fine. I will make some calls for you. Wait here with the Father.'
    I need to write – it's a deal, you see – I write as He reveals to me alone that I never went near to anyone and didn't do it, I didn't, I
    'There there, it's okay. I feel for you. Ali told me a little about your condition. You're in good hands with her. She's getting you the help you need.'
    Deed –
    I need to be writing all of the this down; the dialogue for the section with the priest how would he sound how would the voice of a virtuous voice sound? And how to express the intemperance of my own my mind my how to express it where is my pen and my writing area with peace and quiet
    'It's all right, it's okay. Let it all out if you need to. Say what you need to say. God is always with you.'

    Yes He is
    The Poet and the Priest brought together.
    The creative man and the holy man

A short time on this Earth for the man who makes
Take care of your flock, Holy Man, for they need you more than ever
One sheep has left the fold and can find no way back
And there are wolves out there
The poet's song and the howling wolves
The loss of the poet's sweet song
And the howling wolves
And the song

A voluntary admission was the phrase the men in the lounge had used. They'd surprised him when he'd left the bedroom to use the toilet. They'd called out to him as he'd passed the doorway; he hadn't had the will or the energy to try to evade them. They showed him a brochure for a treatment facility that Ali said would help him sort out his problems once and for all. He noticed that she had already packed a bag for him. He had experienced anger but more profoundly a sense of giving up the fight, of letting go and letting them take him where they pleased.

They are in a 4x4 now, Quentin in the back and the two staff members in the front. He is dressed, which he hasn't been for about a week. It feels strange to him to be in a car rather than lying on or beside his bed. He feels like he has not quite woken up yet. There is no substance to his anger towards Ali. What was the number she rang for them? Where was it on the brochure? It is more like the performance of a feeling. He is hungry and listless and he lacks the energy to consider what awaits him at the facility.

Welcome to the Red Apple Sanatorium

Rest. Recuperation. Tranquility.

I'm not gonna hurt anyone, I'm not gonna touch anyone, I'm not gonna go near anyone. Jerk of the arm. Jerk of the arm. Jerk of the arm. Smooth things over. Touch anyone hurt anyone near anyone touch anyone hurt anyone near anyone Never near anyone. Are we living in a time of plague once again? In that case never touch anyone. Never gonna hurt anyone. I'm never gonna hurt anyone. I will never go near anyone. I, Quentin Carter, will never ever ever ever ever ever go near anyone. Fuck off. The bodies from the plague year of 1625 in a fragment of scented pages. Never never never never to surface with his scribbling a-fucking-way about Buddhas and bloody illnesses fucksake hutment in a car never been done before smash your head smash your head smash your head they're watching Quentin and reading him. Bang bang bang take medication take medication don't know take nonsense never never never ever plague travel uphill road smash through the barrier with your uncle Taleed uncle Taleed uncle Taleed leader of a next generation of fiction writers just take me to the nearest hospital to contain the outbreak I don't want to Bang

Part Nine: Sanatorium Journal

Three weeks later (July 1st 2018)

My room is sparsely furnished but neat and clean. There is a desk. I will speak to the staff about having some of my books delivered along with my laptop (and if not the laptop then at least a typewriter). This person says he was sectioned. He threatened to kill. He has a plant in his room. The bed feels soft and should hopefully be comfortable, while the walls are painted white. Very soothing. A long curtain covers French windows that look out onto a landscape covering itself in ever-falling snow. There is a picture hanging from the main wall. It depicts a mountainous landscape underneath a vast blue sky and a burning sun. It is quite captivating in its way. Look on his laptop and play the games that he plays. The room has no sink or mirror, but it does have a wardrobe where I see some of my own clothes hanging up.

I've already been introduced to some of my fellow patients over dinner (food not too bad at all, and very good coffee from an expensive-looking machine). I was sitting at a table with a patient named Daniels when he suddenly picked up his plate and hurled it at the wall. He then climbed up onto the table and screamed obscenities at the top of his voice. Nurse Waltz and his two colleagues Carmichael and O'Shaunessey came over and helped him down.

'Would you like to spend some time in the quiet room, Mr Daniels?' asked Carmichael with genuine concern. Daniels already seemed quite calm to me by that point.

'Yes, that would be lovely, Mr Carmichael.'

'Come on then,' said Carmichael.

Later in the evening I'm walking around the corridors getting my bearings when I bump into Nurse O'Shaunessey coming the other way. He is around fifty with small, suspicious eyes and thin features. His receding hair is closely cropped and when allied to his stubble it gives him the air of some sort of military reject.

'Mind where you're going,' he says in a gruff cockney accent as he brushes past me.

'You too, Nurse O'Shaunessey,' I grin back at him.

He stops in his tracks. 'Come here you.' He beckons me towards him and I walk over. 'Right now you're stuck right at the top of a fuckin' mountain and you're on my patch. So just make sure you keep on my good side.'

'That's assuming you even have a good side.'

His face goes blank but the snarl quickly returns. 'At least I'm not a fuckin' looney.' He hisses this into my ear. 'I've read your file. Any nasty little thoughts going through that head of yours?' He reaches out and tries to tap my head but I brush his hand away. 'Hmm, violent tendencies,' he says, 'I'd better make a note of that.'

Daniels comes shuffling past in pyjamas, dressing gown and slippers. I had been meaning to speak to him anyway, so I take the opportunity. The holiday camp. Up here in the mountains. Refresh.

'Daniels!' I take him by the arm. 'Please accompany me to the smoking room.' O'Shaunessey watches us go before re-assuming his bearing of sneering authority.

I sit and smoke with Daniels in the pokey but somehow comfortable smoking room with its assortment of armchairs with torn leather that have all seen better days.

'I'm sorry about earlier, man,' he says, 'but sometimes I just get riled up.'

'Don't apologize, friend, I know exactly how you feel. If you have to let it out then feel free to let it out. Say, how long have you been here?' I ask. My brother has contacts and

'A year,' he says. 'But I need to behave 'cos I'm on my last warning, and trust me, man, I don't wanna get kicked out of here.' He coughs out a plume of smoke.

'What are the other patients like?'

Daniels thinks about this for a moment. 'They're all fucking crazy, man,' he says. We both laugh. 'Wail till you meet Cole,' he says, 'he's a hoot. He'll ask you to critique his chosen suit of the day before he even introduces himself.'

'I'll look forward to that pleasure,' I say between drags.

My brother knows people. They deal in tobacco and sub one another cigarettes. This isn't prison but the doors are locked. I ask Mum to take me home but she can't. I have to stay till I'm better. They won't make me better, I tell her. They let me through one door to use the phone. All I say is that I want to go home... the phantom of the deadly plague that Libitina sent upon England... and the hospital...

...I'm never gonna...

...go near anyone...

'Nice talking to you, man,' says Daniels. He offers his hand and I shake it. 'It's getting late and when I'm tired I'm more likely to have... incidents.'

'Night night,' I say, 'glad to meet you. Oh, Daniels, one more thing.'

'Yeah,' he says.

'How do I get books around here?'

'Books? Well, there's a bookshelf in the TV room. Take a few from there. Should be okay so long as no one sees you.'

'What about notebooks?' I ask.

'Notebooks? You can have one of mine. I keep a journal as part of my therapy. You should do the same.'

'I intend to,' I say.

A holiday journal but how can you write, though?

After Daniels has gone to bed, I realize that the late hour to which he was referring is only eight thirty. Nurse Waltz finds me to tell me that it's medication time. Fine, I take my meds. There is no one else around so I take a look in the TV room.

Medication time. I haven't been taking it. I'm never gonna... Does everyone take medication? I was going to the library to study. Are there books here? I will rewind and undo all this. I can. ... hurt anyone... 'Excuse me, can I speak to you about something?'

I switch on the light. It seems that all of the residents go to bed early here. I'm a night owl by habit. I plan to find a couple of books to borrow, make myself a cup of coffee, and then do a little writing before lights out. The TV room has two large leather sofas and a couple of easy chairs. The TV is mounted high on the wall. I switch it on: The Sopranos. I've never watched it but I've always intended to. I suppose I have time to now. I take one of the easy chairs and move it over to the bookcase. The sanatorium's selection of books is nothing if not eclectic: *The Sound and the Fury*, *Norwegian Wood*, all three books of *The Lord of the Rings* in one volume, a novelization of the little-celebrated Spielberg film *Hook*, *The Magic Mountain*, and *The Bluest Eye*, along with four thick Reader's Digest collections.

Sitting on the sofa.

'You had a bad reaction to the medication we gave you.' There was football on the tv. Where's my big Milton book? My friends would've watched the match. A bowl with round sweets in it. For everyone, not just you

I take *The Sound and the Fury* and *Norwegian Wood*, two old favourites, and move over to the DVD rack. Once again it's a curious mix of the classic and the eyebrow-raising: *The Godfather* collection, *Gone in Sixty Seconds* with Nicholas Cage, *Johnny English 2*, *Mr Marjorium's Wonder Emporium* (two copies!), *Mama Mia*, *Rio Bravo* and *Deliverance*. I take the books back to my room and I'm sitting at my desk writing this journal entry. The snow is still

myself am hell

falling steadily outside and I feel quite calm. Never ceases to snow here to night time and sit and watch by myself. I will not go to

'I was running in the park when I just stopped and broke down crying.'

'What were you seeing in that moment? In your head I mean.'

'Just the quick flash and then the bang.'

'The IED?'

'Yeah, the IED. Funny, I don't think I've said that out loud since. IED.'

'Yes?'

'Yeah, sounds so small when you think about the damage it does. It's made by other people and then Boom, and life changes forever.'

Drink your coffee late at night to not to sleep to dream what difference for OT tomorrow? No

I'm woken early by the noise of footsteps. It will be the staff getting ready for morning medication. I check my watch and it's 7:30. Time for a shave and a shower.

I'm looking forward to having a chance to speak to one or both of the doctors today. I'm dressed in jeans, dark green t-shirt and my slippers as I enter the dining room for breakfast. Members of staff come in every day to serve the meals. I could really use a nice juicy fry-up but I'll settle for a big bowl of muesli and a nice black coffee from the pot. I thank the ladies who are serving and head over towards a table where an elderly man in a crisp but old-looking blue suit is sitting. I assume this is Cole and I'm about to introduce myself when O'Shaunessey steps into my path.

'Terribly sorry, sir,' he says in a mock-fawning voice, 'but I'm afraid sanatorium rules prevent the removal of books from the lounge.' I look down and realize that I am indeed carrying the copy of *The Sound and the Fury* (it's an automatic habit with me to pick up a book and take it with me wherever I go, even if I won't get a chance to read it).

'Does it not say in the literature available from the front

desk that this sanatorium believes in a flexible, person-centred approach to patient care?' I don't know for sure that that is the case but it's this sort of rubbish these places usually claim for themselves.

'So what?' he says. His mean eyes narrow a little.

'So, my good man, if it makes me, the patient, happy to remove this book from the lounge, then surely the best thing for you, the carer, to do is allow me to do it, wouldn't you say?' He looks about ready to punch me.

I've started using the cupboard door to hit my head. Maybe it will make things quieter. I want to feel something again but really to feel absolutely none of this at all. Different combinations of meds. Mum brings my Milton book and I read bits of it. Things carrying on. Moving forward while I'm here. Without progress. Some contact to reality. Carry the book around with

'While we're all very pleased to see you settling in so well, Mr Carter, I'm sure somebody as intelligent as you will understand that we need structure here to help the sanatorium function properly.'

'Here, then,' I allow him his little moment of petty triumph by handing the book over. 'Before you put that back you may want to try reading it.' He grunts as if in triumph. I maintain eye contact with him until he exits with the book.

'Hello, my name's Quentin.' I extend my hand to Cole and he takes it. Before he's even begun to shake my hand, he says:

'Tell me honestly, Quentin, do I look silly in this suit?'

'You look great, Cole,' I say. He's still holding my hand and staring at me. I instantly like this man and I wonder what he was like before he became a patient here. I pat his hand, which is still holding mine. 'Don't worry, you're the most stylish person around here by far.'

'What about the sleeves, Quentin, are they too long?'

A young man touches the walls and objects as he walks. He looks sad he does it and he looks so sad why

'Let me see,' I say. Cole releases my hand and holds his arms out in front of him. In fact, his sleeves are a little on the long side, but what of it? I don't want to worry him. 'Perfect length, I'd say. As you can see, I'm no expert but I think your suit can be summed up in one word: cool.' Cole smiles for the first time during our conversation. Just for a moment he seems to have forgotten his worries and he tucks into his toast. I take a sip of my coffee. Cole is extremely thin; his suit is roomy and his gaunt features can't completely obscure a face that I can imagine was once striking. He has a thin covering of bright white hair on top and his blue eyes are still piercing. He has a kindly face, even in the midst of great anxiety. We finish our breakfasts in silence. Cole takes his last mouthful and puts his knife and fork together. He picks up a black Sinatra-style trilby from the chair next to him and pops it on his head with a flourish. He stands up but before he can complete his dandyish exit the demons come again.

'I need a shave, Quentin,' he says. 'I can't get a shave in here. I feel terrible.' His face contorts with worry, its fleeting expression of confidence now destroyed. 'I'm sweating like mad here. Can people see it through the jacket? I just want a shave but I don't think I can get one.' He's leaving the dining room with a look of terrible despair on his face.

'We'll ask Nurse Waltz if he'll help you have a shave, Cole. Okay?' I put my arm round him and guide him out of the dining room in search of Nurse Waltz who's just finishing his paperwork at the medication cupboard. He looks up.

'Hello, I can see you've met Cole, Quentin.'

'Yes, I have, we've been having a nice chat over breakfast. I think Cole might need some help with having a shave.'

'No problem,' says Nurse Waltz, 'let me lock-up here and I'll come and find you in your room, all right?' Cole seems satisfied with this and he walks quite jauntily off down the corridor to his room. Nurse Waltz smiles at me.

'Thanks, Quentin,' he says.

'No problem, I know what that kind of anxiety's like. You must be exhausted at the end of a shift here?'

He grins and puffs out his cheeks. 'That's a really good sign, that you can show concern for the other guys here. The two doctors

myself am hell

would like to meet with you today. At midday?'

'Perfect,' I say.

'Were you right back there – in the park when you were running? Did it feel more like you were back in Afghanistan than running through a park in London?'

'Definitely. I remember all kinds of things that happened over there all the time. Not like this, though. It was like I needed to take shelter from it.'

'It's something the mind does. When exposed to multiple combat traumas, your mind can miss-file some memories and bring them back to you as current experiences. Has this happened before?'

'No, just this one time. I've been reliving that day ever since. It makes me not want to go running anymore, you know? And I love running.'

'You look very physically fit.'

Sometimes I watch the same DVD over and over. While it's playing I don't think about reality. I'm someone else, until something in the film triggers a memory or feeling that I can't keep down. Then I feel so sad I want to die. The man touching the walls. He wants to touch you as well, you can tell. He has to make an effort to stop himself. At night we have strong instant coffee. I spend the morning writing my journal. After an hour I decide to see about taking a walk around the grounds. I check with Nurse Waltz and he says that's fine, but that I should stay within the grounds while it's snowing as it's easy to get lost in the snow on the mountain. It's interesting to know that I'm free to wander further than the hospital grounds. I thank him and wrap up in thick coat, scarf, hat, and gloves. I fetch cigarettes and lighter from my room.

The cold assaults me the instant I set foot outside for the first time in three weeks. The snow is falling gently and for once there's no wind. I decide to take Nurse Waltz's advice and stay within the grounds, so I make my way along the white wall of the building until I come to a tall fence and a narrow passageway, at the end of which is an ornate little gate.

Even under a thick covering of snow, I can see that the

garden has been designed with care. At the rear of the sanatorium there is a path leading from a wooden veranda and winding through the lawn to a lake with an island. I stand on the veranda out of the snow and light my cigarette. It tastes damn good. I'm an occasional smoker and whenever I do smoke these days it invariably makes me think of Ali. I hear the gate click and Nurse Waltz joins me on the veranda. He rubs his gloved hands.

'Does it always snow here?' I ask.

He laughs. 'All winter it does, yes.'

'How do the staff travel up and down the mountain in this?' I ask him.

'We set off early and we drive very carefully.' I offer him a cigarette from the packet but he declines.

'I don't want O'Shaunessey having access to my file. I'm sure it hasn't escaped your attention that he has it in for me.'

'The rules and regulations of places like this are perfect for the bully. The bully doesn't want the patient to get better because then the patient would be regaining control of his life.'

'Yeah, they love the thought that as they drive home from work, people like me are still here suffering. Do people like him start out as bullies? I mean, do they go into this kind of work because they want to feel they have power over others, over people who are vulnerable, or do some of them enter the profession with the best intentions and become somehow institutionalized themselves?'

'I think there's probably a mixture of both of those things. In his case I think he was once a good man but certain events brought out something ugly in him.'

'What events?' I say.

'Just meet the doctors today and keep on keeping your head down, all right?' he says.

We shake hands. As Waltz returns to the warmth of the interior, I take a final drag on my cigarette. It's difficult to distinguish the smoke from my own thick breath. I drop it in the snow and watch the cold silently kill it. As I make my way back to the building, I see a face at the window of one of the rooms. It's a young face, maybe eighteen or nineteen, with disheveled brown hair and a look of the most heartfelt despair. A bare arm pulls the curtain across half of the face but he continues to look at me, or more accurately to look through me at something far beyond here. I raise my hand in greeting but he pulls the rest of the curtain across and disappears from view. So there's Daniels, Cole, this young man, and me.

The plague of 1625. Please tell everyone I'm sorry. I wanted to get well but I couldn't. This is Quentin's tribulation and the end will come soon for all of us. Why do the people look at me? I know why...thou shouldst not know...Where are your music and special effects now, Henry Lawes? Milton Milton Milton... 'Making, in thought, the public woes my own'. Sitting in another room. Here by myself. Others around me.

'Cheers, I work out every day and I was running four times a week.'

'That's great. Don't let this stop you.'

'Easier said than done.'

'What have you learned from the last few weeks?'

'I dunno, I guess I thought I was over the worst of it. I can get around, I've come to terms with what happened. I thought I had anyway. Things were going well, you know?'

'How are the relationships in your life?'

I'm writing at my desk at 22:20 and Daniels and Cole are sitting on my bed and comfy chair respectively. Cole is sipping a mug of coffee with his trilby on his lap. He repeatedly runs his finger round the edge of the rim. At the moment he is calm, tranquil even. Daniels is talking away nine to the dozen, to neither of us in particular, while rummaging through the box of books that arrived today from Tapper, along with my laptop and record player. He didn't send any records but luckily Daniels has a large selection in his room. We're listening to Sgt Pepper and both men are tapping their feet to the beat. Darkness. I met all the people. The man in slippers. The man touching the wall. The man with the room and the plant. This is where you sleep. This is where we serve the coffee. I've made sure the volume isn't too loud to avoid disturbing

Cornelius (for that is his name). He was given a PRN to calm him down after dinner and I would imagine he is fast asleep. I will write more of him in a little while but first I must tell you about my meeting with Doctors Schultz and Landa. Another night alone with the tv and the coffee and the voices from the day and the noise all around me close it off and watch and take yourself back to

At 12:00 sharp I knock on the door with the silver plate that says, 'Dr K Schultz and Dr H Landa'.

'Entaaaaaaaaaaaar!' booms a loud voice. I open the door and see a black leather chair in the Mastermind style. There are two desks on opposite sides of the office.

'Please sit down,' says the same voice from behind the right-hand desk. I do as I'm asked and sit down in the chair. 'Quentin Carter,' says the voice, 'specialist subject: the literature of the mind! Ha! Apologies Mr Carter, my little joke. I'm Dr Landa.' A vast figure emerges from behind the desk and offers me a suitably chunky hand to shake. Firm handshake, always a good sign, I think. You are a young man and your life is not over. Let me leave here let me leave you spend a lot of time alone at night watching films over and over and over. He's wearing an enormous dark blue suit with a waistcoat and pocket watch. His hair is grey verging on white, and it's thin verging on non-existent on top, and long and flowing down the sides. A pair of silver-rimmed reading glasses perches on the end of his aquiline nose. Dr Landa's desk is covered with plants and ornaments. His back wall is full to the brim with copies of the British Journal of Psychiatry and vast tomes on Freud and Jung, as well as one or two crusty looking old hardbacks with his own name running down the spine. 'We are both glad you are feeling ready to begin your therapy with us,' he beams. I trust Dr Landa on first impression. 'Allow me to introduce you to my esteemed colleague.' He gestures towards the opposite desk, behind which sits a thin and small man with slick, side-parted black hair. He hasn't looked up from his typewriter the entire time I've been in the room. That's right, typewriter. This is a gentleman of the old school, as evidenced by his stiff black tie and quill pen and ink well.

'I will be with you in just one moment, gentlemen. Just

allow me to ... there.' He looks up from his typewriter and removes his latest sheaf of paper, placing it onto a neat pile. His desk is the polar opposite of his colleague's, with everything neatly apportioned to its correct place. The Doctor stands up from his chair and walks toward us. He extends his hand to me and gives a somewhat looser and weaker handshake.

'My name is Dr Schultz. I have been reading these letters, which I will now hand over to you.' He holds up two envelopes, one in either hand. 'They are from your friends. I apologise for the invasion of your privacy and I promise it will not happen again. However, when trying to form an initial clinical opinion it is necessary to gather as much unadulterated data as possible. Sometimes in order to do this we must use unconventional methods.' I'm a little irritated that they've read my private correspondence but I've already decided to maintain a positive outlook here come what may.

'I understand,' I say.

'Thank you,' says Dr Schultz.

'Before we begin,' continues Dr Landa, whose English upper-class chumminess makes for a great contrast with the almost mechanical manner of Dr Schultz, 'a few housekeeping notices: Quentin, you don't object to the smell of strong, and I mean very strong, pipe tobacco, do you?' He gives the impression that a great deal hinges on my answer. He has a teacher's manner as he peers at me over the top of his tiny spectacles.

'Not at all,' I say, 'in fact I rather like it.'

Dr Landa claps his hands together. 'Wonderful, wonderful!' He has already begun to fill his curved, Sherlock-style pipe. 'I do find that it improves the quality of my work no end, Quentin.'

'That is debatable,' says Dr Schultz, very pointedly looking at his watch. 'Shall we get on, Dr Landa?'

'Yes, yes, my dear fellow. Just one more item of business before that: hot beverages. What's your poison, Quentin, as it were?'

'Black coffee please,' I say.

'The usual espresso for you, Dr Schultz?'

'Ja,' replies Dr Schultz, moving his chair out from behind his desk.

'And I shall have my usual cappuccino,' continues Dr Landa to no one in particular. 'Get yourself comfortable, Quentin, I will be just one moment.' He maneuvers his bulk past the desk and through to what must be their kitchen. Lacking the presence of Landa, Schultz and I make awkward small talk. I ask him if I may smoke during the consultation, to which he replies in the affirmative. I ask him about their coffee machine, to which he replies sharply that it is a German product and therefore absolutely of the highest possible quality. I tell him I would quite like to see it some time, to which there is no reply. After a prolonged silence he looks at me and says that he is a connoisseur of coffee. It is at this moment that Landa expresses back into the room with three steaming beverages on a tray, each with their own ornate, Italian-style biscuit balanced on a saucer. He hands Schultz's espresso to him and places his own beverage on the desk. He then produces a small coffee table from amongst the detritus of his side of the office and places it next to me.

'Here you are,' he says as he places my coffee down on the table.

'I believe that Mr Carter would like to smoke also,' says Schultz in his monotone.

'Ah, excellent,' says Landa, producing an ashtray after further rummaging. 'Between the two of us we should create quite an atmosphere.' With that he lights his pipe, flings himself down into his chair (which gives a shudder) and picks up a thick fountain pen. 'I prefer to stay behind my desk, Quentin,' he says with pipe in mouth. 'This old thing conceals a multitude of sins. Ready, Quentin?' I nod. 'Then let's begin. Quentin, if I said the word "scrupulosity" to you, what would be your immediate reaction?'

'I don't know, being scrupulous, not being unscrupulous, not doing wrong?'

'Precisely,' says Dr Schultz.

'The fear of sinning,' says Landa.

'Okay,' I say.

'This is very familiar to you personally, no?' says Dr Schultz.

'Yes, in terms of my obsessive thoughts.'

'Tell me,' says Dr Landa, 'are you religious in any way?'

'How many ways are there?' I say with a smile. Schultz scribbles something. 'No. I mean I find religion fascinating in terms of its influence, but I've never subscribed to any particular faith.'

'May I ask why not,' says Landa.

'We live in a largely secular society now. I feel that my interest in religions and their histories informs my own philosophy of life...'

'Which is?' says Landa.

'Oh, I don't know if I can put it into a few words right now,' I say. 'Probably something like doing the least harm to others whilst pursuing one's own free will and choices.' They both nod and scribble a few notes.

'Who determines what is harmful to others?' says Schultz, cutting the atmosphere with his sharp vowels.

'I suppose that's why people need God, to be the one who makes those ultimate judgments,' I say. I wait for them to comment but as no comment seems forthcoming, I continue. 'Without a belief in God, doesn't it all come down to each individual conscience to decide the course of action that causes the least harm?'

'What about sinning in thought and word and deed?' says Schultz.

'Yes, the Anglican doctrine.' I sip my coffee. 'I'm wondering if this approach to sin is too strict for people to live by. Being free of sin in word and deed is hard enough, but to be free of sin in thought is surely impossible?' The doctors share a barely detectable look.

Landa puffs on his pipe and consults some notes. 'Do you feel that you have in the past experienced what we in the business refer to as thought-action fusion?'

'Ja,' agrees Schultz.

'You mean the belief that thinking something equates to doing it, even feels like you have done it?' I say.

'My girlfriend broke up with me, but that was fine. I treated her badly and cheated on her.'

'When was this?'

'Oh, a few months ago. I have a new girlfriend now.'

'That's great.'

'I've been doing talks on life after amputation. I guess life doesn't go in a straight line when you recover. You think everything's fine and then one day you're back in Helmand, but you haven't got your mates sweeping for IEDs with the Vallon detector and you haven't got the casevac there to fly you out. You're just on your own in a park with joggers wondering why the hell you're crying and cowering.'

'You didn't like saying that last word, did you?'

'Precisely,' says Landa. 'The medication will help with this, but what we must also do is train you in how best to respond to these uncomfortable thoughts. We must all work together to free you of your safety behaviours and normalize these thoughts. What you call your conscience is, I think, something else entirely.'

'Sounds good to me,' I smile.

'Dr Landa and I refer to the condition as "the OCD bully". This okay with you, ja?'

'Ja - I mean yes.'

'The only way to defeat the bully is to face it. We cannot appease the bully - this will do us no good. The bully will torment and victimize us for the rest of our life unless we defeat him. The power of the bully lies in the ability he has to trick us into thinking that he and we are one and the same human, ja?'

'Yes, how do you resist doing something that your own mind is telling you to do? I'm.' I don't know if I want them to answer this or not. Another shared look and more scribbling.

I emerge three hours later feeling tired but by no means dispirited. My past meetings with psychiatrists have almost invariably left me feeling raw and exposed. This was different. They ask me the same old questions about how I'm feeling on a scale of 1-10, whether I feel suicidal at the moment etc. I feel almost disappointed in these methods. Tapper would doubtless compare this to Lecter's disappointment with Clarice; 'It won't do, Clarice...'

Landa is relaxed and friendly throughout, while Schultz scribbles furiously in his notebook. The latter's style of questioning is by far the more direct of the two:

'This phrase of yours, "I'm not going to hurt anyone, I'm not going to touch anyone, I'm not going to go near anyone." Do you...'

'Fuck off,' I say.

'I beg your pardon,' says Schultz.

'You missed off the end of the phrase,' I say.

'Ha ha!' chuckles Landa.

'Ah yes,' says Schultz looking a little put out, 'I was trying to be delicate, Mr Carter.'

'No need on my account, doctor,' I say, 'there's no room for delicacy in this business.'

'You can't deny he's got you there, my dear doctor,' laughs Landa again, relighting his pipe. Schultz ignores this and continues with his questioning:

'Do you ever say this phrase out loud anymore, Quentin?'

'Yes. Yes, I do.'

'And why do you think that is?' asks Landa through his pipe.

How is one to answer such a question honestly and without self-consciousness? 'The more threatened I feel by the thought, the more urgent the impulse to say the phrase out loud rather than merely repeat it in my head.'

'Do you think you have taken on that Anglican doctrine of sin in thought and word and deed somehow? Tell me more about what you call your conscience.' Landa says this gently.

'Right and wrong, what you can live with I suppose. The thoughts, words and deeds that allow you to sleep at night. But the OCD gets in the way of that by telling you you've done things that you haven't.'

'Can one sin in thought?' says Landa.

'I know what you're getting at,' I say, 'but clearly for some of us there is a belief buried deep down somewhere that certain thoughts entering our heads equates to a sin.'

'And what do you think of that?' says Landa.

'I think it's completely ridiculous,' I say, 'but I also know the power these thoughts have over me.'

'Is it the thoughts or your responses to the thoughts?'

'Clearly the latter since you're asking the question,' I say. I'm beginning to feel very tired. 'So where do I start?'

'I think it is a question of coming to terms with how the world actually works,' says Landa, taking a moment to sip his cappuccino and replace the cup on its saucer.

'Does anyone really understand that, I mean even you two?' Landa chuckles while Schultz seems to be weighing up his response.

'The more one knows, the more one realizes that we do not live in the world of the Bible or of any other religious text.' Schultz's back is ramrod straight and he makes me feel uncomfortable about slouching in my chair. 'Rather, we are living in the world of the Paradise Lost, Quentin. The world of the fallen language and the fallen nature of man. Your thought without sin, of the pure Anglican doctrine, belongs to Adam and Eve before they encountered the hissing one. The Eden of Paradise Lost before the fall is necessarily fallen, ja? Already? How could it be anything other? Ours is a world polluted by the breath of Satan and by the darkness visible. Men commit unspeakable acts on a daily basis. Men commit evils that John Milton would not have conceived of; we drop bombs on children in the name of oil money; we wage illegal wars for the same. We trample on the already downtrodden in order to appease our insatiable greed. Our leaders are a plague upon this earth the like of which the people of Milton's London would not have seen. If there is a God, do you think he will judge you for your impure thoughts?'

'Are you asking me or is this one of the rhetorical questions?' I say.

'I would like to know,' says Schultz with perhaps a hint of a smile. Landa is puffing away on his pipe. I scan the dense bookshelves to Schultz's right. In amongst the expected books on psychiatry is a copy of Paradise Lost. Was it there all along?

'After my experiences I suppose I don't believe that God cares a damn about my impure thoughts or anyone else's for that matter, if there even is a God.' Schultz is back in note-taking mode.

'I think I would like to say,' says Landa between loud bouts of sucking on his pipe, 'that surely to be human is to have impure thoughts? Does this mean that all humans are impure? In the Paradise Lost sense of the word, yes, I suppose we all are. You know that our capacity for language and creativity are themselves born in original sin. For people of a poetic bent such as yourself, Paradise Lost could be an alternative to the Bible, a holy text in itself. Human beings seem to have needed the guidance of such texts through the ages. But really, what is their relevance to us here and now? Are we to infer from holy texts that we are all evil, all equally deserving of punishment? How could anyone live under such a strain?'

'What's the point of the obsessive thoughts then? What evolutionary purpose do they serve?' If I die before I wake. Meds and meds and meds. Never gonna hurt. Never gonna touch. Shock me, I dare you. Now I have a room, a room with a radio. Days go by, the radio plays, and I stay the same. Death in life. Never near anyone. Not no more. Clothes all around. That smell again. Now someone outside. They bring me food. Never to go near to. Nearness to meness. Schultz dismisses the question with a wave of his hand. The psychiatrists won't let me leave here. Go to OT and then and then and then go to a halfway house

'There is no point and certainly no evolutionary purpose, any more than there is a purpose to the white noise or the inane chatter of children on a train in the summer. They originate in that primitive part of our brains that is alert to danger and kept us safe from predators when human beings faced such things on a daily basis. Here we will work on your beliefs; if you believe you can sin in thought, then the bully has you.' He mimes a hand slowly closing around a neck. 'However, if you can be disabused of such notions, you can free your mind. You are not responsible or accountable for every thought that flies into your head, any more than the two of us are.' He sits back with an air of finality and reads his notes. The smell of Landa's pipe makes me reach into my pocket for my cigarettes. I light up and exhale a blue cloud that seems paltry next to the London fog level of his pipe tobacco. We have certainly succeeded in creating some sort of atmosphere. The smoke engulfs the doctors. Schultz attempts to waft it from his face but only serves to produce fleeting patterns within the cloud.

Singed and smoking matter. Medical bodies subsumed by an atmosphere. They appear still now and preserved. I look out of the large window at the snow slowly journeying. I think of fallen language and falling bodies and angels flung from the heavens to the burning depths. And why the Milton in the shared offices of two eminent psychiatrists, and why not? My hand is on the door handle and I tap it as if it might be hot to the touch. I open the door and take a last look back. The smoke has settled and intensified as if it intends a lengthy stay. Schultz is still scribbling away.

I go to the smoking room and chat to Daniels for an hour. He's in good form. Sometimes he seems to walk around in a daze, while at others, like this afternoon and evening, he's lucid and lively. When I ask him about this, his explanation surprises me:

'ECT, Quentin. Electro-Convulsive Therapy.' Going to OT will not help me. I cannot accept at all I just

'Wow!' I say. 'Did you consent to that?'

He smiles thinly. 'Consent. There's consent and then there's consent, don't you find?'

'What do you mean?'

'Nobody wants to have this treatment. But it seems to work for a lot of patients. It can affect your memory, that's all. What you need to understand is that when I came here a year ago I used to go down the mountain into town, it was part of my treatment. I bet they haven't offered you any time out in the community, have they?'

'No, they haven't,' I say. I start to think about whether I would want such a thing. I find it difficult to think of community activities as part of a programme of treatment. Perhaps my perspective is too black and white, but to me you are either in a treatment facility or you are out in the community, but never both simultaneously. Perhaps that one foot in both camps approach works for some patients. I like the relative solitude of this facility, away from the world out there. Perhaps that in itself is not healthy.

'That's because one day I went to the café where I used to work a couple of hours a day,' continues Daniels, 'and one of the customers called me a retard when I accidentally spilled his drink. You have to understand that I was in a bad place then. I could lose it like that.' He snaps his fingers. 'Look, I was in this place for a reason, right? I was unsure about the whole care in the community thing from the beginning but that's what the docs were big on at the time, forging links between this place and the local community. Anyway, the staff in the cafe could see that I was getting worked up so they sent me on my break. I went for a walk and managed to cool down a bit. When I came back to the café the guy was still there, talking and laughing loudly like he owned the place. I picked up a pot of freshly made tea and chucked it at him.'

'Jesus,' I say.

'The pot smashed in his face. He had cuts and burns. They had to call an ambulance. And that was the end of working in the community for me. The sanatorium managed to persuade the guy not to press charges. He agreed, but only on the proviso that I stay away from the town altogether. Another condition of my continuing here at the sanatorium was to agree to the course of ECT. It takes a few minutes and you have it a couple of times a week. It makes me a bit dozy and forgetful, but it's a last resort. If I hadn't agreed to it, they'd have kicked me out of here and I'd probably have been arrested by now.'

He pats me on the arm and I take a sip of coffee. I smile at him to show support. It's nearly dinner time and there's something else I'd like to ask Daniels:

'Daniels,' I say, 'who's the young man here who we hardly ever see?'

'Ah, Cornelius,' says Daniels ruefully. 'Poor kid, I've tried to look out for him a bit but I think he's still numb from the shock of being where he is, y'know. Anyway, this kid's bright and well-educated, a university man like yourself. I've hardly heard anything that isn't mumbo-jumbo out of him in the month he's been here. Hopefully once they stop screwing around with his meds he'll settle down and realize he's in the best possible place.' I like hearing

Daniels say this, not just for Cornelius' sake but for mine also. 'His Mum visits him regularly and I think he's got a pretty tight family which is always a good thing. Just keep an eye on him, won't you?' says Daniels.

I nod. 'Do you have any family waiting for you in the outside world, Daniels?'

'I was married once. We split up for various reasons, but mainly my problems. We still keep in touch. I don't blame her for ditching me, I wouldn't want to live with me either.'

'But you don't have a choice,' I say.

'Precisely. Yeah, we had a pretty good life together. She was a teacher and I, if you can believe this, was a trader in the city.' Could I believe this? Yes, I suppose I could. You always have to consider the circumstances in which you're getting to know someone and consider that how they are at this moment isn't necessarily how they have always been or will always be. 'In some ways it was the perfect job for me because every trader's an aggressive bastard with no social skills.' We both chuckle. 'The problem was my aggression wasn't restricted to the trading floor. My boss insulted me during a meeting one afternoon and I broke his nose.'

'You must have been an absolute legend?'

'Oh yeah, total hero. Sacked of course, but I'm sure they all still talk about me with reverence to this day.' Daniels sips his coffee. 'If ECT's what it takes to enable me to control myself then fuck it, I'll do it.'

'Well, I can't argue with that,' I say. 'Daniels, do you still think this is the best place for Cornelius to recover, even taking into account some of the people they employ here?'

'You mean one person in particular, I presume?'

'Yeah.' Daniels nods and smokes and seems to get lost in his thoughts. The conversation fizzles out. He heads off, leaving me with my coffee and my thoughts. Strong black instant coffee. A big silver kettle and people gathered in the room. Coffee now but I must sleep. I meet everyone. Holiday camp. Restful. Slippers on for Dinner is a rather pleasant lasagne with salad, then chocolate pudding for dessert. Dinner in tubs that are pre-heated. Same time of the day. Everyone complains. Some people don't want to eat it. All there is. The panic at night when you eat nothing at all to I stay at the table and sip a coffee with *The Sound and the Fury*. At one point I look up from the book and see Cornelius sitting across from me. He has a straggly beard and his hair is unwashed and sticks out at curious angles. He is wearing jeans, t-shirt, and slippers, and he is very thin. I picture him being dragged from the bottom by the river nymphs and brought back to life. Nurse Waltz brings him over some dinner saved from earlier and Cornelius starts, very gingerly, to eat.

'This is my first meal in three days,' he says.

'Yes,' I say, 'this is the first time I've seen you at dinner for ages. Would you like a coffee?'

'Yes please,' he says between mouthfuls. I get up to go to the pot. Instant and vile.

'How do you take it?'

'Black please.' Good. I pour a coffee for him and one for me in the plain white mugs the sanatorium provides.

'First time in a place like this?' I ask him.

'Yes,' he says. He's moved onto the chocolate pudding by now. 'I was at uni when all this started happening.' He points at his head when he says this. 'I can't see myself ever getting out.'

'It's the meds,' I say. 'Once they get the meds right, you'll start seeing some progress, trust me.' He looks at the book. Will you be going to Occupational Therapy?

Cornelius makes eye contact with me for the briefest of moments, and something like comprehension registers in his eyes, before the sadness bubbles up again to the surface.

'What are you reading?' he asks. I show him and he nods. 'I've studied Faulkner.'

'He's my favourite,' I say. 'Listen, whenever you feel like doing a bit of reading, and I know you will one day, you can have this.'

'Thank you,' he says.

'And make sure you bring it in here to annoy O'Shaunessey.'

'I don't like him,' says Cornelius.

'Me neither,' I say. 'Come and listen to some music with myself and some of the others later if you like.' He nods but I doubt he'll come. He's not ready yet. They want me to go to OT but I don't want to. This is not my life.

'Crying?'

'Cowering. It's not a soldier's word, is it?'

'No.'

'Do you ever think about harming yourself?'

'Not at all until recently.'

'It takes courage to say that. We will focus on your trauma and change your relationship with it.'

'Relationship?'

'Yes, how you relate to it. We don't shy away from the traumatic memories. We look at them and bring them into the light.'

I'm finishing this journal entry at my desk in the dead of night. Daniels and Cole have long since departed. Daniels has very kindly loaned me his record player with a few of his favourite albums (according to him he rarely plays them). He confided in me this evening that he's still a pretty wealthy guy (his words) from his time as a city slicker. He said that that's the only reason he was allowed to come to a facility like this. This begs the question of who is paying for Cole and Cornelius, and me for that matter? Such questions are for the outside world, there's no place for them here. To accept the routine is to admit to the reality of the situation and I cannot do that.

I still have Miles Davis' *Kind of Blue* on low volume. I'm going to turn in now. As you can tell, the days in here can be quite draining. I'm glad I was able to speak to Cornelius. I think he'll be okay if he just hangs in there for a while. Nighty night.

Three weeks later

A great deal has happened in the past three weeks. I'm preparing to set off on a journey halfway down the mountain. I'm going to meet Ali and Tapper at a tavern. How did this come about? Well, it all started when I read my two letters from the outside world:

Dear Quentin,
How are you? Please believe me when I say that I sincerely hope you are well. I know that you must have hated me for bringing those people to our home without asking you, but I could not think what else to do. I tell myself that perhaps your feelings towards me have softened a little? Ever since you gave me the strength to do what was necessary, I have tried to carry that principle into every aspect of my life. In the church I knew I had to act in order to help you, even at the risk of losing you. Most people do not live this way, do they? It seems to me that the default human setting is to make easy choices, to take the path of least resistance, keep everyone happy and preserve the status quo. I used to be just like the majority. Meeting and falling in love with you gave me the strength to do what I feel is right regardless of the consequences. The Priest helped me on that day to see that I knew in my heart what to do. I wish there had been another way to get you this treatment without you having to go away from me and our life together.

Have you been able to do any writing? I hope so. Is writing the ultimate sign of health or of insanity? It certainly qualifies as an addiction, does it not. Perhaps a compulsion too?

Can I come and visit you some time, Quentin? If you still care for me at all I would love to see you. If not, then please let me know what I can do to help you get better. Anything, absolutely anything.

Yours always
Ali X

myself am hell

I had been going along to my weekly sessions with the doctors and even enjoying the creative writing sessions hosted by a friendly, timid young lady who teaches English at the secondary school in the town. She was interested in my writing and I was interested in her life as a teacher. Works of art are never finished, just abandoned. Who said that? Can't remember. No OT ever. Anyway, I had just finished one of the creative writing sessions when I decided to read the letters from Ali and Tapper that the doctors had intercepted. They talk of moving me into a halfway house. I don't understand this. Am I ill or not? I read them in the dining room after lunch. After I'd finished Ali's letter, I folded it up and placed it back in its black envelope. I needed time to think.

Dear Quentin,

How are you mate? (Probably a silly question - sorry). But anyway, I hope you're starting to feel a bit better. Sorry Lucy and I haven't been to visit you. What is it with us lot and hospitals? We can't seem to get enough of them. What are the other patients like? I bet there's no one in there who's half as mad as myself and Ali. I still see her quite often, although all we really do is talk about you. When she told me how ill you'd been, I felt angry at myself. We're all so absorbed in our own little worlds. Anyway, I'm sorry mate. I should have been there to help you and to help her; it must have been tough on her to have to deal with that by herself. I believe she did what she did with the best of intentions. I can't wait for you to meet Lucy, although she feels like she already knows you guys pretty well.

Have you been writing at all? I bet you have; there's no way you could ever stop for long. By the way, what's the coffee like there? Anyway, can Ali and I come and visit you, mate? I don't think either of us will be able to rest easy till we've seen you and we know you're okay. You've been a good friend to me, Mr Carter, since the day I broke your nose! And I want you to know that you can rely on me if you need my help.

Cheers!
Hopefully see you soon.

Tapper

I had been thinking about these two a lot in the past few weeks. After I'd read the letters I knew I wanted to see them again, so that much was decided. I needed to think about my course of action in arranging either their visit to me or my visit to them. I decided to broach the subject with nurse Waltz the next time we were taking a cigarette break together. The only contact I had with O'Shaunessey was when we passed one another in the corridor. He would hiss barely audible words at me. You shouldn't be here. You did this. You. I'm so sorry for it ! The first time he did this, it ruined my therapy session. The doctors repeatedly asked me if I was okay, and for the first time in many months, I felt the urge to perform a physical compulsion to offset my discomfort. I tried to resist but in the end I had to perform my old jerk of the arm, go away evil thought compulsion. Both of the doctors naturally noticed this. Dr Landa asked me directly if I had just performed a compulsion, while Dr Schultz scribbled in his notebook. Take the medication and you will get better I answered Landa's question honestly and he asked me the nature of the thought that had troubled me. I told him that the thought had flashed through my mind that I had sexually assaulted him.

'Aha, I see,' was his perfectly unfazed response. 'This is your standard obsessive thought, isn't it.'

'It is,' I replied. I felt so exhausted, I could hardly talk.

'This is okay,' said Schultz, 'the bully can win the occasional battle but he will not win the war.'

'Indeed,' said Landa, 'you have made great progress already, Quentin. This process was never going to be all plain sailing. Tell me, was this obsessive thought an instance of the thought-action fusion we have talked about before?' Relaxation classes on the schedule at OT today. Relaxation. No, thank you. Is this all a joke? Stay in bed and then

'Yes,' I said. Schultz scribbled some more.

'Is it a feeling of shame that you are experiencing?' he said.

'Shame and guilt.'

'This is a great example for us to discuss at our next session. You had the thought, you experienced the thought-action fusion, you performed the physical thought suppression behaviour. Correct?'

'Yes.'

'Now we can see that you are tired so I will only ask you one last question. You want more than anything now to receive reassurance from me that you did not sexually assault me, don't you?'

'Yes, more than anything.'

'But you are not going to seek that reassurance, are you?'

These people here don't know anything. No, they don't. They can't help me. Take me out of here. I can't

'No, I am not.'

'Excellent. Well done.'

Landa prescribed me a light sedative which I took after the session and proceeded to sleep for four hours. By the time I awoke, dinner was being served. It was steak pie and chips, with apple pie and custard for dessert. Ordinarily I would have relished such a meal but on this occasion I felt desolate. An OCD attack can leave you with a sense of emptiness that feels like a black hole growing within and consuming you until all you have left are the thoughts and the compulsions. I sat alone and drank my coffee horrible and bitter and from a silver pot with a big handle, but I did no reading or writing. Those pursuits always were the first to fall by the wayside when the old OCD blues struck. I banged the table in rage but I knew I didn't want to attract the attention of the staff while I was in this agitated state, and the attention of one member of staff in particular. I couldn't believe how easily he'd managed to get inside my head and undermine my progress nothing happens every day the same and every night with the DVds and the remembering and trying not to remember at all.

I woke late the next day feeling groggy from the effects of the sedative. Nurse Waltz was standing outside. He came in once he realized I was awake.

'Morning,' he said. I asked Waltz if he felt like a cigarette out in the snow. I dressed quickly and with plenty of layers; Waltz had on his thick coat with fur lining. We stood on the decking and smoked in silence for a little while. 'Feel like a walk around the grounds?' he asked.

'Sure,' I replied. Once outside there was no time for small talk.

'I need something on him. I need to know where he's vulnerable. He's inside my head so I need to fight dirty.' Waltz thought about this.

'Drugs,' he said. 'He had a daughter who died when she took an E. She was fourteen. He lost his marriage after.' He says his brother knows people and he's coming. Just wait

'A daughter? Him?' I couldn't believe someone like him had ever cared for anyone. The nurses all care here. They do not. They don't know anything here they just my brother can get us all out of here he's

'Yeah,' said Waltz, 'he was a different person then, just a normal guy. But that girl meant everything to him. She made one mistake at a party with her friends and that was that, and he's been taking it out on anyone and everyone ever since.' We can't just take you out of here till you're feeling better, love

'Thank you,' I said.

'Don't thank me, Quentin. I don't feel too good telling you this but suffering a terrible loss doesn't give him a license to behave like he does.' We sat down on a bench and listened to the whistling wind. 'He's a campaigner for drug awareness and education in schools, you know,' said Waltz after a while.

'Really?'

'Oh yeah,' said Waltz, 'it's his whole life. He's appeared on the news talking about it before. You asked me where he's vulnerable, well I'm telling you that's where. I just happened to see him on the breakfast news one morning, this was after we'd been working here together for a couple of years. At that point I knew nothing about any of this, I just knew him as this fairly unpleasant guy from work. Anyway, there he was on the breakfast couch in a smart suit, talking with such passion and emotion about the daughter he lost to drugs. He was a different person to the one I knew; this person was admirable and dignified. You felt his pain and you listened to what he was telling you. The ideal campaigner, right?'

'I'm guessing not?'

'He was effective on camera delivering his message, but when I told him I'd seen him on the TV he absolutely flipped. I just wanted to express my sympathy and admiration for what he was doing but he grabbed me by the throat and told me to mind my own effin' business. I never mentioned it to him again. The campaigning and the TV appearances kept coming. I could never understand why he carried on working here, why he didn't just campaign full-time. I'm sure the financial backing was there. Why not go into politics? He obviously had contacts in high places. They don't know anything they don't help me here You can have my dinner, it's fine. Take deep breaths. Everything he was doing was fueled by anger and hatred. What the campaigning didn't give him was an outlet for his hatred of the world which took his daughter away from him.'

'He needs victims. He needs people over whom he can exercise power and in whom he can see and feel the effects of that power. He needs to inflict harm in order to balance the scales of the irreparable harm the world did to him. That's why he came to work here, and continues to work here, and why he keeps the campaigning as a sort of all-consuming hobby.' Take the food, it's fine. Just try not to panic We both light up another. 'What did he do before his daughter died?'

'I don't know that, Quentin, you'll have to do some digging to find that out. I can imagine that he was a perfectly decent guy and a good Father before she died.'

'Yeah, I think you could be right. Part of that person is still there in all the campaigning. Is that still going on?'

'Oh yeah, more than ever. He fronted a major new campaign aimed at school children, which the government recently rolled out. He was on Question Time a few weeks back. YouTube it, you won't believe your eyes.' Sitting on the computers in the library and then sitting on a computer here just looking not reading sitting up at night with the tv on

'I'll do that. What was he like under questioning on that show?'

'Tetchy. You could tell that some questions got under his skin. He managed to keep himself in check quite well, though. That's quite a lively programme anyway, so he didn't come across as any angrier than the other panelists.' We smoked on in silence. Watching the TV late into the night. Just DVDs, nothing else no programmes at all to never go near to

A plan formed in my head from that day on. I knew that I would need the help of my friends, especially Ali. Waltz agreed to post two letters for me, thus ensuring there was no risk of them falling into the clutches of O'Shaunessey. He told me about the tavern on the mountain and said that if I kept my head down for a couple of weeks, he felt confident that he could persuade the doctors to allow me to hike there by myself as part of my therapy. I wrote to Tapper and Ali asking them to meet me there. A walk out to the pub with some of the other patients but why what's the point in going out to there and coming back to here

During the two weeks it took for Waltz to lay the groundwork, plant the seed, and get the sign-off from the doctors for my solo hike down the mountain, I tried to get myself into some sort of decent physical shape. The hike would be demanding and the conditions extreme. Fortunately, I was already in pretty good conditioning from the running routine that myself and Ali, and latterly Tapper, had developed. I did two runs a day around the grounds of about 5k each. I felt that if I could do these runs in 21-22 minutes that would condition my lungs and heart to handle the hike. He saw me while I was out for the walk he thinks something about me he thinks that I lied to him I also requested a high carb diet and cut my smoking down to a couple a day. One day I had just finished my morning run and was panting hard and leaning on my haunches when I looked up and saw O'Shaunessey watching me from the dining room window. I stared at him and refused to look away until he moved on. A panic for me I need to see him again to tell him that never went near to I'm not well I can't

During that fortnight I often saw Daniels returning from his ECT sessions looking groggy and confused. He was frequently too tired to join myself, Cole, and Cornelius in my room for our evening vinyl sessions. I was delighted when Cornelius started coming along to listen to records, chat about books, and reassure Cole when he became agitated. It looked like the doctors had found the right mix for Cornelius' medication, as he had far more energy and life about him now. I don't know the exact nature of his condition and I don't feel it's my place to pry. They don't know anything in here I'm glad his Mother visits him three times a week because when you're in a vulnerable state you need a strong family network. I've spoken to my parents a few times on the phone but I told them I'm taking good care of myself so there's no need for them to visit me in here. I told them I would visit them when I've been discharged. I think my positivity put their minds at rest. I hope it did. Positivity in here and a future? No your Mum visits every day and brings you things

I felt bad to be leaving the guys to go on my hike, but it would only be for a couple of days. I've become close to them all and their welfare is important to me. Waltz smuggled in a few beers for our last gathering before I set off. We had a lovely evening drinking beer, listening to The Beatles, Miles Davis, and Bob Dylan, and chatting about anything and everything. Go to the pub? How can you all go out to the pub together Daniels was in great form and he proposed a toast to my safe return and to good mental health, to which we all drank. Cole wore a snazzy purple suit, which we all praised profusely to the point where he beamed with pride. Naturally I couldn't help a little point scoring against my favourite nurse at medication time.

'How's the family?'

'What did you say?'

'The family,' I answered, 'how's the family?' He visibly shrank and his face was hollow and pale. 'I have to say you're the least likely TV star I've ever seen, but fair play to you. What do your family make of it all?' Game to Quentin. 'I think the fact that you still come and work here and give your time to all of us makes us extremely lucky.' Will you come for your meds please? Evening meds and nighttime meds always the same on a daily basis I extended my hand to him, and with Carmichael there he was forced to shake it. I took my meds and thanked them both. O'Shaunessy wasn't going to let me have the last word though.

'Bandmaster to the Attendant's Orchestra at Worcestershire County Lunatic Asylum,' he said as if suddenly remembering the answer to a quiz question.

'What?'

'That was a post held by Edward Elgar during his career. I hear you're quite a fan of his, Quentin?'

'As classical composers go, I can tolerate him, yes. But what interests me is how you came to know about my interest in Elgar?' The music that played when

'Don't be so paranoid, Quentin.' He busied himself with some of the medication paperwork, ignoring me like a teacher who's just dismissed a naughty pupil. Connections to the outside world that

'Since you mentioned Elgar, don't you find it interesting that he actually moved to Hampstead, which as you know was the home of the great poet John Keats, but instead of setting one of Keats' odes to music he instead chose an ode by a second-rate poet called Arthur O'Shaughnessy. Isn't that interesting?'

'In what way?'

'Well, a second-rater called O'Shaughnessy?' He continued with his paperwork. 'Relax, I'm just kidding. Keats and Elgar both died on February 23rd. Did you know that?'

'I'm actually rather busy, if you don't mind.' Suddenly he was the consummate professional. Reading and music and connection to

'Hey, you brought the subject up.'

'I wonder what day your cards are marked for, Mr Carter?'

'You know, nurse O'Shaunessey, I don't look at life in such a fatalistic way. I don't believe we're all set on unalterable paths. We are all capable of change.' I laughed and slapped him on the back. He flinched and dropped his pen. Come and have some dinner. They heat it in trays and it is wheeled in and served. Processed food. If you want to talk about what I think you do, that's all right, I've already heard it

And so we come to this morning. The guys all form a farewell party except for Daniels who has another ECT session. I must look quite a sight dressed up in my thick winter clothes, variously scrounged from and donated by the staff and patients. I have on an improvised cloth balaclava and a Clint Eastwood-style poncho over the top of a thick and rough leather overcoat that my good friend Waltz had hanging in his closet (apparently it belonged to his father, who was something of a hunter and outdoorsman on this very mountain). Pyjamas and slippers and I have snowshoes on over my walking boots and all in all I feel ready for my trip, if a touch over-insulated against the elements (which I know won't be the case once I'm out there). Sit in the living room and wait for them both to come something good for you to look forward to

I've been walking for an hour. I have my compass out, the first time I've used one since school. The snow hits my face hard in the howling wind but the compass and directions tell me I'm on the right track. I'm heading north on a trail that will take me deep into the woods until I get to a huge tree which the locals call the Major Oak (possibly as some sort of nod to the Robin Hood legend?). The snow is soft beneath my snowshoes and makes that lovely crunching noise with each step. I see few other footsteps, but there are blotches of snow on some of the trees where snowballs have been thrown. This seems to bode well for the rest of my journey for some reason. I make my way between the trees when a sudden gust of wind nearly blows me off my feet. I feel pain all down the left side of my body and my mouth has filled with snow. Weather forecast on the tv in the lounge

As I move on, I can barely see my hand in front of me; it's all I can do to place one foot in front of another. I imagine I hear cries of pain and screeches of malicious laughter swirling within the never-ceasing orchestra of the wind. I check my pocket watch and see that it's 11:30. It's still morning but I feel surrounded by darkness amidst the trees and this blizzard. The daytime tv in the lounge and the others moving in and out I find a nook within the base of a thick tree. The trail has become overgrown and every piece of branch feels like someone reaching out to accost me, to stop me in my tracks. Ali, Tapper, the doctors, Cole, Daniels, Cornelius ... As I brush the branches aside, I feel them resist and try to claim me. Are you going to get dressed for your visitors My struggle to free myself becomes more frenzied and I can't help but repeat the tired OCD mantra that goes along with the physical movement: *I'm not gonna hurt anyone, I'm not gonna touch anyone, I'm not gonna go near anyone*. An image enters my mind without warning of a bear fighting a pack of wolves. Suddenly they become aware of my presence and turn their fearsome eyes and teeth upon me. The blizzard is getting worse. I trip and fall and lash out at the branches in front of me. Jerk your arm and rid yourself before your visitors what will they think of me

    I fall face first into the snow and from what little I can see it seems I've come through this stretch of woods. I scramble up onto my knees as best I can in the snowshoes and I look around for the Major Oak. It isn't hard to find, standing apart from the woods and dominating the immediate landscape will you please come for your meds I stumble over to the enormous base of the tree. It's like a building with a vast basement car park. I take a blanket from my pack and wrap myself in it. I create a nest in the snow at the bottom of the tree. I use the snow to pack myself in tight. I'm shivering - my teeth are chattering, but before long I fall into a feverish semi-sleep. Try to stay awake in the day You stay up all night by yourself watching TV, no, only DVDs

    I wake with a shudder to the sound of birds singing in the branches of the Major Oak. I push my way out of my little nest and realize that everything is brighter. How long have I been asleep? Is it the next morning? No, impossible. I check my watch - 13:30. I'm dressed now and ready will Neighbours be on will they come in the middle of The brightness is because the snow has ceased. I'm still on schedule to make the lake by night fall. I look back and see the peak of the mountain far above the woodland canopy.

'So how's life?'

'I seem to be back there more and more often.'

'In Afghanistan?'

'Yeah. More memories. More of those memories that seem like you're right back there, like it's all happening again right now.'

'What triggered them this time?'

'It can be anything. I got a call from my ex's Mum?'

'Does that happen often?'

'More often than you'd think. Mary's a lovely lady. I reckon she thinks my soul is her responsibility.'

'Is that a nice feeling?'

'It's nice to know people care about you. I used to take that for granted, y'know. Yeah, it is nice.'

    I like the idea of a quest, always have. I could be Gawain or Beowulf on an heroic mission; an expert dragon-slayer setting off to fulfil his destiny. There's a pass through the mountains and then a big lake where I'll set up camp for the night. I take a deep breath of the cold mountain air and look around. What time are they coming to see me? The cold doesn't seem so harsh anymore and life is slowly returning to my limbs. The wind is whistling and it seems to lift and scatter a flock of birds from the trees. I close my eyes and forget for a moment and it's a great feeling. Is this what people mean by 'mindfulness'? Or is this more like mindlessness, losing oneself? I've never really been one for that whole Wordsworthian communing with nature thing. But then I've also never experienced a landscape quite like this. The wicker chairs in the lounge and the plastic sofas and the tv never off nearly time for a hot drink and biscuit

    My movements are regular and easy now but the terrain is becoming bumpy. I decide it would be easier to remove the snowshoes for now and just walk in my boots. The landscape changes rapidly as small rocks make way for large. It takes three hours to make it through the pass. I want to go back to my bed to sleep please try to stay up during the day what for The snow is falling again just as darkness begins to descend. I put the snowshoes back on and keep following the trail as it returns to sparse woodland and snow-covered grassland. The thought occurs to me that hiking and the outdoors might be very good for the management of my OCD in the future. I've arrived at the frozen lake and my campsite for the night. I couldn't imagine myself being very good at putting up a tent, particularly in the freezing cold. Fortunately, I had the foresight to order a self-erecting tent online long enough in advance to have it delivered to the sanatorium. It's absolutely freezing so I find a nice flat area in front of a small clump of trees and bushes and I pull the cord. The tent springs up, ready for use. I'll try to warm up a bit in the tent before I attempt to make a fire and cook my dinner of sausages and beans. It's quite spacious in the tent, even with the enormous backpack. I get my sleeping bag out and climb in. I zip up the tent and settle in for a little sleep. Stay awake during the day for to sleep at night and then wake up again in the morning to have breakfast and morning meds and then

I wake with a start, imagining a mountain fiend smashing aside my tent and tearing me limb from limb. I get out of the sleeping bag and find my hat and gloves. I put on my boots, wrap my blanket around me, and step outside. I check my watch: it's midnight. I snap some low twigs and a couple of thin branches off a nearby tree. They feel strangely dry amidst the snow. I form the wood into a rough wigwam outside the tent and introduce my lighter. Using my rucksack as a shelter from the wind, and after about ten frustrating minutes, the fire finally takes hold and a thin plume of smoke rises. As a few small flames lick up I fill my pan with four thick sausages and a tin of baked beans.

The food looks ready so, with the pan in my hand, I find my coffee flask and pour half of the remainder into my cup (saving the rest for the morning). Would you like a tea or a coffee and a biscuit while you wait for them I heat it over the fire while I tuck into my first sausage. As the flames dance, I allow my thoughts to roam away from here. If O'Shaunessey is being allowed to victimize people seeking treatment for mental health problems in return for him being the grieving Father at the forefront of a government drug education programme, then that must be exposed. Have your meds before they come I take my medication with the last dregs of my coffee. I stamp out the fire and take a last look out over the lake. Its patterns are mysterious in the darkness. It feels like I'm trespassing on a sacred covenant between the lake and the night.

    I wake up and free myself from the cosy sleeping bag. It's seven thirty and there's a covering of fog on the lake that's quite beautiful. There are a few birds chirping away and it looks like there has been more snow during the night. I decide to skip breakfast and get moving. Last night was the first I have ever spent out in the open with only a tent separating me from the elements. It's amazing how safe one feels under a tent, as if this wafer-thin material will provide protection from whatever is out there. It's an example of the power of positive thinking and faith in a benign Nature. Be patient and just wait I flatten the wood and ash from the fire and pack away the pan. I get dressed quickly and shove the rolled up sleeping bag and flattened tent into my rucksack. I take my wash bag down to the side of the lake and give myself a shave with my electric razor while I stare into the ice. Would it support me? I'm certainly not going to risk it. I imagine people sunbathing and congregating around the lake here when the weather's nicer. Is the weather ever nicer on the mountain? Nature programmes on the TV in the lounge always on I brush my teeth with the aid of some water from the canteen. I think the first order of the day when I arrive must be to have a shower. Something doesn't smell too good around here and I'm pretty sure it's me. The old smell from the university room and

    As I walk away from the lake, I pack a snowball together and hurl it as far as I can and it lands with a disappointing plop. I'm on a clearly marked path. I think back to the pass between the two ridges and my mind considers the gaps, the spaces between things. A further half an hour of tramping finds me pondering the nature of the sanatorium and the Red Apple group. There must be other mental health treatment facilities under the same umbrella. Do Landa and Schultz oversee the goings on in these places too? What kind of organization would invest in a man like O'Shaunessey? Surely all I need is concrete proof that the Group are knowingly allowing him to abuse patients? Visiting hours just phone up and book in

Just over the rise in the landscape there should be...yes, there it is. Behind a clump of trees, I can see part of what looks at a distance like a rather large cottage. There is smoke coming from the chimney and already the place is making me feel its warmth. It's not until I'm up close that I can really see the tavern in any detail. It looks like quite an old building. It's built on a slope and thus appears to be almost a natural feature of the landscape. I imagine an interior packed with rocks and snow along with thirsty punters. There is a car park on the other side of the tavern with several 4 x 4's parked there. It disappoints me a little to see actual cars here. I was hoping for stables and maybe the odd stagecoach. Videos at night on the TV in the corner I stand before the ancient-looking wooden front door. As I look up, I notice that the tavern has a sign that flaps gently in the breeze as it hangs over one of the windows: *'The Mountain Bear Tavern and Resting Place',* is its appealing name. There's an image of a big grizzly bear sitting at a bar with a pint of beer.

Wood is the dominant motif as I find myself standing before The Mountain Bear's reception desk. There are two varnished blocks of oak at either end of the thick wooden desktop. It has circles on it which I trace with my still-gloved hand. Embedded in the blocks are hatchets. Are they not just asking for a disgruntled customer to pull a hatchet out and attack them one day? I remove my gloves and put down my rucksack. It's a relief to be free of that weight. I ring the hand bell and a woman with bright pink hair appears almost instantly as if brought forth out of the air. She has a ring in her lip, one in her nose, and piercings all up and down both ears.

'Hello there,' her manner is warm and welcoming.

'Hello, my name's Quentin Carter.' No response. 'I've got a room reserved, staying one night, with breakfast in the morning.'

'Ah yes, Mr Carter,' she says while looking closely at her computer screen. 'Your room is ready for you now.' She clicks her mouse a few more times. She looks up at me as if doing a reappraisal. 'And I see your stay is all paid for.'

'That's right.' So the look she gave me was an "I see the sanatorium is paying for your room, please don't grab a hatchet and chop me to death" look. Or maybe I'm just being a little sensitive. I haven't been out and about in the world for a while so I'm bound to be a bit rusty when it comes to the whole social niceties thing. You are fortunate to have a bed here the demand is I don't want it I just when will they be here I feel so tired the idea of being fortunate to be here

'I'll show you to your room now if you like.' Her voice is clipped and clear.

'Thank you. Oh, could I also make a dinner reservation for three for this evening please?'

'It's already been made, Mr Carter. Reservation for three at eight tonight.'

'Great. Would you be able to tell me if either of my friends have arrived yet, Miss Cooper and Mr...?'

'Let's have a look. Errrrr, no not yet. I have their reservations, but they haven't checked in yet.'

'Thank you.'

My brother has got...he will...he's coming to...just wait and see everyone has a plan for leaving here but nobody does maybe I'll go out when it stops snowing

The room is spacious and it has a stunning wintery view, facing back up the mountain. I note the presence of a bathtub and I think a relaxing soak might be very much in order. The lady from reception, whose name is Maya, gave me a token for a free drink at the bar which I'll cash in when I have my lunch. There's a kitchen area with a breakfast bar. I could wash my clothes while I'm here. The hotel part of the tavern is vast. I'd pictured a ramshackle barroom with a couple of cramped rooms upstairs, but the accommodation area extends far back on an incline and there are twenty rooms for paying guests. Why would we all go out to the pub? We're not...it's not a normal There's a cafetiere and a bag of ground coffee so I strip off my clothes and throw them in the washer, flick the kettle on and run myself a bath. From the silver pot with the spout, the coffee, so bitter

The hot water is so invigorating. I light a cigarette although I know I shouldn't smoke in the room. Waiting for them both in the smoking room with... I give myself a good scrub and try to formulate a mental list of research areas:

1. The history of the Red Apple Group: who started it, who's in charge, where did they come from?
2. How did O'Shaunessey come to be associated with them? Have they recruited other people like him?
3. Financial situation. Can I do all of this, or do I need to hire an investigator for this kind of work? I need to find out anything dodgy this company has ever done. Maybe this isn't even about O'Shaunessey anymore. Is he a mere tool, a puppet?
4. How many facilities do they have? I need full lists of their employees. Do they have similar arrangements with members of staff at their other mental health facilities?

I clamber out and dry myself quickly. My limbs feel good from the exertions of the hike and from the bath. I dress in jeans, t-shirt, and green flash pumps. There's a set of three computers together in the reception area. An internet session at OT...Look up what you like, love Lunch first, then research. I decide to eat at the bar with my complimentary pint of nicely fizzy lager. Maya is serving behind the bar as well, presumably the other staff are only on when it's busier during the evenings. I treat myself to a pie and chips, which goes down very nicely after my several weeks of getting in shape. I see a man dressed in black carrying a crate of bottles. For a second, I could swear I saw the word 'Attendant' on the back of his polo shirt, but after he's gone I can't be sure. Research, then another pint, then a snooze before the guys arrive. Stay awake please for us until your guests get here

I wake from my sleep and spray on some of the hotel's very nice complimentary cologne. That smell again from the university and the room I try to arrange my hair into some sort of style but it just looks like a bit of a mop, not helped by the sleep. My initial attempt at research was not fruitful, as of course I knew it wouldn't be. I was allotted an hour on the hotel's computer, so I typed 'Red Apple Group' into a search engine. I'm anxious about seeing the guys and I had a couple of obsessive thoughts about people who walked past and sat next to me while I was on the computer. I feel a little uncomfortable now *I'm not gonna hurt anyone I'm not gonna touch anyone I'm not gonna go near anyone Fuck off*

Anyway, the fruits of my research:

1. An invented cigarette brand featured in the films of writer and director Quentin Tarantino. Click here for images. Make your own packet of Red Apple cigarettes. Click here for list of films and scenes featuring the Red Apple brand.
2. Multinational corporation founded in Tokyo in 1973, with headquarters in London, New York, Paris, Shanghai. One of the founders, Mr Toshiro Hanzo, is still Chief Executive Officer. The Group is known for its extensive charity work. Click here for a list of the Red Apple Group's charitable partnerships, associations, and donations.

I click on the website link and the background is the familiar company logo. The prose on the site is lively and the tone welcoming. It reads as if written by a young person. There's a list of the organizations owned by the Group: four mental health treatment facilities in the UK; ten in the US; one in Japan. There's nothing very comprehensive here, just the usual blurb about the benefits of quiet, seclusion and a "person-centred approach" to care. This is the very outer layer of any research, the company propaganda. There's a link to the construction activities of the Group, with pictures of some of the buildings they've been responsible for putting up throughout the world; it's impressive stuff. And clearly now they've moved into schools. On a whim, I type in "Red Apple Group" and "Food" and discovered that the Group owns one of the major school catering companies in the UK.

They clearly have their foot in the door in terms of becoming major players in an increasingly privatized education sector. Below the link to the catering company is a picture of a group of school kids surrounding a man in a Red Apple Group t-shirt. They are all smiling and cheering. Beneath the picture the caption reads, 'The Red Apple Group has completed work on its first school in Uganda, with a lot of help from some fantastic volunteers of course!' I click on the link and it takes me to the webpage of a major global children's charity. So Red Apple are already building in association with a big player in international aid. The picture with the children is from 2011 so it's safe to assume the Group now have schools all over Africa. I go to the bar and order another pint. There's half an hour left on the timer. I don't bother asking if it's okay to drink at the computer. Sometimes I think life becomes simpler when you just don't bother asking permission. Lose yourself in the screen...Look at things and read them...I'm sure they'll come if they said they would

So what's The Group's angle here? Good PR of course but I think they're after more than just PR opportunities. Perhaps they build the schools, pay for the education, and then continue the funding through university for the brightest students? Then they have graduate positions within The Group's companies waiting for the best of these students, which they naturally feel obligated to accept because The Group paid for their entire education, and probably still makes payments to their families. Or have I taken a leap too far? I don't think so. I might be off with the specifics, but the methodology is exactly that of The Group; it sticks to a long-term strategy and reaps the rewards of investing in people over many years. I'm prepared to bet that building schools isn't all they're up to in Africa. It's been on the news for years that the Chinese are buying up swathes of land in Africa and putting factories and plants and God knows what else there. Have The Group got their fingers in that pie? And what about vaccines? The Group would want a slice of the cash available from AIDS medicines and a host of other expensive treatments. They could get their tentacles into a community and quietly start to exert control.

Someone sits down at the computer next to me. I have my slippers on, so

My tiredness is overwhelming all of a sudden and I don't feel comfortable sitting this close to someone. I could be back at uni all those years ago in the library, looking up OCD and depression on the computers. *Not gonna hurt anyone, touch anyone, go near, off...* But I'm not there, I'm just tired and my head's spinning from all this Red Apple stuff. I want to run back to my room, but don't run. Don't give the thoughts the time of day. But I'm so tired. Five more minutes on the clock. Use your five minutes, then go to your room and sleep. OCD does not rule your life. It doesn't tell you when you can and can't sit next to someone. But get out of there. This Red Apple stuff. Just get away. Please stay in the lounge and wait for them

'Like when you were in the army? I mean in terms of having people in your corner?'

'I always thought of the army as fun. Does that sound crazy?'

'Not at all. What else could come close to those experiences and those bonds?'

'When I think about it now, it wasn't just the experience and the adrenaline. It was more like family.'

'Family, yes. A feeling of belonging?'

'Yeah, you notice it when it's gone.'

It's eight twenty pm and I'm down in the lobby on the lookout for my friends. I have this strange fear that they won't show up. I'm still being nagged by thoughts but I'm doing my level best to ignore them. Maya greets me and points out my two friends, already seated around a table in the bar. 'Hey, you two, what's a man gotta do to get an emotional reunion hug around here?'

Tapper beams broadly, leaps to his feet, and envelops me in the biggest, manliest, grizzly bear hug ever. Ali looks positively timid by comparison. Once he finally stops clapping me on the back and ruffling my hair, I open my arms wide to her. Your friends are here to see you...The tears well up for me For just a moment she looks unsure. 'Come here,' I say. We embrace warmly. The feel of her skin and the smell of her hair are a heady combination that set my senses tingling, but more than that there's a feeling of safety, of being amongst friends. I step back to take her in; her hair is longer than I remember and tied in a messy topknot. Her face is lean and angular; I think she's lost a little weight. She's wearing a flowing red skirt and sandals (clearly my friends have not hiked up the mountain this evening). She has on an orange top that shows off toned arms. I notice her trademark leather jacket hanging on the back of one of the tavern's green easy chairs. Ali's apprehension has changed to happiness. I recognize this as the kind of happiness that people would give anything for, but that seems so impossible that they dare not even hope for its arrival. We've obviously been staring at one another for some time.

'Just get a room already, you two,' says Tapper. We all laugh. They look at the tv...the bowl of sweets for everyone what to say now after all this time

'We all have rooms,' I say for want of anything either meaningful or amusing to contribute. In all honesty, I'm nervous as hell and the situation isn't helping my OCD. I pull up an easy chair and pretend to be reading the dinner menu while Tapper chatters away. He's talking in a roundabout way about my situation with O'Shaunessey.

'This is a global corporation you're dealing with here, Quentin, and they're not messing around. I've been doing some research since you wrote to us, and I think I've found out some useful avenues to pursue on this Red Apple Group investigation.' He sounds like a private eye, and it both amuses me slightly and gives me a nice feeling of being supported and taken seriously. 'They work with NGOs all over the world, you know,' he continues at a rapid pace, 'and wherever there's a disaster area or a massive relief effort required, you can bet your bottom dollar the Red Apple Group will be there in the background putting up new buildings in double quick time, lending manpower to the NGO efforts, and working with the bigger charities to get medical aid to those in need. They're absolutely ubiquitous, and yet you'd have to look extremely carefully to notice their presence in Haiti or Syria or any of these places. You've probably found all this out yourself, haven't you?' In the sessions in OT on the computer with...The snooker is on the TV so we talk about it just to...

'Not at all, mate, the vast majority of this is news to me. Please tell me more.'

'Once I knew a bit more about the corporation, I felt I had the basis to dig out the whiff of any scandal that might be lingering around them. No one becomes that big and that omnipresent without getting their hands a bit dirty, right?' Ali and I both nod in agreement. 'Well, with them they always make sure the air in their vicinity is kept pretty fresh, but if you dig far enough into the barrel there are one or two rotten apples.'

He loves having a captive audience like this. He's clearly managed to find out a lot more than me so far. Applause from the crowd I remember watching this in the sunshine of last year with friends

'Let's hear about your rotting apples then,' I say. 'By the way, my Sherlockian powers of observation tell me that you two did not hike your way up this here mountain today.' Tapper is wearing new-looking jeans and an expensive-looking polo shirt.

'How do you know we didn't hike?' says Tapper, taking a sip of his cider.

'Because Ali's wearing that colourful skirt and sandals,' Ali smiles at this, 'and you look like you've just been out with your personal shopper.' He looks himself up and down as if noticing the clothes for the first time.

'Ah yes,' he says, 'Lucy's influence. She's trying her best to smarten up my image. They're not really my choice, but she's the one with the eye for fashion. She likes taking care of things like that for me.'

'Is she going to do something about your hair next?' says Ali, interrupting him and ruffling it.

'Never mind my hair, let's get back to these rotten apples. Have you guys been following this scandal of aid workers in Haiti in 2011 using prostitutes and the organizations they worked for

myself am hell

covering it up?'

I must admit this story has escaped my notice. Relaxing snooker making me feel sleepy...The meds and

'I saw it on the news, yes,' says Ali. 'Disgusting. That kind of corruption is what you get when charities become big businesses. What is the connection to The Red Apple Group?'

'Exactly that,' says Tapper, 'big business. The...'

'By the way, Quentin, can I please take this opportunity to apologise for placing you at the mercy of this possibly evil corporation.' I can't help but laugh. 'Seriously,' she says with a glint in her eye, 'the sanatorium has an excellent reputation for getting results.'

'Don't worry at all, it is an excellent facility.'

'Please continue,' she says to Tapper. They will not help me because they...Just try to keep calm I want to go home but When you're better just try to have a nice time with your friends

'Yes, right, well like you said Ali, charities are big business these days. When this scandal came out it tainted anyone associated with it. These people who'd gone to a disaster area and exploited the local women for sex, some of whom might possibly have been under-age, then just been allowed to resign and leave the country without any consequences; well, my research showed me that four of the seven involved went to work for the Red Apple Group on school building projects in Kenya, Zambia, and Uganda. It's like they were taken out of the disaster relief field and placed in safe posts where they wouldn't cause any more trouble or attract any more attention. The charity hoped that the whole thing would never come out so there'd be nothing to explain, and of course our friends at The Red Apple Group were only too happy to help by giving these bad eggs jobs in their school building projects. They also now had considerable leverage over one of the big players in international aid. They were never going to play that card straight away, they just let it be known that one day the favour would have to be returned.'

'That's them to a tee,' I chip in, 'they're patient and purposeful.' Maybe I don't need a professional investigator after all, perhaps a tenacious amateur will do. 'What happened when the manure hit the electrical appliance?' Someone comes in and changes the channel but it's okay...a cowboy film...he touches the walls and everything in the lounge and they both watch him and what are they thinking about

'Well, that's the really interesting part. I'm only beginning to skim the surface of that myself. By the way, I'm starving, shall we eat?'

'Yes, let's,' says Ali, taking a sip of her scotch. 'If I'm going to have to listen to you all evening I might as well be full as well as drunk.'

'The thing is, The Group thought they were just being party to covering up the prostitution scandal, bad enough in itself but no bigger than anything they or any other corporation had covered up before, right?' We both nod. 'But once those three guys had been placed in Uganda by the Group, all three were subsequently arrested for child sex offences as part of a UN-led investigation. What happened in Haiti was the tip of a particularly vile iceberg.'

'Heavens,' says Ali, 'you read about these things but this is still difficult to take it in.' As our dinner arrives the mood is quite somber. In the past I've always tried to avoid hearing about things like this because of my OCD, but I've learned you can't hide from horror. He touches the walls and his face is in pain and we look at him and the staff come in and he touches the arm of the sofa and he wants to touch us and I feel for him

'So, arrests were made?' I say.

'Yeah.' Tapper is busily eating. 'The investigation uncovered a paedophile ring operating throughout international aid agencies. In all, sixteen convictions were handed down for child rape and pornography cases by people employed as aid workers in the third world. Three of them had a direct connection to The Red Apple Group. These three scumbags are now rotting in jail, but nothing ever happened to the people at The Red Apple Group who enabled their actions.'

'So no connection was ever made public between these people and The Group?' I ask.

myself am hell

'Not publically, no. Not in the mainstream media at all. There are rumours on the internet. That's how I got onto the story. I'll do some more digging, but this is how you get them, mate. There's a pattern in how they protected these paedophile aid workers and how they're protecting your bully of a nurse.'

'Very good work, my friend,' I say.

'Of course, the fact that they can throw money at any legal challenge helps them keep things like this quiet.'

'Guys,' says Ali, 'far be it from me to be the voice of doom here but all of this is a long way from Quentin's situation at the sanatorium. Maybe all you have to do is report this nurse and either get him sacked or suspended.'

I look at Tapper.

'You mean we don't bring down the evil corporation?' He sounds disappointed.

'Perhaps taking on a corporation is asking rather a lot of Quentin at present.'

They continue the conversation while I drift away. Tapper is stressing how exciting it will be to take on a massive corporation. He's talking about films now. I hear 'The Insider' and 'All the President's Men'. I've written him into a major conspiracy movie and he's playing the part for all he's worth. It's actually quite nice to hear them bickering about my welfare. They are beside me and I wonder what they think of this place

'To friendship,' says Ali finally. We toast and I finish my brandy and move onto my pint of ale. I take a sip and make a loud expression of enjoyment.

'Presumably the sanatorium is a dry facility?' says Ali.

'It is,' I say, 'although I have a friend on the inside who can provide a nice single malt for me and the guys every now and then.' He says his brother is coming here

'Glad to hear it,' she says. She finishes her own measure of single malt and points our empty glasses out to Tapper who is busy texting. He looks mildly put out, but bounces off to the increasingly crowded bar, nonetheless. As the evening gets into full swing, the Mountain Bear Tavern is drawing quite a crowd of hikers and serious-looking mountaineer types. He talks away and it's nice to hear his voice again Ali explains to me that two of the outbuildings also serve as accommodation in addition to the rooms upstairs. Tapper returns with the drinks. I tell her the names of the other patients

'I'll be right back,' I tell my two amigos. I walk past the busy bar which has ample room for a pool table and a big old classic jukebox that's currently pumping out a Jimi Hendrix track; good luck to anyone who wants to get an early night here. The sounds at night here On the right-hand wall of the bar room is a large landscape painting of a mountain range. It's all greys and browns and the effect is magnificent. I walk up to the painting to take a closer look. The bottom half of the picture is encased in mist and snow, but upon a close-up study I can see a pass winding up into the mountains as well as a small, glistening stream that is just about managing to make its way along against the immobilizing cold. Most striking of all, though, is the shadowy shape of a figure in the bottom right-hand corner. He (for I'm assuming it is a he from what little features the painter provides) is holding his ribs with his left hand, although his hand itself is obscured by a small splurge of the brightest red. The effect of a man suffering from a serious wound is emphasized by the torso tilting over to the left. Is this man fleeing from an unseen assailant? And if so, what hope can he have in this barren landscape? I move over to the bottom left corner to see if there are any other significant details there. There are no more human figures but I do notice some very feint impressions in the snow all along the bottom edge of the painting. These could be paw prints. Are we looking at the victim of a wolf attack here? I'm happily absorbed in studying the painting when some people walk past having a loud conversation that snaps me out of my reverie. With my return to the here and now comes a return of my need to urinate.

More laughter and toasts follow. Tapper has a pint of warm English ale, while Ali has switched to a chamomile tea. I'm on the black coffee now.

'Did you guys see that painting near the pool table?' I ask.

'Mmmm,' says Ali, 'very nice.' Her mind sounds elsewhere. Tapper is too busy stuffing his face to respond. Oh well. I have a part of my life now that Ali and Tapper know very little about. This excursion away from the sanatorium has shown me that when I leave the place I will miss Daniels, Cole, Cornelius, and Waltz. What will happen to us all what happens to people who don't get better I'll have to enjoy their company while I can. This mountain is like a world in and of itself. It's almost like I don't want to leave the sanatorium. Is this just a sign that my treatment hasn't finished yet? It's hard to think of your life as being part of a treatment programme. But mine is, a series of them. Or is it one continuous programme? We reach the end of a period of time or of treatment and we think we're "better". But even in the so-called healthy and functional times, I'd still have my OCD flashes every day. I always will.

'We keeping you up, mister?' I nod. 'Time for more drinks, methinks.' Before I can protest, he's ordered another round of drinks and resumed his conversation with Ali. The dining room and bar are full and are awash with conversations of different volumes and tones. To me they are white noise. Back on my own again please. I can't let this happen. Join in. Speak. Maybe it's just an accumulation of some hard days and nights. Don't be so tough on yourself, Quentin. Humans need sleep.

I bid the two of them goodnight. They protest initially but they can see how tired I am. I give them both a hug and take my leave. As I get up from the table: *I'm not gonna touch anyone, I'm not gonna go near anyone, Fuck Off* I just need to get back to my room. I feel uncomfortable but I know it will pass. It's truly lovely to see the guys again, but now it's time for sleep.

Back in my room I warm up some of the coffee from earlier in a white china mug in the microwave. I climb into bed and settle down to a few pages of 'The Magic Mountain'. The bedside lamp is large and bright. I feel calmer and happier now. The discomfort will fade, it always does. I didn't run away, I was tired. Just tired.

'And what about recovery at Headley?'

'I was just about to mention that.'
'Go on.'
'Well, eventually, you know, at first it wasn't, it was awful...But towards the end that place started to feel like the army again, you know.'
'And what happened when you left?'
'It was tough at first. My folks helped out with everything. It had all gone wrong with Ali as you know. Back then I couldn't see everything she'd done for me.'

I wake early to the sound of knocking. I flick the kettle on before I open the door to find Tapper gasping for air and nearly collapsing. Panic and sweat during the night and little relief on waking

'Have you been running?' I ask somewhat redundantly as he sprawls onto a stool and all over the breakfast bar. I open the fridge. 'Drink?' Asking stupid questions can be quite liberating. He nods and I throw him a can of Coke, which he of course opens immediately and covers himself in fizzy foam. He groans and gulps at the same time. I can't help laughing at this sticky, sweating mess in front of me with his hair on end and his cheeks and nose bright red.

'That was fucking horrific.'

'It's the air up here, mate, it kills your lungs.' Throat dry. Don't want to get up but they are coming again to see me

'That was twenty-five minutes, all I could manage.'

'That's pretty good. It took me a few weeks to build up to longer runs up here. Higher up it's even worse. It's like there's not enough air to sustain life, let alone runners. Coffee?'

'Please.' I make the coffee while he mops up the mess on the breakfast bar. We convene in the lounge with our beverages. 'These apartments are lovely. I wish we were all staying longer.' Instant from the silver pot. No one else minds it, or maybe I just haven't noticed how they feel.

'Well, why don't we?' I say on impulse. He makes the universal sign for money. 'Sod that, I'll bill your stay to the sanatorium.'

He laughs. 'Well, I'm certainly up for an extended break up here. Let's see what Ali reckons.'

The coffee tastes crisp and deep this morning. I wonder where they get their beans. 'Cheers.' We clink mugs. He trundles back to his room for a much-needed shower. Downstairs there's a terrific spread on offer. As well as the full English option, there's an array of different-flavoured yoghurts, fruit conserves, mueslis, granolas, croissants, breads, cheeses, and cold meats. I opt for the yoghurt and fruit while Tapper rewards himself for his physical efforts with a big plate of bacon and pancakes with lashings of maple syrup. Toast and cornflakes today. They smile at me like getting up for breakfast in your pyjamas is an achievement. Ali, never a great breakfast eater, sticks to two pieces of buttered toast. We're all dressed in plenty of layers and our hiking boots as we're going for a walk after breakfast.

Ali has agreed to stay with us for a further week and I've organized it with the staff here. I'll put a call in to the sanatorium later as they'll be expecting me back tomorrow. I look around at some of the other guests as Ali and Tapper engage in conversation. There's a very eclectic clientele: a group of leather-clad bikers tucking into their cooked breakfasts; a bunch of school children excitedly munching on their cereal with two of their teachers; and various traveler-types with their coloured hair and stringy bracelets. I wonder if any of these guys have ever volunteered or worked on a project in Africa run by the Red Apple Group? The fact that I'm asking the question suggests to me that it's very possible. I get up for another coffee and I'm behind one of the bikers in the queue. What are they doing up a snowy mountain? What are we all doing here? Is it good to be able to ask the question? Is it a good sign?

It's invigorating as we set off. The mists of our breathes combine as we head further down the mountain. I think about taking the guys to the lake and proudly showing off my camping spot. Just before I open my mouth, though, I remember how uninterested they were in the painting in the tavern and I decide to preserve the lake for myself. Some of the others have gone for a walk with one of the nurses to the duck pond in the park. My guests are coming again later. I think different meds started last night again and walking out to the shop to buy chocolate and a newspaper for myself

'Can you believe they have a cinema and a café further down the mountain?' says Ali.

'What?' This is not at all in keeping with my idea of the mountain or my feelings about it.

'Yes, we saw the signs on the way up, remember, Tapper?'

'Mmmm,' says Tapper. He's on his phone.

'Lucy?' Ali says to me.

'Lucy,' I confirm instantly.

'Must be nice being that in love,' says Ali.

Tapper puts away his phone.

'Should be about a twenty-five-minute walk,' he says.

'What's on?' I ask.

'They show old movies,' says Ali, 'today's is The Third Man.'

'That is a classic,' I say.

'I hear you,' says Tapper.

'Never seen it,' says Ali.

'You are in for a treat, Miss Cooper. Black and white, Orson Welles, Vienna, zither music,' says Tapper.

'Sounds great,' she says with a raised eyebrow.

'Oh, it is,' he continues, 'back me up, Quentin.'

'He's right,' I say, 'it's a beautiful film. We'll take a trip to bombed-out Vienna.'

'It starts in two hours,' says Tapper.

'Hot chocolates in the café beforehand then,' says Ali in her cheeriest voice. We both look at her. 'Okay, coffee then. I just like the idea of hot chocolate in the snow.'

'Coffee and a cigarette,' I say.

A couple of miles from the café and the cinema signs begin to appear. Tapper's back on his phone, while Ali hasn't been able to wait until our arrival for a cigarette. She offers one to me, but I'll wait until we get to the café and I can have a nice hot coffee with it. I can imagine herds of noisy, littering tourists blundering up here for the café and cinema, and the walks and the scenery. We enter an enclosure in some pine trees and discover a semi-circular path that takes in a sizeable café with benches for outdoor seating and a tiny wooden building with a sign that says, 'The Mountain-top Movie Theatre.' I overlook the obvious problem with this name as we file into the café. It's nearly full of parents and children as well as mountain hikers with rucksacks and boots. There's one little table free so Ali and Tapper secure three spare chairs while I order the drinks.

 The girl who takes my order is young, pretty and Asian. I flash her one of my smiles, which she returns, revealing in the process an immaculate set of teeth. I'm a bit out of practice at trying to be charming but she seems to like me well enough. Would you all like a cup of coffee and a biscuit? Yes please. It's coffee time, I say. I'm sorry, it won't be very good. We don't care, we are just here to see you, she says. I will bring you a grinder and a bag of beans, he says. Do they have a cafetiere? A cupboard full of them, I say. We laugh. Are you reading the paper?

 'You're very busy today,' I say.

 'We're always really busy this time of day. What can I get for you?' Her accent is English with just a hint of somewhere else that I can't quite place.

 'Three flat whites please.' The guys seem to like these. I've never had one, but I'm trying to embrace change. She's short, with a pleasingly curvy figure which I can't help but notice as she prepares the drinks with the rapid care common to the best baristas. We could go out for a coffee today we could all go out the three of us

 Ali and I are outside at a bench with an ashtray between us. We're on our second flat white and our fourth or fifth cigarette since we arrived. It's snowing a little, and every so often a gust of wind sends a mini avalanche of powder shooting out of the trees and off the roof of the café and the cinema. Tapper's still inside on his phone texting Lucy. I asked him to go and get the second round of drinks; I've had enough interactions with strangers for one day.

'Can I offer you some advice?' she says.

'You know you can,' I say with a smile.

'Forget about The Group. Tapper wants to be in a conspiracy movie. Keep your head down, get discharged and come back to your life.' It's so nice to be out

'That's what I'd like to do.'

'Then do it. He will soon find something else to occupy him.' We smoke in silence for a moment. 'Look after yourself. Put your recovery first.'

'It's funny, the plot of The Third Man involves a shocking conspiracy.' Where is the snow today the temperature is mild and we sit and talk together no need for snow shoes and layers and boots today

'Really?' She nods her head as if to music. 'Any lovers in the film?'

She looks me in the eye. I could almost kiss her. 'Yes. But doomed. There are also lots of sewers and lots of shadows.' She looks away. I feel like I've been cruel. I move over on the bench and put my arm around her. She rests her head on my shoulder.

'I talk to Tom sometimes,' I say.

She lifts her head. 'Why?'

'For information, for the writing. We actually get on quite well. Is that okay with you?'

She seems to think about this. 'Yes, it is. Probably more than okay. It could be very good for both of you. Are you going to meet him?' I just want to feel well, that's all. You already seem better than yesterday

'We sort of agreed that he might come and pick me up from the facility when the time comes.'

'And then?'

'And then just spend some time together and have some conversations that I can use as research.'

'I have not seen him in several years,' she says. 'Is he well?' I may do more writing or I may not

'I think he's surviving, getting by the best he can like we all are,' I say. I want to survive. They both think I'm looking better today

    A shadow falls on the waters of the sewer and a rat scuttles by. A big rat, but dirty? Yes, surely. Is this Vienna or the other side of the mountain? There's an air of refinement even among the squalor and ruins and rubble. There was a third man, but is there anything beyond the sanatorium worth exploring? Should I even be asking that? Ali thinks it's not worth it and I'm inclined to agree with her. Life's no film and I'm no one-man army. Let things settle in my mind and hopefully everything will become clear Tapper would do a quote from Big Trouble in Little China here but I'm not going to. The rat notices me and there's a moment of recognition. He doesn't look low or ashamed, he actually looks quite proud in his bearing. The water pours on. If you don't look at it too closely or listen to it too intently, it doesn't seem dirty. I lean up against the damp wall and light a cigarette. The rat seems to like it. He's sniffing the air. I blow the smoke in his direction and he sniffs the air. Friends for life.

    'Did you love her?'

    'No. I don't think I've ever been in love. What am I saying? I know I haven't. I cared about her. I know now that she loved me.'

    'Did she smother you?'

    'With the benefit of years, no, I wouldn't say that.'

    'Really?'

    'Is that how you feel?'

    'I felt like that sometimes, sure.'

    'Is it weird for you talking about this with me?'

    'You would think it would be, wouldn't you? But I think the three of us have been through so much since then. Especially you.'

    'I haven't been through anything more than you have. Different scars, that's all.'

    'Thank you for saying that.'

    'I mean it. Is this whole thing has taught me anything it's that the scars you can't see hurt just as much as the ones you can.'

    'I think you're right. Do you ever feel sorry for yourself?'

    'Of course, but you can't do it. Let other people feel sorry for you if they want. If you're still breathing, you're not doing too badly.

That's one of the benefits of being a soldier.'
  'Milton was blind when he wrote Paradise Lost.'
  'Who?'

The film finishes and my visitors leave, saying that they will return in a couple of days. I was able to sit and watch the film and enjoy it. I am beginning to feel a fog clearing from my head. I can hold possibility in my head and feel its power. I eat my dinner of some sort of meat with damp vegetables and stodgy potatoes. I feel hungry so I eat, and then I feel okay. I sip the coffee and wince a little. I should call Tapper and take him up on the offer of the beans and grinder. But then, how much longer will I be here? People come and go from the hospital. If my parents came and took me out for the day, I could buy a cafetiere.

I refill my cup and take it to the smoking room. There are Daniels and Cole and several others. But I don't know now if I've really seen any of these people before. Where is the man who touches the wall and the man who has a brother? Where is my friend from school? We all sit and talk for a while. We go out to take our meds when we are called by O'Shaunessey. But that is not this man's name. Where do I know that name from? My head hurts if I start to think about things too much. I just enjoy the new feelings and try not to worry where they come from. My parents will take me to the shops tomorrow. They sounded so happy when I called them. Some of the others are going out to the pub this evening. I wonder if it's still snowing out there on the mountain?

ABOUT THE AUTHOR

Henry Wright lives in Kent with his wife and their two cats. He has OCD. 'myself am hell' is his first novel.

Printed in Great Britain
by Amazon